Keep Me
The Twist Me Trilogy: Book 2

Anna Zaires

♠ Mozaika Publications ♠

Copyright © 2014 Anna Zaires
www.annazaires.com

Published by Mozaika Publications, an imprint of Mozaika LLC.
www.mozaikallc.com

Cover by Najla Qamber Designs
najlaqamberdesigns.com

e-ISBN: 978-1-63142-020-7
Print ISBN: 978-1-63142-009-2

PART I: THE ARRIVAL

CHAPTER ONE

❖ JULIAN ❖

There are days when the urge to hurt, to kill, is too strong to be denied. Days when the thin cloak of civilization threatens to slip at the least provocation, revealing the monster inside.

Today is not one of those days.

Today I have her with me.

We're in the car on the way to the airport. She's sitting pressed against my side, her slim arms wrapped around me and her face buried in the crook of my neck.

Cradling her with one arm, I stroke her dark hair,

delighting in its silky texture. It's long now, reaching all the way down to her narrow waist. She hasn't cut her hair in nineteen months.

Not since I kidnapped her for the first time.

Inhaling, I draw in her scent—light and flowery, deliciously feminine. It's a combination of some shampoo and her unique body chemistry, and it makes my mouth water. I want to strip her bare and follow that scent everywhere, to explore every curve and hollow of her body.

My cock twitches, and I remind myself that I just fucked her. It doesn't matter, though. My lust for her is constant. It used to bother me, this obsessive craving, but now I'm used to it. I've accepted my own madness.

She seems calm, content even. I like that. I like to feel her cuddled against me, all soft and trusting. She knows my true nature, yet she still feels safe with me. I have trained her to feel that way.

I have made her love me.

After a couple of minutes, she stirs in my arms, lifting her head to look at me. "Where are we going?" she asks, blinking, her long black lashes sweeping up and down like fans. She has the kind of eyes that could bring a man to his knees—soft, dark eyes that make me think of tangled sheets and naked flesh.

I force myself to focus. Those eyes fuck with my concentration like nothing else. "We're going to my home in Colombia," I say, answering her question. "The place where I grew up."

I haven't been there for years—not since my parents were murdered. However, my father's compound is a fortress, and that's precisely what we need right now. In the past few weeks, I've implemented additional security measures, making the place virtually impregnable. Nobody will take Nora from me again— I've made sure of that.

"Are you going to be there with me?" I can hear the hopeful note in her voice, and I nod, smiling.

"Yes, my pet, I'll be there." Now that I have her back, the compulsion to keep her near is too strong to deny. The island had once been the safest place for her, but no longer. Now they know of her existence—and they know she's my Achilles' heel. I need to have her with me, where I can protect her.

She licks her lips, and my eyes follow the path of her delicate pink tongue. I want to wrap her thick hair around my fist and force her head down to my lap, but I resist the urge. There will be plenty of time for that later, when we're in a more secure—and less public— location.

"Are you going to send my parents another million dollars?" Her eyes are wide and guileless as she looks at me, but I can hear the subtle challenge in her voice. She's testing me—testing the bounds of this new stage of our relationship.

My smile broadens, and I reach over to tuck a strand of hair behind her ear. "Do you want me to send it to them, my pet?"

She stares at me without blinking. "Not really," she says softly. "I would much rather call them instead."

I hold her gaze. "All right. You can call them once we get there."

Her eyes widen, and I see that I surprised her. She was expecting that I would keep her captive again, cut off from the outside world. What she doesn't realize is that it's no longer necessary.

I've succeeded in what I set out to do.

I've made her completely mine.

"Okay," she says slowly, "I'll do that."

She's looking at me like she can't quite figure me out—like I'm some exotic animal she's never seen before. She often looks at me like that, with a mixture of wariness and fascination. She's drawn to me—she's been drawn to me from the very beginning—yet she's still afraid of me on some level.

The predator in me likes that. Her fear, her reluctance—they add a certain edge to the whole thing. It makes it that much sweeter to possess her, to feel her curled up in my arms every night.

"Tell me about your time at home," I murmur, settling her more comfortably against my shoulder. Brushing back her hair with my fingers, I look down at her upturned face. "What have you been up to all these months?"

Her soft lips curve in a self-deprecating smile. "You mean, besides missing you?"

A warm sensation spreads through my chest. I don't

want to acknowledge it. I don't want it to matter. I want her to love me because I have a sick compulsion to own all of her—not because I feel anything in return. "Yes, besides that," I say quietly, thinking of the many ways I'm going to fuck her when I get her alone again.

"Well, I met with some of my friends," she begins, and I listen as she gives me a general overview of her life over the past four months. I already know much of this, since Lucas had taken the initiative to put a discreet security detail on Nora while I had been in a coma. As soon as I woke up, he gave me a thorough report on everything, including Nora's daily activities.

I owe him for that—and for saving my life. Over the past few years, Lucas Kent has become an invaluable part of my organization. Few others would've had the balls to step up like that. Even without knowing the full truth about Nora, he had been smart enough to infer that she means something to me and take steps to ensure her safety.

Of course, the one thing he didn't do was restrict her activities in any way. "So did you see him?" I ask casually, lifting my hand to play with her earlobe. "Jake, I mean?"

Her body turns into stone in my arms. I can feel the rigid tension in each muscle. "I ran into him briefly, after dinner with my friend Leah," she says evenly, looking up at me. "We had some coffee together, the three of us, and that was the only time I saw him."

I hold her gaze for a second, then nod, satisfied. She didn't lie to me. The reports had mentioned that particular incident. When I first read about it, I wanted to kill the boy with my bare hands.

I still might do that, if he approaches Nora ever again.

The thought of another man near her fills me with white-hot fury. According to the reports, she didn't date during our time apart—with one notable exception. "How about that lawyer?" I ask softly, doing my best to control the rage boiling inside me. "Did the two of you have a good time?"

Her face turns pale underneath her golden skin tone. "I didn't do anything with him," she says, and I can hear the apprehension in her voice. "I went out that night because I was missing you, because I was tired of being alone, but nothing happened. I had a couple of drinks, but I still couldn't go through with it."

"No?" Much of the anger drains out of me. I can read her well enough to know when she's lying—and right now she's telling the truth. Still, I make a mental note to have this investigated further. If the lawyer touched her in any way, he'll pay.

She looks at me, and I can feel her own tension dissipating. She can discern my moods like no one else. It's as if she's attuned to me on some level. It's been that way with her from the very beginning. Unlike most women, she's always been able to sense the real me.

"No." Her mouth tightens. "I couldn't let him touch me. I'm too fucked up to be with a normal man now."

I lift my eyebrows, amused despite myself. She's no longer the frightened girl I brought to the island. Somewhere along the way, my little pet grew some sharp claws and was starting to learn how to use them.

"That's good." I run my fingers playfully across her cheek, then bend my head to inhale her sweet scent. "Nobody is allowed to touch you, baby. Nobody but me."

She doesn't respond, just continues looking at me. She doesn't need to say anything. We understand each other perfectly. I know I will kill any man who lays a finger on her, and she knows it too.

It's strange, but I've never felt possessive about a woman before. This is new territory for me. Before Nora, women were all interchangeable in my mind— just soft, pretty creatures passing through my life. They came to me willingly, wanting to be fucked, to be hurt, and I indulged them, satisfying my own physical needs in the process.

I fucked my first woman when I was fourteen, shortly after Maria's death. She was one of my father's whores; he sent her to me after I dispatched two of the men who murdered Maria by castrating them in their own homes. I think my father was hoping the lure of sex would be enough to distract me from my path of vengeance.

Needless to say, his plan didn't work out.

She came into my room wearing a tight black dress, her makeup perfectly done and her lush, full mouth painted a glossy red. When she began to strip in front of me, I reacted just like any teenage boy would—with instant, violent lust. But I wasn't any teenage boy at that point. I was a killer; I had been one since I was eight.

I took the whore roughly that night, partly because I was too inexperienced to control myself, partly because I wanted to lash out at her, at my father, at the whole fucking world. I took my frustrations out on her flesh, leaving behind bruises and bite marks—and she came back for more the next night, this time without my father's knowledge. We fucked like that for a month, with her stealing into my room every chance she got, teaching me what she liked . . . what she claimed many women liked. She didn't want sweet and gentle in bed; she wanted pain and force. She wanted someone to make her feel alive.

And I found that I liked that. I liked hearing her scream and beg as I hurt her and made her come. The violence crawling under my skin had found another outlet, and it was one I used every chance I got.

It wasn't enough, of course. The rage dwelling deep within me couldn't be pacified so easily. Maria's death changed something inside me. She had been the only pure, beautiful thing in my life, and she was gone. Her death accomplished more than my father's training ever could: it killed any remaining conscience I might've possessed. I was no longer a boy reluctantly following in my father's footsteps; I was a predator who craved blood and vengeance. Ignoring my father's orders to let the matter drop, I hunted down Maria's killers one by one and made them pay, drinking in their screams of agony, their pleas for mercy and for quicker death.

After that, there were retaliations and counter-retaliations. People died. My father's men. His rival's men. The violence kept escalating until my father decided to pacify his associates by removing me from the business. I was sent away, to Europe and Asia . . . and there I found dozens more women like the one who had introduced me to sex. Beautiful, willing women whose proclivities mirrored my own. I gave them their dark fantasies, and they gave me momentary pleasure—an arrangement that suited my life perfectly, especially after I came back to take up the reins of my father's organization.

It wasn't until nineteen months ago, during a business trip to Chicago, that I found *her*.

Nora.

My Maria reincarnated.

The girl I intend to keep forever.

CHAPTER TWO

❖ NORA ❖

Sitting there in Julian's embrace, I feel the familiar hum of excitement mixed with trepidation. Our separation hasn't changed him one bit. He's still the same man who almost killed Jake, who didn't hesitate to kidnap a girl he wanted.

He's also the man who nearly died rescuing me.

Now that I know what happened to him, I can see the physical signs of his ordeal. He's leaner than before, his tan skin stretched tightly over sharp cheekbones. There is a ragged pink scar on his left ear, and his dark hair is extra-short. On the left side of his skull, the growth pattern of that hair is a bit uneven, as though it's concealing a scar there as well.

Despite those tiny imperfections, he's still the most gorgeous man I've ever seen. I can't tear my eyes away from him.

He's alive. Julian is alive, and I'm with him again.

It still seems so surreal. Up until this morning, I thought he was dead. I was convinced he had died in the explosion. For four long, excruciating months, I had been forcing myself to be strong, to get on with my life and try to forget the man sitting next to me right now.

The man who stole my freedom.

The man I love.

Raising my left hand, I gently trace the outline of his lips with my index finger. He's got the most incredible mouth I have ever seen—a mouth made for sin. At my touch, his beautiful lips part, and he catches the tip of my finger with his sharp white teeth, biting down on it lightly, then sucking my finger into his mouth.

A tremor of arousal runs through me as his warm, wet tongue laves my finger. My inner muscles clench, and I can feel my underwear getting damp. God, I'm so easy when it comes to him. One look, one touch, and I want him. My sex feels swollen and slightly sore after the way he fucked me earlier, but my body aches for him to take me again.

Julian is alive, and he's taking me away again.

As that fact begins to sink in, I pull my finger away

from his lips, a sudden chill feathering over my skin and cooling my desire. There's no turning back now, no possibility of changing my mind. Julian is again in charge of my life, and this time I'd willingly flown into the spider's web, placing myself at his mercy.

Of course, it wouldn't have mattered if I had been unwilling, I remind myself. I remember the syringe in Julian's pocket, and I know that the outcome would've been the same regardless. Conscious or sedated, I would've been accompanying him today. For some messed-up reason, that fact makes me feel better, and I place my head back on Julian's shoulder, letting myself relax against him.

It's futile to fight against one's destiny, and I'm starting to accept that fact.

* * *

With traffic, our ride to the airport takes a little over an hour. To my surprise, we don't go to O'Hare. Instead we end up at a small airstrip where a sizable plane awaits our arrival. I can make out the letters 'G650' on its tail.

"Is that yours?" I ask as Julian opens the car door for me.

"Yes." He doesn't look at me or elaborate further. Instead his gaze appears to be scanning our surroundings, as though looking for hidden threats. There is an alertness to his manner that I don't remember seeing before, and for the first time, I realize that the island was his sanctuary as well, a place where he could truly relax and let down his guard.

As soon as I climb out, Julian grips my elbow and ushers me toward the plane. The driver follows us. I didn't see him before, as a panel separated the backseat area of the car from the front, so now I sneak a glance at him as we walk toward the plane.

The guy must be one of Julian's Navy SEALs. His blond hair is cut short, and his pale eyes are ice-cold in his square-jawed face. He's even taller than Julian, and he moves with the same athletic, warrior-like grace, his every movement carefully controlled. There is a huge assault rifle in his hands, and I have no doubt that he knows exactly how to use it. Another dangerous man . . . one that many women would undoubtedly find attractive, with his regular features and muscular body. He doesn't appeal to me, but I'm spoiled. Few men can hold a candle to Julian's dark-angel allure.

"What kind of a plane is this?" I ask Julian as we walk up the steps and enter a luxurious cabin. I don't know anything about private jets, but this one looks fancy. I'm doing my best not to gawk at everything, but I'm failing miserably. The cream-colored leather seats inside are huge, and there is an actual couch with a coffee table in front of it. There is also an open door leading to the back of the airplane, and I catch a glimpse of a king-size bed sitting there.

My mouth falls open in shock. *The plane has a*

bedroom.

"It's one of the higher-end Gulfstreams," he replies, turning me so he can help me take off my coat. His warm hands brush against my neck, sending a pleasant shiver through me. "An ultra-long-range business jet. It can take us directly to our destination without needing to make a fuel stop."

"It's very nice," I say, watching as Julian hangs my coat in the closet by the door and then takes off his own jacket. I can't take my eyes off him, and I realize that a part of me still fears that this is not real—that I'll wake up and find out that this was all just a dream . . . that Julian had truly died in the explosion.

The thought causes a shudder to run through me, and Julian notices my involuntary movement. "Are you cold?" he asks, stepping toward me. "I can have the temperature adjusted."

"No, I'm fine." Nevertheless, I enjoy Julian's warmth as he pulls me toward him and rubs my arms for a few seconds. I can feel the heat of his body seeping through my clothes, chasing away the memory of those awful months when I thought I'd lost him.

Wrapping my arms around Julian's waist, I hug him fiercely. He's alive, and I have him with me. That's all that matters now.

"We're ready for takeoff." An unfamiliar male voice startles me, and I let go of Julian, looking back to see the blond driver standing there, watching us with an unreadable expression on his hard face.

"Good." Julian keeps his arm around me, pressing me against his side when I try to step away. "Nora, this is Lucas. He's the one who dragged me out of the warehouse."

"Oh, I see." I beam at the man, my smile wide and genuine. This man had saved Julian's life. "It's very nice to meet you, Lucas. I can't even begin to thank you for what you did—"

His eyebrows arch a little, as though I said something that surprised him. "I was just doing my job," he says, his voice deep and slightly amused.

The corner of Julian's mouth lifts in a faint smile, but he doesn't respond to that. Instead he asks, "Is everything ready for us at the estate?"

Lucas nods. "All set." Then he looks at me, his face as expressionless as before. "It's nice to meet you too, Nora." And turning around, he disappears into the pilot's area at the front.

"He drives *and* flies planes for you?" I ask Julian after Lucas is gone.

"He's very versatile," Julian says, leading me toward the plush seats. "Most of my men are."

As soon as we sit down, a strikingly beautiful dark-haired woman comes into the cabin from somewhere in the front. Her white dress appears to have been poured on her curves, and with the full layer of makeup she has on, she looks as glamorous as a movie star—except for the tray with a champagne bottle and two glasses she's holding in her hands.

Her gaze lands on me briefly before sliding over to Julian. "Would you like anything else, Mr. Esguerra?" she asks as she bends down to place the tray on the table between our seats. Her voice is soft and melodic, and the hungry way she looks at Julian sets my teeth on edge.

"This should suffice for now. Thank you, Isabella," he says, giving her a brief smile, and I feel a sudden sharp stab of jealousy. Julian told me once that he hadn't fucked anyone else since meeting me, but I still can't help wondering if he had sex with this woman at some point in the past. She looks like a bombshell, and her manner makes it clear she would be more than willing to bring Julian anything he wants—including herself, naked on a silver platter.

Before my thoughts can travel any further down that road, I take a deep breath and force myself to look out the window at the slowly falling snow. A part of me knows that this whole thing is insane, that it's illogical to feel so possessive about Julian. Any rational woman would be overjoyed to have her kidnapper's attention deflected away from her, but I'm no longer rational when it comes to him.

Stockholm Syndrome. Capture-bonding. Traumatic bonding. My therapist had used all of these terms during our few brief sessions together. She had been trying to get me to talk about my feelings for Julian, but it had been too painful for me to discuss the man I'd thought I lost, so I stopped going to her. I did look up the terms later, though, and I can see why they would be applicable to my experience. I don't know if it's as simple as that, though, or if it even matters at this point. Naming something doesn't make it go away. Whatever the cause of my emotional attachment to Julian, I can't turn it off. I can't make myself love him any less.

By the time I turn back to face Julian, the flight attendant is gone from the main cabin. I can hear the jet engines roaring to life, and I automatically fasten my safety belt, as I'd been taught to do my whole life.

"Champagne?" he asks, reaching for the bottle at the table.

"Sure, why not," I say, and watch him deftly pour me a glass.

He hands it to me, and I sit back in my spacious seat, sipping the bubbly drink as the plane starts rolling.

My new life with Julian has begun.

CHAPTER THREE

❖ JULIAN ❖

Sipping from my own glass, I study Nora as she looks out the window at the rapidly shrinking ground below. She's wearing jeans and a blue fleece sweater, her small feet clad in a pair of chunky-looking black sheepskin boots. Uggs, I think they're called. Despite that off-putting footwear, she still looks sexy—though I far prefer seeing her in summer dresses, her smooth skin glowing in the sun.

Watching her calm expression, I wonder what she's thinking, if she has any regrets.

She shouldn't. I would've taken her regardless.

As though sensing my gaze on her, she turns toward me. "How did they find out about me?" she asks quietly. "The men who kidnapped me, I mean. How did they learn of my existence?"

At her question, my entire body tenses. My mind flashes back to those hellish hours after the attack on the clinic, and for a moment, I'm gripped by that same volatile mix of burning fury and paralyzing fear.

She could've died. She would've died, if I hadn't found her in time. Even if I'd given them what they wanted, they would've still killed her to punish me for not giving in to their demands sooner. I would've lost her, just like I lost Maria.

Just like we both lost Beth.

"It was the nursing assistant at the clinic." My voice comes out sounding cold and distant as I place my champagne glass back on the tray. "Angela. She was on Al-Quadar's payroll all along."

Nora's eyes glitter brightly. "That bitch," she whispers, and I can hear the pain and anger in her voice. Her hand shakes as she puts down her own glass on the table. "That fucking bitch."

I nod, trying to control my own rage as images from the video Majid sent me slide through my mind. They tortured Beth before killing her. They made her suffer. Beth, whose life had held nothing but suffering since her asshole of a father sold her to a brothel across the Mexican border at the age of thirteen. Who had been one of the very few people whose loyalty I never questioned.

They made her suffer . . . and now I will make them suffer worse.

"Where is she now?" Nora's question brings me out of a pleasurable reverie where I have each member of Al-Quadar strung up and at my mercy. When I look at her blankly, she clarifies, "Angela."

I smile at her naïve question. "You don't have to worry about her, my pet." All that remains of Angela are ashes, scattered on the lawn of the clinic in the Philippines. Peter's brand of questioning is brutal but effective, and he always disposes of the evidence afterwards. "She paid for her betrayal."

Nora swallows, and I know she understands exactly what I mean. She's no longer the same girl I met in that club in Chicago. I can see the shadows in her eyes, and I know I'm responsible for putting them there. Despite my best efforts to keep her sheltered on the island, the ugliness of my world touched her, tainted her innocence.

Al-Quadar will pay for that as well.

The scar on my head begins to throb, and I touch it lightly with my left hand. My head still aches occasionally, but other than that, I'm almost back to my normal self. Considering that I spent a good portion of the last four months as a vegetable, I'm quite content with this state of affairs.

"Are you all right?" There is a concerned expression on Nora's face as she reaches up to touch the area above my left ear. Her slender fingers are gentle on my scalp. "Does it still hurt?"

Her touch sends pleasure streaking down my spine. I want this from her. I want her to care about my well-being. I want her to love me even though I stole her freedom—even though, by all rights, she should hate me.

I have no illusions about myself. I'm one of those men they show on the news—the ones that everyone fears and despises. I took a young woman because I wanted her and for no other reason.

I took her, and I made her mine.

I make no excuses for my actions. I feel no guilt either. I wanted Nora, and now she's here with me, looking at me like I'm the most important person in her world.

And I am. I am exactly what she needs now . . . what she craves. I will give her everything, and I will take everything from her in return. Her body, her mind, her devotion—I want it all. I want her pain and her pleasure, her fear and her joy.

I want to be her entire life.

"No, it's fine," I say in response to her earlier question. "It's almost healed."

She pulls her fingers away, and I catch her hand, not ready to forego the pleasure of her touch. Her hand is slim and delicate in my grasp, her skin soft and warm. She tries to tug it away reflexively, but I don't let her, my fingers tightening around her small palm. Her strength is insignificant compared to mine; she can't make me release her unless I choose to let her go.

She doesn't really want me to let her go, anyway. I can feel the excitement rising within her, and my body hardens, a dark hunger awakening within me again. Reaching across the table, I slowly and purposefully unbuckle her safety belt.

Then I stand up, still holding her hand, and lead her to the bedroom at the back of the airplane.

* * *

She's silent as we enter the room and I close the door behind us. The area is not soundproof, but Isabella and Lucas are at the front of the plane, so we should have some privacy. I don't normally care if someone hears or sees me having sex, but what I do with Nora is different. She's mine, and I don't intend to share her. In any way.

Letting go of her hand, I walk over to the bed and sit down on it, leaning back and crossing my legs at the ankles. A casual pose, though there's nothing casual in the way I feel as I look at her.

The desire to possess her is violent, all-consuming. It's an obsession that goes beyond a simple sexual need, though my body burns for her. I don't just want to fuck her; I want to imprint myself on her, to mark her from the inside out, so that she will never belong to any man but me.

I want to own her completely.

"Take off your clothes," I order, holding her gaze. My dick is so hard, it's as though it's been months, instead of hours, since I had her. It takes all of my self-restraint not to rip off her clothes, bend her over the bed, and pound into her flesh until I explode.

I control myself because I don't want a quick fuck. I have other things in mind for today.

Taking a deep breath, I force myself to stay still, watching as she slowly begins to disrobe. Her face is flushed, her breathing coming faster, and I know she's already aroused, her pussy hot and slick, primed for me. At the same time, I can feel the hesitation in her movements, see the wariness in her eyes. There is a part of her that still fears me, that knows what I'm capable of.

She's right to be afraid. There is something within me that thrives on the pain of others, that wants to hurt them.

That wants to hurt *her.*

She takes off her fleece sweater first, revealing a black tank top underneath. Her pink bra straps peek through, and the innocent color excites me for some reason, sending a fresh surge of blood straight to my cock. The tank top comes off next, and by the time she's pulled off her boots and jeans, I'm all but ready to explode.

In her pink matching bra-and-panties set, she's the most delectable creature I have ever seen. Her petite body is fit and toned, the muscles in her arms and legs subtly defined. Despite her slenderness, she is undeniably feminine, her ass perfectly curved and her small breasts surprisingly round. With her long hair flowing down her back, she looks like a Victoria's Secret model in miniature. The only flaw is a small scar on the right side of her flat stomach—the reminder of her appendectomy.

I have to touch her.

"Come here," I say hoarsely, my cock straining painfully against the fly of my jeans.

Staring at me with her huge dark eyes, she approaches cautiously, uncertainly, as though I might attack her at any time.

I suck in another deep breath to prevent myself from doing exactly that. Instead, when she reaches me, I lean forward and firmly grip her waist, drawing her toward me so that she's standing between my legs. Her skin is cool and smooth to the touch, her ribcage so narrow that I can almost encircle her waist with my hands. It would be so easy to damage her, to break her. Her vulnerability turns me on almost as much as her beauty.

Reaching up, I find the clasp of her bra and release her breasts from their confinement.

As the bra slips down her arms, my mouth goes dry and my entire body tightens. Even though I've seen her naked hundreds of times, each time is a revelation. Her nipples are small, pinkish-brown in color, and her breasts are the same light golden hue as the rest of her body. Unable to resist, I cup those soft, round mounds in my hands, squeezing them, kneading them. Her flesh is sleek and firm, her nipples stiff against my palms. I can hear the catch in her breathing as my thumbs rub across those hardened peaks, and my hunger intensifies.

Releasing her breasts, I hook my fingers into the waistband of her underwear and push it down her legs, then cup her sex with my right hand. My middle finger pushes into her small opening, and the warm moisture I find there makes my cock jerk. She gasps as my callused thumb presses against her clit, and her hands reach up to grab my shoulders, her sharp little nails digging into my skin.

I can't wait any longer. I must have her.

"Get on the bed." My voice is thick with lust as I withdraw my hand from her pussy. "I want you on your stomach."

She scrambles to obey as I rise to my feet and begin to disrobe.

I've trained her well. By the time I've removed my own clothes, she's lying on her stomach fully naked, a pillow propping up her curvy little ass. Her arms are folded under her head, and her face is turned toward me. She's watching me with those thickly lashed eyes of hers, and I can sense her nervous anticipation. She both desires and fears me in this moment.

It turns me on, that look, but it also awakens

another kind of hunger in me. A darker, more perverse need. Out of the corner of my eye, I spot the belt from my jeans lying on the floor. Picking it up, I wind the buckle end around my right hand and approach the bed.

Nora doesn't move, though I can see the anxious tension in her body. My lips twitch. *Such a good girl.* She knows it would go worse for her if she resists. Of course, by now she also knows that I will temper her pain with pleasure, that she will derive enjoyment from this too.

Pausing at the edge of the bed, I extend my free hand and trail my fingers along her spine. She trembles under my touch, a reaction that sends dark excitement surging through me. This is exactly what I want, what I need—this deep, twisted connection that exists between us. I want to drink in her fear, her pain. I want to hear her screams, feel her helpless struggles—and then have her melt in my arms as I bring her to ecstasy again and again.

For some reason, this small girl brings out the worst in me, makes me forget whatever shreds of morality I possess. She's the only woman I've ever forced into my bed, the only one I've wanted this much . . . and in such a wrong way. Having her here, at my mercy, is beyond heady—it's the most powerful drug I've ever tasted. I've never felt this way about another human being before, and the knowledge that she's mine, that I can do anything I want to her, is a rush unlike any other.

With all those other women, it was a game we played, a way to scratch a mutual itch, but with Nora, it's different. With her, it's something more.

"Beautiful," I murmur, stroking the soft skin of her thighs and buttocks. Soon it will be marked, but for now I'm enjoying its smoothness. "So very, very beautiful . . ." Bending over her, I press a gentle kiss to the base of her spine, inhaling her warm female scent and letting the anticipation build. A shiver ripples through her, and I smile, adrenaline surging through my veins.

Straightening, I take a step back and swing the belt.

I don't use a lot of force, but she still jumps when the belt lands on the round globes of her ass, a soft whimper escaping her lips. She doesn't try to move or crawl away; instead her small fists grip the sheets tightly, and her eyes squeeze shut. I swing harder a second time, then again and again, my movements taking on a hypnotic, trance-like rhythm. With each stroke of the belt, I sink deeper and deeper into the blackness, my world narrowing until all I see, all I hear, all I feel is her. The reddening of her tender flesh, the pained gasps and sobs that issue from her throat, the way her body quivers and trembles under each stroke of my belt—I drink it all in, letting it feed my addiction, soothe the desperate hunger gnawing at my insides.

Time blurs and stretches. I don't know if it's been minutes or hours. When I finally stop, she's lying limp and unmoving, her buttocks and thighs covered with pink welts. There is a dazed, almost blissful expression on her tear-wet face, and her slender body is shaking, small tremors rippling over her skin.

Letting the belt drop to the floor, I carefully pick her up and sit down on the bed, holding her cradled on my lap. My own heart is hammering in my chest, my mind still reeling from the incredible rush I just experienced. She shudders, hiding her face against my shoulder, and begins to cry. I stroke her hair, slowly, soothingly, letting her come down from her endorphin-induced high as I come down from mine.

This is what I need now—to comfort her, to feel her in my arms. I want to be her everything: her protector and her tormentor, her joy and her sorrow. I want to bind her to me physically and emotionally, to brand myself so deeply on her mind and soul that she will never think about leaving me.

As her sobs begin to ease, my sexual hunger returns. My soothing caresses become more purposeful, my hands starting to roam over her body with an intent to arouse, not just to calm. My right hand slips between her thighs, my fingers pressing against her clit, and at the same time, my other hand grips her hair and pulls on it, forcing her to meet my gaze. She still looks dazed, her soft lips parted as she stares at me, and I lean down, taking her mouth in a deep, thorough kiss. She moans into my mouth, her hands clutching at my shoulders, and I can feel the heat rising between us. My balls draw up tightly against my body, my cock aching for her slick, warm flesh.

I stand up, still holding her in my arms, and place her on the bed. She winces, and I realize the sheets are rubbing against her welts, hurting her. "Turn over, baby," I whisper, wanting only her pleasure now. She obediently rolls over onto her stomach, in the same position as before, and I position her so that she's on her hands and knees, her elbows bent.

On all fours, with her ass tilted up and her back slightly arched, she's the hottest thing I've ever seen. I can see everything—the folds of her delicate pussy, the tiny hole of her anus, the delicious curves of her cheeks, pink with marks from the belt. My heart is pounding heavily in my chest, and my cock is throbbing painfully as I grasp her hips, line the head of my dick up against her opening, and push inside.

Hot, wet flesh envelops me, sheathing me in tight, slick perfection. She moans, arching toward me, trying to take me deeper, and I oblige, withdrawing partially and then slamming back in. A cry escapes her throat, and I repeat the move, my spine prickling with pleasure at the clinging grip of her tight channel. Waves of heat roll through me, and I begin to thrust with abandon, barely cognizant of my fingers digging into the soft skin of her hips. Her moans and cries increase in volume, and then I feel her peaking, her inner muscles contracting around my cock, milking it. Unable to hold on any longer, I explode, my vision blurring from the force of my release as my seed erupts into her warm depths.

Panting, I collapse onto my side, pulling her with me. Our skin is damp with sweat, gluing us together, and my heart is racing. She's breathing heavily too, and I can feel her pussy clenching around my softening cock as one last orgasmic shudder ripples through her.

We lie joined together as our breathing begins to ease. I'm holding her spooned against me, the soft curve of her ass pressing into my groin, and a sense of peace, of contentment, slowly steals over me. It's always like that with her. Something about her calms my demons, makes me feel almost normal. Almost . . . happy. It's not something I can explain or rationalize; it's just there. It's what makes my need for her so acute, so desperate.

So dangerously fucked up.

"Tell me you love me," I murmur, stroking her outer thigh. "Tell me you missed me, baby."

She shifts in my arms, turning over to face me. Her dark eyes are solemn as she meets my gaze. "I love you, Julian," she says softly, her delicate palm curving around my jaw. "I missed you more than life itself. You know that."

I do—but I still need this from her. In recent months, the emotional aspect has become as necessary to me as the physical. It amuses me, this strange quirk of mine. I want my little captive to love me, to care about me. I want to be more than just the monster of her nightmares.

Closing my eyes, I draw her deeper into my embrace and let myself relax.

In a few hours, she's going to be mine in every sense of the word.

CHAPTER FOUR

❖ NORA ❖

I must've fallen asleep in Julian's arms because I wake up when the plane begins to descend. Opening my eyes, I stare at the unfamiliar surroundings, my body sore and aching from the sex we just had.

I had forgotten what it was like with Julian, how devastating and cathartic the roller coaster ride of pain and ecstasy could be. I feel both empty and exhilarated at the same time, wrung out, yet invigorated by the maelstrom of emotions.

Sitting up gingerly, I wince as my bruised bottom touches the sheets. That had been one of the more intense belting sessions; I won't be surprised if these bruises last a while. Casting a glance around the room, I spot a door that I assume leads to the bathroom. Julian is not in the room, so I get up and go over there, feeling the need to wash up.

To my surprise, the bathroom contains a small shower, as well as a real sink and toilet. With all these amenities, Julian's jet seems more like a flying hotel than any commercial plane I've been on. There is even a plastic-wrapped toothbrush, toothpaste, and mouthwash tucked inside a little shelf on the wall. I use all three and follow up with a quick shower. Then, feeling infinitely more refreshed, I go back into the bedroom to get dressed.

When I enter the main cabin, I see Julian sitting on the couch, an open laptop on the table in front of him. The sleeves of his shirt are pushed up, exposing tan, muscular forearms, and there is a frown of concentration on his face. He looks serious—and so devastatingly beautiful that my breath catches for a moment.

As though sensing my presence, he looks up, his blue eyes gleaming. "How are you, my pet?" he asks, his voice low and intimate, and I feel a hot flush moving over my entire body in response.

"I'm fine." I don't know what else to say. *My butt hurts because you whipped me, but that's okay because you trained me to enjoy it?* Yeah, sure.

His lips curl in a slow smile. "Good. I'm glad to hear

it. I was just about to come get you. You should get into your seat—we'll be landing soon."

"Okay." I follow his suggestion, trying not to flinch at the pain caused by the simple act of sitting down. I will definitely have bruises for the next few days.

Strapping myself in, I look out the window, curious about our destination. As the plane breaks through the cloud cover, I see a large city spread out below, with mountains looming on the edge of it. "What city is that?" I ask, turning towards Julian.

"Bogotá," he replies, closing his laptop. Picking it up, he walks over to sit down next to me. "We'll only be there for a few hours."

"You have business there?"

"You could say that." He looks vaguely amused. "There is something I'd like to get done before we fly to the estate."

"What?" I inquire warily. An amused Julian is rarely a good sign.

"You'll see." And opening the laptop again, he focuses on whatever he was doing before.

* * *

A black car similar to the one that dropped us off at the airport waits for us when we get off the plane. Lucas assumes the role of our driver again, while Julian continues working on his laptop, seemingly absorbed in his task.

I don't mind. I'm too busy staring at everything as we drive through the crowded streets. Bogotá has a certain 'Old World' vibe that I find fascinating. I can see traces of its Spanish heritage everywhere, mixed with a uniquely Latino flavor. It makes me crave arepas—corn cakes that I used to get from a Colombian food truck in downtown Chicago.

"Where are we going?" I ask Julian when the car pulls up in front of a stately old church in a wealthy-looking neighborhood. Somehow I hadn't pictured my captor as the church-going type.

Instead of answering, he climbs out of the car and extends his hand to me. "Come, Nora," he says. "We don't have a lot of time."

Time for what? I want to question him further, but I know it's futile. He's not going to answer me unless he feels like it. Placing my hand in Julian's large palm, I climb out of the car and let him lead me toward the church building. For all I know, we're meeting some of his associates here—though why he wants me with him for that is anyone's guess.

We enter through a little side door and find ourselves in a small, but beautifully decorated room. Old-fashioned wooden benches line the sides of it, and there is a pulpit with an intricate cross toward the front.

For some reason, the sight of it makes me nervous. An insane, improbable thought occurs to me, and my palms begin to sweat. "Um, Julian . . ." I look up to find him gazing at me with a strange smile. "Why are we here?"

"Can't you guess, my pet?" he says softly, turning to face me. "We're here to get married."

For a moment, all I can do is stare at him in mute shock. Then a nervous laugh escapes my throat. "You're joking, right?"

He lifts his eyebrows. "Joking? No, not at all." He reaches for my hand again, and I feel him sliding something onto my left ring finger.

My heart racing, I look down at my left hand in numb disbelief. The ring looks like something a Hollywood star might wear—a thin, diamond-encrusted band with a large, round stone sparkling in the center. It's both delicate and ostentatious, and the fit is utterly perfect, as though it had been made just for me.

The room fades in front of my eyes, spots of light dancing in the corners of my vision, and I realize that I literally stopped breathing for a few seconds. Desperately sucking in air, I look up at Julian, my entire body beginning to shake. "You . . . you want to marry me?" My voice comes out in a kind of horrified whisper.

"Of course I do." His eyes narrow slightly. "Why else would I bring you here?"

I have no response to that; all I can do is stand there and stare at him, feeling like I'm hyperventilating.

Marriage. Marriage to Julian.

It simply doesn't compute. Marriage and Julian are so far apart in my mind, they might as well be on opposite poles of the planet. When I think of marriage, it's in the context of a pleasant, yet distant future—a future that involves a doting husband and two noisy children. In that picture, there is a dog and a house in the suburbs, soccer games and school picnics. There is no killer with the face of a fallen angel, no beautiful monster to make me scream in his arms.

"I can't marry you." The words tumble out before I can think better of it. "I'm sorry, Julian, but I can't."

His face turns black. In a flash, he's on me, one arm wrapped around my waist, pressing me against him, and the other hand gripping my jaw. "You said you loved me." His voice is soft and even, but I can feel the dark rage underneath. "Was that a lie?"

"No!" Shaking, I hold Julian's furious gaze, my hands pushing helplessly against his powerful chest. I can feel the weight of the ring on my finger, and it adds to my panic. I don't know how to explain, how to make him understand something that I can barely comprehend myself. I want to be with Julian. I can't live without him, but marriage is something else entirely, something that doesn't belong in our twisted relationship. "I do love you! You know that—"

"So why would you refuse?" he demands, his eyes dark with fury. His grip on my jaw tightens, his fingers biting into my skin.

My eyes begin to burn. How can I explain my

reluctance? How can I say that he's not someone I can picture as my husband? That he's part of a life I never imagined, never wanted, and that marrying him would mean giving up that vague, far-off dream of a normal future? "Why do you want to marry me?" I ask desperately. "Why do you want something so traditional? I'm already yours—"

"Yes, you are." He leans down until his face is mere inches from mine. "And I want a legal document to that effect. You will be my wife, and no one will be able to take you from me."

I stare at Julian, my chest tightening as I begin to understand. This is not a sweet, romantic gesture on his part. He's not doing this because he loves me and wants to start a family. That's not the way Julian operates. Marriage would legitimize his possession of me—it's as simple as that. It would be a different form of ownership, a more permanent one . . . and something within me shudders at the very idea.

"I'm sorry," I say evenly, gathering my courage. "I'm not ready for this. Can we discuss it again at some point later?"

His expression hardens, his eyes turning into chips of blue ice. Abruptly releasing me, he takes a step back. "All right." His voice is as cold as his gaze. "If that's how you want to play it, my pet, we'll do it your way."

Reaching into his pocket, he pulls out a smartphone and begins typing on it.

A sick sensation curls low in my stomach. "What

are you doing?" When he doesn't answer, I repeat my question, trying not to sound as panicked as I feel. "Julian, what are you doing?"

"Something I should've done a long time ago," he finally replies, looking up at me as he pockets his phone. "You still dream of him, don't you? Of that boy you once wanted?"

My heart stops beating for a second. "What? No, I don't! Julian, I promise you, Jake has nothing to do with this—"

He interrupts with a curt, dismissive gesture. "I should've removed him from your life a long time ago. Now I will remedy that oversight. Maybe then you will accept that you are with me now, not him."

"I *am* with you!" I don't know what to say, how to convince Julian not to do it. Stepping toward him, I grip his hands, the heat of his skin burning my frozen fingers. "Listen to me, I love *you*, only you . . . He doesn't mean anything to me—he hasn't for a long time!"

"Good." His expression doesn't soften, though his fingers fold around mine, imprisoning them in his grasp. "Then you shouldn't care what happens to him."

"No, that's not how it works! I care because he's a human being, an innocent bystander in all of this, and for no other reason!" I'm shaking so hard now, my teeth are chattering. "He doesn't deserve to be punished for my sins—"

"It doesn't matter to me what he deserves." Julian's

voice lashes at me like a whip as he uses his grip on my hands to pull me closer. Leaning down, he grits out, "I want him out of your mind and out of your life, do you understand me?"

The burning in my eyes intensifies, my vision blurring from unspilled tears. Through the haze of panic clouding my mind, I realize there's only one thing I can do to stop this—only one way I can prevent Jake's death.

"All right," I whisper in defeat, staring at the monster I'd fallen in love with. "I will do it. I will marry you."

* * *

The next hour feels surreal.

After calling off his henchmen, Julian introduces me to a wizened old man wearing a Catholic priest's robes. The man doesn't speak English, so I nod and pretend to follow along as he chatters at me in rapid-fire Spanish. It's embarrassing to admit, but the only Spanish I know is from my classes in high school. When I was growing up, my parents spoke English in the house, and I didn't spend enough time with my abuela to pick up anything more than a few basic phrases.

When my introduction to the priest is over, Julian leads me to another room—a small office that has a desk and two chairs. As soon as we get there, two young women enter the room. One of them brings in a long white dress, while the other one carries shoes and accessories. They're friendly and excited, chatting with me in a mix of Spanish and English as they start doing my hair, and I try to respond in kind. However, my answers come out awkward and wooden, the growing knot of dread in my chest preventing me from acting like the eager young bride they expect to see. Noticing my lack of enthusiasm, Julian shoots me a dark glare, then disappears, leaving the women to fuss over me.

By the time they're done prettifying me, I'm both mentally and physically exhausted. Even though Chicago and Bogotá are in the same time zone, I feel jet-lagged and utterly drained. A strange numbness steals over me, easing the churning tension in my stomach.

It's happening. It's really happening. Julian and I are getting married.

The panic that gripped me earlier is gone, having mellowed into a type of weary resignation. I don't know what I expected from a man who held me captive for fifteen months. A reasonable discussion on the pros and cons of getting married at this point in our relationship? I mentally snort. *Yeah, sure.* In hindsight, it's clear that our four-month separation had dulled my memories of those initial terrifying weeks on the island—that I had somehow managed to romanticize my abductor in my mind. I had foolishly begun to think that things could be different between us, to believe I had some say in my life.

"All done." The woman who was working on my hair gives me a beaming smile, interrupting my thoughts. "Beautiful, señorita, very beautiful. Now, please, the dress, and then we make your face nice."

They give me silk undergarments to go with the dress, and then tactfully turn away, giving me some privacy. Not wanting to drag it out, I swiftly change and pull on the dress—which, like the ring, fits me perfectly.

Now all that remains is makeup and accessories, and the two women make short work of that. Ten minutes later, I'm ready for my wedding.

"Come look," one of them says, leading me toward the corner of the room. There is a full-length mirror there that I hadn't noticed before, and I stare in stunned silence at my reflection, hardly recognizing the image I see.

The girl in the mirror is beautiful and sophisticated, with her hair styled in an artful updo and her makeup tastefully done. The mermaid-style dress is just right for her slim frame, with a sweetheart bodice exposing the graceful slope of her neck and shoulders. Teardrop-shaped diamond earrings decorate her small earlobes, and a matching necklace sparkles around her neck. She's everything a bride should be . . . especially if one ignores the shadows in her eyes.

My parents would've been so proud.

The thought pops out of nowhere, and I realize for

the first time that I'm getting married without my family there, that my parents won't get to see their only child on that special day. A dull ache spreads through my chest at the thought. There will be no wedding-dress shopping with my mom, no cake-tasting with my dad.

No bachelorette party with my friends at an all-male strip club.

I try to imagine how Julian might react to something like that, and an unexpected snicker escapes my lips. I have a strong suspicion those poor strippers would leave the club in body bags if I so much as ventured near them.

A knock on the door interrupts my semi-hysterical musings. The women rush to answer it, and I hear Julian speaking to them in Spanish. Turning toward me, they wave goodbye and quickly leave.

As soon as they're gone, Julian enters the room.

Despite everything, I can't help staring at him. Dressed in a crisp black tuxedo that hugs his tall, powerful frame to perfection, my husband-to-be is simply breathtaking. My mind flashes to our sex session on the plane, and wet heat gathers between my thighs even as my bruises begin to throb at the reminder. He's studying me too, his gaze hot and proprietary as it moves over my body.

"Isn't it bad luck for the groom to see the bride before the ceremony?" I inject as much sarcasm into my voice as I can, trying to ignore the effect he has on my senses. At this moment, I hate him almost as much as I love him, and the fact that I want to jump his bones bothers me to no small degree. I should be used to it by now, but I still find it disturbing, the way my brain and my body don't communicate in his presence.

A small smile tugs at the corner of his sensual mouth. "It's okay, my pet. I think you and I are past such concerns. Are you ready?"

I nod and walk toward him. There's no point in delaying the inevitable; one way or another, we're getting married today. Julian offers me his arm, and I loop my hand through the crook of his elbow, letting him lead me back into the beautiful room with the pulpit.

The priest is already waiting for us, as is Lucas. There is also a sizable camera sitting on top of a tall tripod.

"Is that for wedding pictures?" I ask in surprise, stopping in the entryway.

"Of course." Julian's eyes gleam at me. "Memories and all that good stuff."

Uh-huh. I can't fathom why Julian wants this—the dress, the tux, the church. The entire thing is confusing to me. We're not entering into a loving union; he's simply binding me to him tighter, formalizing his ownership. All these accoutrements are meaningless, especially since Lucas is the only one who'll witness the event.

The thought makes my chest ache again. "Julian," I

say quietly, looking up at him, "can I call my parents now? I want to tell them about this. I want to let them know I'm getting married." I'm almost certain he will refuse my request, but I feel compelled to ask regardless.

To my surprise, he smiles at me. "If you wish, my pet. In fact, after you talk to them, they can watch our ceremony on a live video feed. Lucas can set that up for us."

I gape at him in shock. He wants my parents to watch the wedding? To see *him*—the man who kidnapped their daughter? For a moment, I feel like I entered an alternate universe, but then the sheer genius of his plan dawns on me.

"You want me to introduce you to them, don't you?" I whisper, staring at him. "You want me to tell them that I came with you of my own free will, to show them how happy we are together. Then you won't have to worry about the authorities or anyone else coming after you. I'll be just another girl who fell for a handsome, wealthy man and ran off with him. These pictures . . . that video . . . it's all about staging a show . . ."

His smile widens. "How you act and what you say to them is entirely up to you, my pet," he says silkily. "They can witness a joyous occasion, or you can tell them you were abducted again. It's your choice, Nora. You can do whatever you wish."

CHAPTER FIVE

❖ JULIAN ❖

Her dark eyes are wide and unblinking as she stares at me, and I know exactly what her choice will be. As far as her parents are concerned, she'll be the happiest bride in the world.

She'll put on the best act of her life.

Anger and something else—something I don't care to examine closely—churns in my gut at the thought. Rationally I understand her hesitation. I know what I am, what I have done to her. A smart woman would run as fast as she could—and Nora has always been smarter, more perceptive than most.

She's also young. I forget that sometimes. In the comfortable world of middle-class America, few women get married at her age. It's possible that marriage is not something she thought about yet; in fact, it's likely, given that she had been in high school when I met her.

Rationally I understand all that . . . but rationality has nothing to do with the savage emotions seething under my skin. I want to string her up, whip her, and then fuck her until she's raw and begging for mercy— until she admits that she's mine, that she can't fucking live without me.

I don't do any of that, though. Instead I smile coolly and wait for her decision.

She inclines her head in a small nod. "All right." Her voice is barely audible. "I'll do it. I'll tell them all about our love affair."

I conceal my satisfaction. "As you wish, my pet. I'll have Lucas set up a secure connection for you."

And leaving her standing there, I walk over to Lucas to discuss the logistics of that specific operation.

* * *

I ask Padre Diaz to give us an hour before starting the ceremony and then sit down on one of the benches, giving Nora some privacy to talk to her parents. Of course, I'm monitoring her conversation through a little bluetooth device in my ear, but she doesn't need to know that.

Leaning back against the wall, I get comfortable and prepare to be entertained.

Her mother picks up on the first ring.

"Hi Mom . . . it's me." Nora's voice is cheerful and upbeat, practically brimming with excitement. I stifle a smile; she's going to be even better at this than I thought.

"Nora, honey!" Gabriela Leston's voice is filled with relief. "I'm so glad you called. I tried calling you five times today, but your phone kept going to voicemail. I was about to go over there in person—oh, wait, what number are you calling from?"

"Mom, don't freak out, but I'm not at home, okay?" Nora's tone is soothing, but I wince internally. I don't know much about normal parents, but I'm pretty sure saying the words 'don't freak out' ensures that they do exactly that.

"What do you mean?" Her mother's voice immediately sharpens. "Where are you?"

Nora clears her throat. "Um, I'm in Colombia, actually."

"WHAT?" I flinch at the earsplitting shout. "What do you mean, you're in Colombia?"

"Mom, you don't understand, it's great news . . ." And Nora launches into an explanation of how we had fallen in love on the island, how devastated she had been when she'd thought I was dead—and how ecstatic she was to learn that I'm alive.

After she's done, there is only silence on the phone. "Are you telling me that you're with him now?" her mother finally asks, her voice hoarse and strained. "That he came back for you?"

"Yes, exactly." Nora's tone is jubilant. "Don't you see, Mom? I couldn't really talk to you about any of this before because it was too difficult—because I thought I'd lost him. But now we're together again, and there's something . . . something *amazing* that I have to tell you."

"What is it?" Her mother sounds understandably wary.

"We're getting married!"

There is another long silence on the other end of the line. Then: "You're getting married . . . to *him*?"

I suppress another smile as Nora starts trying to convince her mother that I am not as bad as they think—that it was a combination of unfortunate circumstances that resulted in her kidnapping and that things are very different between us now. I'm not sure if Gabriela Leston is buying this, but she doesn't really need to. The recording of this conversation will be distributed to key individuals in certain government agencies, helping soothe their ruffled feathers. I'm too valuable for them to fuck with, but it still doesn't hurt to play along. Perception is everything, and Nora as my wife is much more palatable to them than Nora as my captive.

I could've married her earlier, but I was trying to

keep her hidden, keep her safe. That's why I abducted her and took her to my island: so no one would find out about her existence and her importance to me. Now that the secret is out, however, I want the entire world to know that she's mine—that if they dare touch her, they will pay. News of my vendetta against Al-Quadar is starting to filter through the sewers of the underworld, and I've made sure that the rumors are even more brutal than the reality.

It's those rumors that will keep Nora's family safe—that and the security detail I put on her parents. It's unlikely anyone would try to get to me through my in-laws—I'm not exactly known as a family man—but I am not taking any chances. The last thing I want is for Nora to grieve for her parents the way she's still grieving for Beth.

By the time Nora is wrapping up her conversation, Padre Diaz starts getting impatient. I give him a warning look, and he immediately stops fidgeting, all visible traces of annoyance fading from his features. The good Padre has known me since I was a boy, and he knows when he should exercise caution.

When I glance in Nora's direction again, she waves to me, motioning for me to approach. I get up and walk over to her, turning off my bluetooth device on the way. As I get close, I hear her saying, "Listen, Mom, let me introduce you to him, okay? I'll ask him to put us on video—that way it'll be almost like we're all meeting in person . . . Yeah, we'll connect with you in a couple of minutes." And hanging up, she looks up at me expectantly.

"Lucas." I barely raise my voice, but he's already there, carrying a laptop with a secure connection. Placing it on a windowsill, he props it up so that the little camera points at us. A minute later, the video call is established, and Gabriela Leston's face fills the screen. Tony Leston—Nora's father—is behind her. Both pairs of dark eyes immediately turn toward me, studying me with a peculiar mix of hostility and curiosity.

"Mom, Dad, this is Julian," Nora says softly, and I incline my head with a small smile. Lucas walks back to the other end of the room, leaving us alone.

"It's very nice to meet you both." I purposefully keep my voice cool and steady. "I'm sure Nora has already filled you in on everything. I apologize for the speed with which this is happening, but I would love it if you could be a part of our wedding. I know it would mean a great deal to Nora to have her parents present, even if it is remotely." There is nothing I can say to the Lestons to justify my actions or make them like me, so I don't even try. Nora is mine now, and they will have to learn to accept that fact.

Nora's father opens his mouth to say something, but his wife elbows him sharply. "All right, Julian," she says slowly, staring at me with eyes eerily similar to her daughter's. "So you are marrying Nora. May I ask where you're going to be living after that, and whether we're going to see her again?"

I smile at her. Another smart, intuitive woman. "For the first few months, we'll probably be here, in Colombia," I explain, keeping my tone light and friendly. "There are certain business matters that I have to take care of. After that, however, we'd be more than happy to come for a visit—or to have you visit us."

Gabriela nods. "I see." The tension on her face remains, though relief briefly flickers in her eyes. "And what about Nora's future plans? What about college?"

"I will make sure she gets a good education and has a chance to pursue her art." I give the Lestons a level look. "Of course, I'm sure you realize that Nora doesn't need to worry about money anymore. Neither do you. I am more than comfortable, financially, and I always take care of my own."

Tony Leston's eyes narrow with anger. "You can't buy our daughter—" he starts saying, only to be elbowed into silence again by his wife. Nora's mother clearly has a better grasp on the situation; she realizes that this conversation could just as easily not be happening.

I lean closer to the camera. "Tony, Gabriela," I say quietly, "I understand your concern. However, in less than a half hour, Nora will be my wife—my responsibility. I can assure you that I will take care of her and do my best to ensure her happiness. You have nothing to worry about."

Tony's jaw tightens, but he remains silent this time.

It's Gabriela who speaks next. "We would appreciate it if we could talk to her on a regular basis," she says evenly. "To make sure she's as happy as she seems today."

"Of course." I have no problem making that concession. "Now, the ceremony is starting in a few minutes, so we need to set up a better video feed for you. It was a pleasure meeting you both," I say politely, then close the laptop.

Turning, I see Nora watching me with some bemusement. In the long white dress and with her hair all done, she looks like a princess—which I suppose makes me the evil dragon stealing her away.

Inexplicably amused by the thought, I lift my hand and run my fingers down her baby-soft cheek. "Are you ready, my pet?"

"Yes, I think so," she murmurs, staring up at me. They did something to her eyes, those women I hired, making her eyes seem even larger and more mysterious. Her mouth also looks softer and shinier than usual, utterly fuckable. A sharp surge of lust catches me off-guard, and I force myself to take a step back before I do something sacrilegious at my own wedding.

"The video is all set up," Lucas informs me, coming up to us.

"Thank you, Lucas," I say. Then, turning toward Nora, I take her hand and lead her toward Padre Diaz.

CHAPTER SIX

❖ NORA ❖

The ceremony itself takes only about twenty minutes. Cognizant of the camera trained on us, I smile widely and do my best to look like a happy, glowing bride.

I still don't fully understand my own reluctance. After all, I'm marrying the man I love. When I thought he was dead, I wanted to die myself, and it took all of my strength to survive from one day to the next. I don't want to be with anyone but Julian . . . and yet I can't shake the chill deep inside.

He handled my parents smoothly, I will give him that. I'm not sure what I had been expecting, but the calm, almost civil conversation that took place hadn't been it. He had been in control the entire time, his matter-of-fact attitude leaving no room for tearful accusations and recriminations. He had apologized for the rushed wedding, but not for abducting me in the first place—and I know it's because he feels no guilt about that. In his mind, he has a right to me. It's as simple as that.

After a lengthy speech in Spanish, Padre Diaz begins speaking to Julian. I catch a few words—something about spouse, love, protection—and then I hear Julian's deep voice responding "Sí, quiero."

It's my turn next. Looking up at Julian, I meet his gaze. There is a warm smile on his lips, but his eyes tell a different story. His eyes reflect hunger and need, and underneath it all, a dark, all-consuming possessiveness.

"Sí, quiero," I say quietly, repeating Julian's words. *Yes, I do. Yes, I want.* My rudimentary Spanish is good enough to translate that at least.

Julian's smile deepens. Reaching into his pocket, he takes out another ring—a slim, diamond-studded band that matches my engagement ring—and slides it onto my nerveless finger. Then he presses a platinum band into my palm and extends his left hand to me.

His palm is almost twice the size of mine, his fingers long and masculine. He has a man's hands—strong and roughened with calluses. Hands that can pleasure or hurt with equal ease.

Taking a deep breath, I slide the wedding band onto

Julian's left ring finger and look up at him again, only half-listening as Padre Diaz concludes the ceremony. Staring at Julian's beautiful features, all I can think about is that it's done.

The man who kidnapped me is now my husband.

* * *

After the ceremony, I say goodbye to my parents, assuring them that I will speak to them again soon. My mom is crying, and my dad is wearing a stony expression that usually means he's extremely upset.

"Mom, Dad, I promise I'll be in contact," I tell them, trying to hold back my own tears. "I won't disappear on you again. Everything is going to be fine. You have nothing to worry about . . ."

"I promise she will call you very soon," Julian adds, and after a few more tearful goodbyes, Lucas disconnects the video feed.

The next half hour is spent taking pictures all over the beautiful church. Then we change back into our regular clothes and head back to the airport.

At this point, it's evening and I'm completely exhausted. The stress of the past couple of hours, combined with all the travel, has made me nearly comatose, and I close my eyes, leaning back against the black leather seat as the car winds its way through the dark streets of Bogotá. I don't want to think about anything; I just want to empty my mind and relax.

Shifting, I try to find a better position, one that doesn't place too much weight on my still-tender bottom.

"Tired, baby?" Julian murmurs, placing his hand on my leg. His fingers squeeze lightly, massaging my thigh, and I force my heavy eyelids to open.

"A bit," I admit, turning toward him. "I'm not used to this much flying—or marrying."

He grins at me, his teeth flashing white in the darkness. "Well, luckily you won't have to go through this experience again. The marrying, I mean. I can't promise anything about the flying."

Maybe I'm overly tired, but that strikes me as ridiculously funny for some reason. A giggle escapes my throat, first one, then another, until I'm laughing uncontrollably, all but rolling on the backseat of the car.

Julian watches me calmly, and when my laughter finally begins to quiet down, he pulls me into his lap and kisses me, claiming my mouth with a long, fierce kiss that literally steals my breath away. By the time he lets me come up for air, I can barely remember my own name, much less what I was laughing about before.

We're both panting, our breath intermingling as we stare at each other. There's hunger in his gaze, but there's also something more—an almost violent longing that goes deeper than simple lust. A strange tightness squeezes my chest, and I feel like I'm falling further, losing even more of myself. "What do you want from me, Julian?" I whisper, lifting my hand to cradle the hard contours of his jaw. "What do you need?"

He doesn't answer, but his large hand covers mine, holding it pressed against his face for a few moments. He closes his eyes, as though absorbing the sensation, and when he opens them, the moment is gone.

Shifting me off his lap, he drapes a heavy arm over my shoulders and settles me comfortably against his side. "Get some rest, my pet," he murmurs into my hair. "We still have a ways to go before we get home."

* * *

I fall asleep on the plane again, so I have no idea how long the flight is. Julian shakes me awake after we land, and I follow him sleepily off the plane.

Warm, humid air hits me as soon as we disembark, so thick it feels like a damp blanket. Bogotá had been much warmer than Chicago, with the temperature somewhere in the high sixties, but this . . . this feels like I stepped into a wet sauna. With my winter boots and a fleece sweater, I feel like I'm being cooked alive.

"Bogotá is at a much higher elevation," Julian says, as though reading my mind. "Down here, it's tierra caliente—the low-elevation hot zone."

"Where are we?" I ask, waking up a bit more. I can hear the chirping of insects, and the smell in the air is that of lush green vegetation, of the tropics. "Which part of the country, I mean?"

"The southeast," Julian replies, leading me toward an SUV waiting on the other side of the runway. "We're actually right on the edge of the Amazon rainforest."

I lift my hand to rub at the corner of my eye. I don't know much about Colombian geography, but that sounds very remote to me. "Are we near some villages or towns?"

"No," Julian says. "That's the beauty of this location, my pet. We're completely isolated and safe. Nobody will bother us here."

We reach the car, and he helps me inside. Lucas joins us a couple of minutes later, and then we're off, driving down an unpaved road through a heavily wooded area.

It's pitch-black outside, the headlights of the car our only source of illumination, and I peer curiously through the darkness, trying to discern our destination. All I can see, however, are trees and more trees.

Abandoning that futile effort, I decide to get more comfortable instead. It's cooler in the car with the air conditioning working full-blast, but I'm still too hot, so I take off my sweater. Thankfully, I'm wearing a tank top underneath. As the chilly air blows across my heated skin, I sigh with relief, fanning myself to accelerate the cooling process.

"I have clothes for you here that are more weather-appropriate," Julian says, observing my actions with a half-smile. "I probably should've thought to bring them with me, but I was far too eager to retrieve you."

"Oh?" I glance at him, absurdly pleased by his admission.

"I came after you as soon as I could," he murmurs, his eyes gleaming in the dark interior of the car. "You didn't think I'd leave you alone for long, did you?"

"No, I didn't," I say softly. And it's the truth. If there's one thing I've always been sure of, it's that Julian wants me. I'm not sure if he loves me—if he's capable of loving anyone—but I've never doubted the strength of his desire for me. He risked his life for me back at that warehouse, and I know he would do so again. It's a certainty that goes bone-deep and fills me with a peculiar sense of comfort.

Closing my eyes, I lean back against the seat with another sigh. The dichotomy of my emotions makes my head hurt. How can I be upset with Julian for forcing me to marry him and at the same time be glad that he couldn't wait to abduct me again? What sane person feels that way?

"We've arrived," Julian says, interrupting my musings, and I open my eyes, realizing that the car had stopped.

In front of us is a sprawling two-story mansion surrounded by several smaller structures. Bright outdoor lights illuminate everything in the vicinity, and I can see wide green lawns and lush, meticulously maintained landscaping. Julian wasn't exaggerating when he called this place an estate.

I can also see some of the security measures, and I gaze around curiously as Julian helps me out of the car and leads me toward the main building. On the far edges of the property, there are towers spaced a few dozen yards apart, with armed men visible at the top of each one.

It's almost as if we're in prison, except that these guards are meant to keep the bad people out, not in.

"You grew up here?" I ask Julian as we approach the house. It's a beautiful white building with stately columns at the front. It reminds me a bit of Scarlett O'Hara's plantation from *Gone with the Wind*.

"I did." He shoots me a sidelong glance. "I spent most of my time here until I was about seven or eight. After that, I was usually in the cities with my father, helping him with business."

After we walk up the porch steps, Julian stops at the doorway and bends down to lift me into his arms. Before I can say anything, he carries me over the threshold, setting me back on my feet once we're inside. "No reason why we can't observe this little tradition," he murmurs with a mischievous grin, maintaining his hold on my sides as he looks down at me.

My lips twitch in an answering smile. I can never resist Julian when he's being playful like this. "Ah, yes, I forgot that you're Mr. Traditional today," I tease, purposefully trying not to think about the forced nature of our marriage. It's important for my sanity to keep the good times separate from the bad, to live in the moment as much as possible. "And here I thought you just felt like picking me up."

"I did," he admits, his grin widening. "It's the first time my inclinations and tradition have coincided, though, so why don't we go with 'observing tradition'?"

"I'm game," I say softly, gazing up at him. In this moment, my mind is firmly in the 'good times' camp, and I would gladly go along with anything he wants, do anything he wants.

"Señor Esguerra?" An uncertain female voice interrupts us, and I turn to see a middle-aged woman standing there. She's wearing a black short-sleeved dress, with a white apron wrapped around her rounded frame. "Everything is ready, just as you requested," she says in accented English, watching us with barely restrained curiosity. "Should I serve you dinner?"

"No, thank you, Ana," Julian replies, his hand resting possessively on my hip. "Just bring a tray with some sandwiches to our room, please. Nora is tired from our travels." Then he looks down at me. "Nora, this is Ana, our housekeeper. Ana, this is Nora, my wife."

Ana's brown eyes widen. Apparently the 'wife' bit is as much of a shock to her as it had been to me. She recovers quickly, though. "Very pleased to meet you, Señora," she says, giving me a wide smile. "Welcome."

"Thank you, Ana. It's nice to meet you too." I smile

back, ignoring the sharp pain squeezing my chest. This housekeeper is nothing like Beth, but I can't help thinking of the woman who had become my friend—and of her cruel, pointless death.

No, don't go there, Nora. The last thing I need is to wake up screaming from another nightmare.

"Please make sure we're not disturbed tonight," Julian instructs Ana, "unless it's something urgent."

"Yes, Señor," she murmurs, and disappears through the wide double doors leading out of the entryway area.

"Ana is one of the staff here," Julian explains as he guides me toward a wide, curved staircase. "She's been with my family in one capacity or another for most of her life."

"She seems very nice," I say, studying my new home as we walk up the stairs. I've never been inside such a lavish residence, and I can hardly believe I'm going to be living here. The decor is a tasteful mix of old-fashioned charm and modern elegance, with gleaming wooden floors and abstract art on the walls. I suspect the gilded picture frames alone are more expensive than anything I had in my studio apartment back home. "How many people are on the staff?"

"There are two who always take care of the house," Julian answers. "Ana, whom you've just met, and Rosa, who's the maid. You'll probably meet her tomorrow. There are also several gardeners, handymen, and others who oversee the property as a whole." Pausing in front of one of the doors upstairs, he opens it for me. "Here we are. Our bedroom."

Our bedroom. That has a very domestic ring to it. On the island, I had my own room, and even though Julian slept with me most nights, it still felt like my private space—something I apparently wouldn't have here.

Stepping inside, I cautiously survey the bedroom.

Like the rest of the house, it has an opulent, old-fashioned feel to it, despite several modern touches. There is a thick blue rug on the floor, and a massive four-poster bed in the center. Everything is done in shades of blue and cream, with some gold and bronze mixed in. The drapes covering the windows are thick and heavy, like in a luxury hotel, and there are a few more abstract paintings on the walls.

It's beautiful and intimidating, like the man who is now my husband.

"Why don't we take a bath?" Julian says softly, stepping up behind me. His powerful arms fold around me, his fingers reaching for my belt buckle. "I think we could both use one."

"Sure, that sounds good," I murmur, letting him undress me. It makes me feel like a doll—or maybe a princess, given our surroundings. As Julian tugs off my shirt and pushes down my jeans, his hands brush against my bare skin, causing tingles of heat to ripple down to my core.

Our wedding night. Tonight is our wedding night. My breathing quickens from a combination of arousal and nerves. I don't know what Julian has in store for me, but the hard ridge pressing against my lower back leaves no doubt that he intends to fuck me again.

When I am completely naked, I turn to face him and watch as he takes off his own clothes, his well-defined muscles gleaming in the soft light coming from the recessed ceiling. His body is slightly leaner than before, and there is a new scar near his ribcage. Still, he's the most striking man I have ever seen. He's already fully erect, his thick, long cock jutting out at me, and I swallow, my sex clenching at the sight. At the same time, I am cognizant of a faint soreness deep inside and the continued tenderness of my bruised bottom.

I want him, but I don't know if I can handle any more pain today.

"Julian . . ." I hesitate, unsure how to best phrase it. "Is there any way . . . Can we—?"

He steps toward me, framing my face with his large hands. His eyes glitter brightly as he looks down at me. "Yes," he whispers, understanding my unspoken question. "Yes, baby, we can. I will give you the wedding night of your dreams."

CHAPTER SEVEN

❖ JULIAN ❖

Bending down, I hook my arm under her knees and pick her up. She barely weighs anything, her small frame impossibly light as I carry her to the bathroom, where Ana prepared the jacuzzi for us.

My wife. Nora is now my wife. The fierce satisfaction I feel at the thought makes no sense, but I don't intend to dwell on it. She's mine, and that's all that matters. I will fuck her and pamper her, and she will fulfill my every need, no matter how dark and twisted. She will give me all of herself, and I will take it.

I will take it all, and then I'll demand more.

Tonight, though, I will give her what she wants. I will be sweet and gentle, as tender as any husband with his new bride. The sadist inside me is quiescent for now, content. There will be plenty of time later to punish her for her reluctance at the church. At this moment, I have no desire to hurt her—I just want to hold her, to stroke her silky skin and feel her shuddering with pleasure in my arms. My cock is hard, throbbing with need, but the hunger is different now, more controlled.

Reaching the large round jacuzzi, I step in and lower both of us into the bubbling water, sitting down with Nora ensconced on my lap. She lets out a blissful sigh and relaxes against me, closing her eyes and putting her head on my shoulder. Her glossy hair tickles my skin, the long ends floating in the water. I shift slightly, letting the strong jets pummel my back, and feel the tension gradually draining out of me despite my lingering arousal.

For a couple of minutes, I am content to just sit there, holding her cradled in my arms. Despite the sweltering heat outside, the temperature inside the house is cool, and the hot water feels good on my skin. Soothing. I imagine it feels good to Nora too, easing the soreness from the bruises I inflicted earlier.

Lifting my hand, I lazily stroke her back, marveling at the smoothness of her golden skin. My dick twitches, clamoring for more, but I'm in no rush this time. I want to prolong this moment, to heighten the anticipation for us both.

"This is nice," she murmurs after a while, tilting her head back to gaze at me. Her cheeks are flushed from the heat of the water and her lids are partially lowered, making her look like she's already been thoroughly fucked. "I wish I could take a bath like this every day."

"You can," I say softly, shifting her off my lap so she's facing me and reaching under the water to pick up her right foot. "You can do whatever you want here. It's your home now."

Applying light pressure to her sole, I begin to massage it the way she likes, enjoying the quiet moans that escape her lips at my touch. Her feet are small and pretty, like the rest of her. Sexy even, with the pink polish on her slender toes. Giving in to a sudden urge, I lift her foot to my mouth and suck on it lightly, swirling my tongue around each toe. She gasps, staring at me, and I can hear her breathing picking up, see her eyes darkening with arousal. This turns her on, I realize, and the knowledge makes my dick harden further.

Holding her gaze, I reach for Nora's other foot and give it the same treatment. Her toes curl at the touch of my tongue and her breathing becomes unsteady, her own tongue coming out to moisten her lips. The ache in my groin intensifying, I release her foot and slowly slide my hand up the inside of her leg, feeling her thigh muscles quivering with tension as I approach her sex. My fingers brush against her pussy, parting the soft folds. Then I push the tip of my middle finger into her small opening, using my thumb to press on her clit at the same time.

Inside, she's impossibly hot and slick, her inner walls gripping my finger so tightly that my cock jumps in response. She lets out a soft moan, lifting her hips toward me, and my finger slides deeper into her, causing a choked cry to issue from her throat. She scoots back reflexively, as though trying to pull away, but I wrap my free hand around her arm and pull her toward me, gathering her against my side. "Don't fight it, baby," I murmur, holding her still as I begin to fuck her with my finger, my thumb applying even, rhythmic pressure to her clit. "Just let yourself feel . . . Yes, that's it . . ."

Her head falls back and her eyes close, an expression of intense rapture appearing on her face as she lets out another moan.

Beautiful. She's so fucking beautiful. I can't tear my gaze away, drinking in the sight of her coming apart in my arms. Her slim body arches and tightens, and then she cries out as her flesh ripples around my finger in release, the squeezing motion making my dick throb in agonized need.

I can't take this much longer. Withdrawing my finger, I slide my hands under her body and pick her up as I rise to my feet. She opens her eyes and loops her arms around my neck, watching me intently as I step out of the jacuzzi and begin carrying her back to the bedroom. We're both dripping with water, but I can't bear to stop for even a moment. I don't give a fuck about getting our sheets wet right now—I don't give a fuck about anything except her.

Reaching the bed, I put her down, my hands shaking with violent lust. On any other night, I would already be inside her, pounding her tight little pussy until I explode, but not tonight. Tonight is for her. Tonight I will give her what she asked for—a wedding night with a lover, not a monster.

She watches me, her dark eyes slumberous with desire as I climb onto the bed between her legs and bend over her soft, tender flesh. Ignoring my aching cock, I begin with small kisses on the insides of her thighs and then move up until I reach my goal: her wet cleft, pink and swollen from her earlier orgasm.

Pulling her folds apart with my fingers, I lick the area directly around her clit, tasting her essence, then push my tongue inside, penetrating her as deeply as I can. She shudders, her hands finding their way down to my head, and I feel her nails digging into my skull. One of her fingers brushes against my scar, sending a bolt of pain through me, but I ignore that too, focusing solely on pleasuring her, on making her come. I revel in every drop of moisture I wring from her body, every gasp and moan that escapes her lips as my tongue works over the bundle of nerves at the peak of her sex. She begins to tremble, her thighs vibrating with tension, and I taste a spurt of salty-sweet moisture as she comes with a helpless cry, her hips lifting off the bed and her pussy grinding against my tongue.

When she finally goes limp, breathing heavily from her release, I crawl over her and kiss the delicate shell of her ear. I'm not done with her yet, not by a long shot.

"You're so sweet," I whisper, feeling her shiver at the heat of my breath. My cock throbs harder at her response, my balls full to bursting, and my next words come out low and rough, almost guttural. "So fucking sweet . . . I want to fuck you so badly, but I won't"—I tongue the underside of her earlobe, causing her hands to clutch convulsively at my sides—"not until you come for me again. You think you can come for me, baby?"

"I . . . I don't think so . . ." She gasps, twisting in my arms as my mouth moves down to the smooth column of her throat, leaving a warm, damp trail on her skin.

"Oh, I think you can," I murmur, my right hand slipping down her body to feel her soaking-wet pussy. As my lips travel over her shoulders and upper chest, I massage her swollen clit with my fingers, and she begins to pant again, her breathing becoming erratic as my mouth approaches her breasts. Her rosy nipples are hard, practically begging for my touch, and I close my lips over one taut bud, sucking on it strongly. She lets out a sound that's halfway between a moan and a whimper, and I turn my attention to the other nipple, sucking on it until she's trembling underneath me, the moisture from her sex inundating my hand. Before she can reach her peak, however, I slither down her body and taste her again, my tongue pushing inside her just as her contractions begin anew.

I lick her until her orgasm is fully over, then I move up over her again, supporting myself with my right elbow. Using my left hand, I grasp her jaw, forcing her to meet my gaze. Her eyes look unfocused, clouded with the aftermath of pleasure, and I lower my head, claiming her mouth with a deep, thorough kiss. I know she can taste herself on my lips, and the thought excites me, causing my pulse to spike. At the same time, her arms fold around my neck, embracing me, and I feel her breasts pushing against my chest, her nipples like hard little pebbles.

Holy fuck. I have to have her. Now.

My self-control fraying, I continue kissing her as I use my knees to spread open her thighs. Pressing the head of my cock against her opening, I slide my left hand into her hair to cradle the back of her skull.

Then I begin to push into her body.

She's small inside too, her pussy tighter than any I've known before. I can feel her wet flesh gradually engulfing me, stretching for me, and my spine tingles, my balls drawing up against my body. I'm not even fully inside her yet, and I'm about to explode from the mind-numbing pleasure. *Slow*, I harshly remind myself. *Go slow.*

She tears her mouth away from mine, her breath

coming in soft little pants against my ear. "I want you," she whispers, her legs coming up to clasp my hips. The movement brings me deeper into her, making me groan in desperate need. "Please, Julian . . ."

Her words destroy whatever shreds of restraint I still possess. *To hell with going slow.* A low growl vibrates deep within my chest, and my hand fists in her hair as I begin to thrust into her, savagely, relentlessly. She cries out, and her arms tighten around my neck, her body eagerly welcoming my ruthless assault.

My mind explodes with sensations, with overwhelming ecstasy. This, right here, is what I want, what I need. Why I will never let her go. Our bodies strain together on the bed, wet sheets tangling around our limbs as I lose myself in her, in the sounds and smells of hot, no-holds-barred sex. Nora is like liquid fire in my arms, her slim body arching against me, her legs twining around my thighs. Each thrust brings me deeper into her until I feel like we're fusing together, melding into one another.

She reaches her peak first, her pussy squeezing me even tighter. I hear her strangled cry as she bites my shoulder in the throes of her orgasm, and then I'm there, shuddering over her as my seed shoots out in continuous heated spurts.

Breathing harshly, I sink down on top of her, my arms no longer able to support my weight. Every muscle in my body is shaking from the force of my release, and I'm covered with a thin veil of sweat. After a few moments, I muster the strength to roll over onto my back, pulling her to lie on top of me.

It shouldn't be this intense again, not after the way we fucked earlier, but it is. It always is. There's never a moment when I don't want her, when I don't think about her. If I ever lost her—

No. I refuse to think about that. It won't happen. I won't let it.

I will do whatever it takes to keep her safe.

Safe from everyone but me.

CHAPTER EIGHT

❖ NORA ❖

When I wake up in the morning, Julian is already gone.

Climbing out of bed, I head straight for the shower, feeling grimy and sticky after last night. We both fell asleep right after sex, too worn out to bother washing up or changing the wet sheets. Then, just before dawn, Julian woke me up by sliding inside me again, his skilled fingers bringing me to orgasm before I was fully awake. It's as if he can't get enough of me after our long separation, his already-strong libido going into overdrive.

Of course, I can't get enough of him either.

A smile curves my lips as I remember the searing passion of last night. Julian promised me the wedding night of my dreams, and he certainly delivered. I don't even know how many orgasms I've had over the past twenty-four hours. Of course, now I'm even more sore, my insides raw from so much fucking.

Still, I feel immeasurably better today, both physically and mentally. The bruises on my thighs are less tender to the touch, and I'm no longer feeling quite as overwhelmed. Even the idea of being married to Julian doesn't seem as frightening in the morning light. Nothing has truly changed, except that now there is a piece of paper joining us together, letting the world know that I belong to him. Captor, lover, or husband— it's all the same; the label doesn't alter the reality of our dysfunctional relationship.

Stepping under the shower spray, I tilt my head back, letting the hot water flow over my face. The shower is as luxurious as the rest of the house, the circular stall big enough to accommodate ten people. I wash and scrub every inch of my body until I begin to feel human again. Then I go back into the bedroom to get dressed.

I find an enormous closet in the back of the room, filled mostly with light summer clothes. Remembering the stifling heat outside, I select a simple blue sundress, then slide my feet into a pair of brown flip-flops. It's not the most sophisticated outfit, but it'll do.

I'm ready to explore my new home.

* * *

The estate is huge, much bigger than I thought yesterday. Besides the main house, there are also barracks for the two-hundred-plus guards who patrol the perimeter, and a number of houses occupied by other employees and their families. It's almost like a small town—or maybe some type of military compound.

I learn all this from Ana over breakfast. Apparently Julian left instructions that I was to be fed and shown around when I woke up. Julian himself is occupied with work, as usual.

"Señor Esguerra has an important meeting," Ana explains, serving me a dish she calls *Migas de Arepa*— scrambled eggs made with pieces of corn cakes and a tomato-onion sauce. "He asked me to look after you today, so please let me know if you need anything. After breakfast I can have Rosa give you a tour if you like."

"Thank you, Ana," I say, digging into my food. It's incredibly delicious, the sweetness of the arepas complementing the zesty flavor of the eggs. "A tour would be great."

We chat for a bit as I finish up my meal. In addition to learning about the estate, I find out that Ana has lived in this house most of her life, having started as a young maid working for Julian's father. "That's how I learned English," she says, pouring me a cup of frothy hot chocolate. "Señora Esguerra was American, like you, and she didn't speak any Spanish."

I nod, remembering Julian telling me about his mother. She had been a model in New York City before marrying Julian's father. "So you knew Julian when he was a child?" I ask, sipping the hot, rich drink. Like the eggs, it's unusually flavorful, with hints of clove, cinnamon, and vanilla.

"I did." Ana stops there, as though afraid of saying too much. I give her an encouraging smile, hoping to prod her into telling me more, but she begins to clear off the dishes instead, signaling an end to the conversation.

Sighing, I finish my hot chocolate and get up. I want to learn more about my husband, but I have a feeling Ana may be just as close-mouthed on this topic as Beth.

Beth. The familiar pain shoots through me again, bringing with it a burning rage. Memories of her violent death are never far from my mind, threatening to drown me in hate if I let them. When Julian first told me about what he did to Maria's attackers, I had been horrified . . . but now I understand it. I wish I could somehow lay my hands on the terrorist who killed Beth, make him pay for what he did to her. Even the knowledge that he's dead doesn't pacify my anger; it's always there, eating at me, poisoning me from within.

"Señora, this is Rosa," Ana says, and I turn toward the dining room entrance to see a young dark-haired woman standing there. She looks to be about my age, with a round face and a bright smile. Like Ana, she's wearing a short-sleeved black dress with a white apron. "Rosa, this is Señor Esguerra's new wife, Nora."

Rosa's smile brightens further. "Oh, hello, Señora Esguerra, it's a pleasure to meet you." Her English is even better than Ana's, her accent barely noticeable.

"Thank you, Rosa," I say, taking an immediate liking to the girl. "It's very nice to meet you too. And, please, call me Nora." I look toward the housekeeper. "You too, please, Ana, if you don't mind. I'm not used to the 'Señora' bit." And it's true. It's especially strange to hear myself addressed as Señora Esguerra. Does this mean that Julian's last name is now mine? We haven't discussed this yet, but I suspect Julian would want to follow tradition in this case as well.

Nora Esguerra. My heart beats faster at the thought, some of yesterday's irrational fear returning. For nineteen-and-a-half years, I have been Nora Leston. It's a name that I'm used to, that I'm comfortable with. The idea of changing it makes me deeply uneasy, as though I'm losing another part of myself. As though Julian is stripping me of everything that I used to be, transforming me into someone I barely recognize.

"Of course," Ana says, interrupting my anxious musings. "We're happy to call you anything you wish." Rosa nods vigorously in agreement, beaming at me, and I take a few deep breaths to calm my racing heartbeat.

"Thank you." I manage to give them a smile. "I appreciate it."

"Would you like to see the house before we go outside?" Rosa asks, smoothing her apron with her palms. "Or would you prefer to start outdoors?"

"We can start indoors, if that's okay with you," I tell her. Then I thank Ana for the breakfast, and we begin the tour.

Rosa shows me the downstairs first. There are over a dozen rooms, including a large library stocked with a variety of books, a home theater with a wall-sized TV, and a sizable gym filled with high-end exercise equipment. I'm also pleased to discover that Julian remembered my painting hobby; one of the rooms is set up as an art studio, with blank canvasses lined up in front of a huge south-facing window. "Señor Esguerra had all of this put in a couple of weeks before you came," Rosa tells me, leading me from room to room. "So everything is brand-new."

I blink, surprised to hear that. I had assumed that the art studio was new, since Julian is not into painting, but I didn't realize he'd redone the entire house. "He didn't have a pool put in too, did he?" I joke as we walk down the hall.

"No, the pool was already there," Rosa says in absolute seriousness. "But he did have it renovated." And leading me toward a screened back porch, she shows me an Olympic-sized pool surrounded by tropical greenery. In addition to the pool itself, there are lounge chairs that look amazingly comfortable, huge umbrellas that provide shade from the sun, and several outdoor tables with chairs.

"Nice," I murmur, feeling the hot, humid air on my skin. I have a feeling the pool will come in quite handy in this weather.

Going back indoors, we head upstairs. Besides the master suite, there are a number of bedrooms, each one bigger than my entire apartment back home. "Why is the house so big?" I ask Rosa after we view all the lavishly decorated rooms. "There are only a few people living here, right?"

"Yes, that's true," Rosa confirms. "But this house was built by the older Señor Esguerra, and from what I understand, he entertained a lot here, frequently inviting his business associates to stay over."

"How did you come to work here?" I give Rosa a curious look as we go down the curving staircase. "And learn to speak English so well?"

"Oh, I was born here, on the Esguerra estate," she says breezily. "My father was one of the older Señor's guards, and my mother and older brother also worked for him. Señor's wife—she was American, you see— taught me English when I was a child. I think she was maybe a bit bored here, so she gave lessons to the entire household staff and anyone else who wanted to learn the language. Then she insisted that we speak only

English in the house, even among ourselves, so we could practice."

"I see." Rosa seems chattier than Ana, so I ask her the same question I posed to the housekeeper earlier. "If you grew up here, did you know Julian back then?"

"No, not really." She glances at me as we exit the house onto the front porch. "I was very young, only four years old when your husband left the country, so I don't remember much from when he was a boy. Up until a couple of weeks ago, I saw him here for only a short time after . . ." She swallows, looking down at the ground. "After it all happened."

"After his parents' death?" I ask quietly. I remember Julian telling me that his parents were killed, but he never explained how it happened. He just said it was one of his father's rivals.

"Yes," Rosa says somberly, her bright smile nowhere in sight. "A few years after Julian left, one of the North Coast cartels tried to take over the Esguerra organization. They struck at many of its key operations and even came here, to the estate. A lot of people died that day. My father and brother, too."

I stop in my tracks, staring at her. "Oh God, Rosa, I'm sorry . . ." I feel terrible that I brought up such a painful subject. For some reason, it hadn't occurred to me that people here might've been impacted by the same events that had shaped Julian. "I'm so sorry—"

"It's okay," she says, her expression still strained. "It happened almost twelve years ago."

"You must've been very young then," I say softly. "How old are you now?"

"Twenty-one," she replies as we begin walking down the porch steps. Then she shoots me a curious look, some of her somberness fading. "What about you, Nora, if you don't mind me asking? You seem young as well."

I grin at her. "Nineteen. Twenty in a few months." I'm glad she feels comfortable enough with me to ask personal questions. I don't want to be 'Señora' here, don't want to be treated like some lady of the manor.

She grins back, her former zest for life apparently restored. "I thought so," she says with evident satisfaction. "Ana thought you were even younger when she saw you last night, but she's almost fifty and everyone our age looks like a baby to her. My guess this morning was twenty, and I was right."

I laugh, charmed by her frankness. "You were, indeed."

During the rest of the tour, Rosa peppers me with questions about me and my life back in the States. She's apparently fascinated with America, having watched a number of American movies in an effort to improve her English. "I hope to go there someday," she says wistfully. "See New York City, walk in Times Square among all the bright lights . . ."

"You should definitely go," I tell her. "I only visited New York once, and it was great. Lots of things to do as a tourist."

As we talk, she shows me around the estate, pointing out the guards' barracks that Ana mentioned earlier, and the men's training area on the far side of the compound. The training area consists of an indoor fighting gym, an outdoor shooting range, and what appears to be an obstacle course on a large, grass-covered field. "The guards like to keep in top shape," Rosa explains as we pass by a group of hard-faced men practicing some type of martial arts. "Most of them are former military, and all are very good at what they do."

"Julian trains with them too, right?" I ask, watching in fascination as one man knocks out his opponent with a powerful kick to the head. I know a little self-defense from the lessons I took back home, but it's kid stuff compared to this.

"Oh, yes." Rosa's tone is somewhat reverential. "I've seen Señor Esguerra on the field, and he's as good as any of his men."

"Yes, I'm sure he is," I say, remembering Julian rescuing me from the warehouse. He had been completely in his element, arriving in the night like some angel of death. For a moment, the dark memories threaten to swamp me again, but I push them away, determined not to dwell on the past. Turning away from the fighters, I ask Rosa, "Do you know where he is today, by any chance? Ana said he's in a meeting."

She shrugs in response. "He's probably in his office, in that building over there." She points toward a small modern-looking structure near the main house. "He had it remodeled as well, and he's been spending a lot of time there since his return. I saw Lucas, Peter, and a few others go in there this morning, so I assume Julian is meeting with them."

"Who's Peter?" I ask. I already know Lucas, but I'm hearing Peter's name for the first time.

"He's one of Señor Esguerra's employees," Rosa replies as we walk back toward the house. "He came here a few weeks ago to oversee some of the security measures."

"Oh, I see."

By the time we arrive at the house, my clothes are sticking to my skin from the extreme humidity. It's a relief to be back indoors, where the air-conditioning keeps the temperature nice and cool. "That's Amazonia for you," Rosa says, smiling as I gulp down a glass of cold water I grab from the kitchen. "We're right next to the rainforest, and it's always like a steam bath outside."

"Yeah, no kidding," I mutter, feeling in dire need of another shower. It had been hot on the island as well, but the breeze coming from the ocean had made it tolerable, even pleasant. Here, however, the heat is almost smothering, the air still and thick with moisture.

Placing the empty glass on the table, I turn toward Rosa. "I think I might use that pool you showed me," I tell her, deciding to take advantage of the amenities. "Would you like to join me?"

Rosa's eyes widen. She's clearly surprised by my invitation. "Oh, I'd love to," she says sincerely, "but I need to help Ana prepare lunch and then clean the bedrooms upstairs . . ."

"Of course." I feel slightly embarrassed because, for a moment, I forgot that Rosa is not here solely to keep me company—that she has actual duties and responsibilities around the house. "Well, in that case, thank you for the tour. I really appreciate it."

She grins at me. "It was my pleasure, happy to do it anytime."

And as she busies herself in the kitchen, I head upstairs to change into a swimsuit.

CHAPTER NINE

❖ JULIAN ❖

I find Nora by the pool, lounging with a book under one of the umbrellas. Her slim legs are crossed at the ankles, and she's wearing a strapless white bikini, her golden skin gleaming with droplets of water. She must've been swimming recently.

Hearing my footsteps, she sits up and places her book on a side table. "Hi," she says softly when I approach her lounge chair. Her sunglasses are too big for her small face, making her look a bit like a dragonfly, and I make a mental note to buy her a more fitting pair on the next trip to Bogotá.

"Hello, my pet," I murmur, sitting down on her chair. Raising my hand, I pull the sunglasses off her nose and lean forward to take her mouth in a short, deep kiss. She tastes like sunlight, her lips soft and yielding, and my cock instantly stiffens, reacting to the proximity of her almost-naked body. Tonight, I promise myself as I reluctantly lift my head. I will have her again tonight.

"What was your meeting about this morning?" she asks, her breathing slightly uneven after the kiss. Her dark eyes hold curiosity and just a hint of caution as she looks at me. She's testing the waters again, trying to determine how much I'm willing to share with her now.

I consider that for a moment. It's tempting to continue keeping her in the dark. Despite everything, Nora is still so naïve, so ignorant of the real world. She got a small taste of it back in that warehouse, but it was nothing compared to the things I deal with every day. I want to continue shielding her from the brutal nature of my reality, but there is no safety in ignorance any longer—not when my enemies know about her. Besides, I have a feeling my young wife is tougher than her delicate appearance would suggest.

She has to be, to survive me.

Arriving at a decision, I give her a cool smile. "We just got intelligence on two Al-Quadar cells," I say, watching her reaction. "Now we're figuring out how we can wipe them out and capture some of their members in the process. The meeting was to coordinate the logistics of that operation."

Her eyes widen slightly, but she does a good job of controlling her shock at my revelations. "How many cells are there?" she asks, shifting forward in the chair. I can see her right palm curling into a fist next to her leg, though her voice remains calm. "How big is their organization?"

"Nobody knows, except their top leaders. That's why it's so hard to eradicate them—they're scattered all over the world, like vermin. They made a mistake, though, when they tried to play hardball with me. I am very good at exterminating vermin."

Nora swallows reflexively, but continues holding my gaze. *Brave girl.* "What did they want from you?" she asks. "Why did they decide to play hardball?"

I hesitate for a second, then decide to fill her in. She might as well know the full story at this point. "My company developed a new type of weapon—a powerful explosive that's almost impossible to detect," I explain. "A couple of kilos is all it would take to blow up a mid-sized airport, and a dozen kilos could take out a small city. It's got the explosive force of a nuclear bomb, but it's not radioactive, and the substance that it's made of resembles plastic, so it can be molded into nearly anything . . . even children's toys."

She stares at me, her face turning pale. She's beginning to understand the implications of this. "Is that why you didn't want to give it to them?" she asks.

"Because you didn't want to place such a dangerous weapon in the hands of terrorists?"

"No, not really." I give her an amused look. It's sweet of her to ascribe noble motives to me, but she should know better at this point. "It's simply that the explosive is difficult to produce in large quantities, and I already have a long list of buyers waiting. Al-Quadar was at the very bottom of that list, so they would've had to wait years, if not decades, to get it from me."

To Nora's credit, her expression doesn't change. "So who is at the top of your list?" she says evenly. "Some other terrorist group?"

"No." I laugh softly. "Not even close. It's your government, my pet. They put in an order so large, it will keep my factories busy for years."

"Oh, I see." Initially she appears relieved, but then a puzzled frown creases her smooth forehead. "So legitimate governments buy things from you too? I thought the US military developed their own weapons . . ."

"They do." I grin at her naïveté. "But they would never pass up a chance to get their hands on something like this. And the more they buy, the less I can sell to others. It's an arrangement that works well for everyone."

"But why don't they just take it from you by force? Or simply shut down your factories?" She stares at me in confusion. "In general, if they know of your existence, why do they allow you to produce illegal weapons?"

"Because if I didn't do it, somebody else would—and that person might not be nearly as rational and pragmatic as I am." I can see the disbelieving look on Nora's face, and my grin widens. "Yes, my pet, believe it or not, the US government would rather deal with me, who bears America no particular ill will, than to have someone like Majid in charge of a similar operation."

"Majid?"

"The motherfucker who killed Beth." My voice hardens, my amusement disappearing without a trace. "The one responsible for stealing you at the clinic."

Nora tenses at the mention of Beth, and I see her hands balling into fists again. "The Suit—that's what I called him in my mind," she murmurs, her gaze appearing distant for a moment. "Because he was wearing a suit, you see . . ." She blinks, then focuses her attention on me again. "That was Majid?"

I nod, keeping my expression impassive despite the rage churning inside me. "Yes. That was him."

"I wish he hadn't died in the explosion," she says, surprising me for a moment. Her eyes glitter darkly in the sunlight. "He didn't deserve such an easy death."

"No, he didn't," I agree, now comprehending her meaning. Like me, she wishes that Majid had suffered. She hungers for revenge; I can hear it in her voice, see it on her face. It makes me wonder what would happen if she somehow ended up with Majid at her mercy.

Would she be able to truly hurt him? To inflict such pain that he would beg for death?

It's an idea I find more than a little intriguing.

"Did you ever bring Beth here?" she asks, interrupting that train of thought. "To this compound, I mean?"

"No." I shake my head. "Before she came to stay on the island, Beth traveled with me, and I didn't come here for a long time."

"Why not?"

I shrug. "It wasn't my favorite place, I guess," I say casually, ignoring the dark memories that flood my mind at her innocent question. The estate was where I'd spent most of my childhood, where my father's belt and fists reigned supreme until I was old enough to fight back. It was where I killed my first man—and where I came to retrieve my mother's bloodied corpse twelve years ago. It wasn't until I renovated the house completely that I could stand the thought of coming to live here again, and even then, it's only Nora's presence that makes it bearable for me to be here.

She places her hand on my knee, bringing me back to the present. "Julian . . ." She pauses for a moment, as though unsure whether to proceed. Then she apparently decides to forge ahead. "There's something I would like to ask you," she says quietly, but firmly.

I lift my eyebrows. "What is it, my pet?"

"I took lessons back home," she says, her hand unconsciously tightening on my knee. "Self-defense and shooting, that sort of thing . . . and I'd like to resume them here, if possible."

"I see." A smile curves my mouth. My earlier speculations had been right, it seems. She's not the same frightened, helpless girl I brought to the island. This Nora is stronger, more resilient . . . and even more appealing. I remember reading about her lessons in Lucas's report, so her request is not totally unexpected. "You would like me to train you how to fight and use weapons?"

She nods. "Yes. Or maybe have someone else teach me, if you're busy."

"No." The thought of any one of my men laying his hands on her, even in a teaching capacity, makes me see red. "I will teach you myself."

* * *

I decide to start Nora's training that afternoon, after I catch up on a few business emails. For some reason, I like the idea of teaching her self-defense. I don't intend for her to ever be in a dangerous situation again, but I still want her to know how to protect herself if the need arises.

The irony of what I'm doing doesn't escape me. Most people would say I'm the one she needs protection from, and they would probably be right. I don't give a fuck, though. Nora is mine now, and I will do whatever it takes to keep her safe—even if it involves teaching her how to kill someone like me.

When I'm done with my emails, I go searching for her back at the house. This time I find her in the house gym, running on the treadmill at full speed. Judging by the sweat trickling down her slender back, she's been going at this pace for a while.

Making sure not to startle her, I come up to her from the side.

Spotting me, she reduces the speed on the treadmill, slowing down to a jog. "Hi," she says breathlessly, reaching for a small towel to wipe her face. "Is it time for the training?"

"Yes, I have a couple of hours now." My words come out low and husky as a familiar surge of arousal hardens my cock. I love seeing her like this, all out of breath, with her skin damp and glowing. It reminds me of how she looks after a particularly messy bout of sex. Of course, the fact that she's wearing only a pair of running shorts and a sports bra doesn't help. I want to lick the droplets of sweat off her smooth, flat belly, then throw her on the nearest mat for a quick fuck.

"Excellent." She gives me a huge smile and hits the 'Stop' button on the treadmill. Then she hops off the machine, grabbing her water bottle. "I'm ready."

She looks so excited that I decide to hold off on the mat fucking for now. Delayed gratification can be a good thing, and I did carve out this time specifically for her training.

"All right," I say. "Let's go." And taking her hand, I

lead her out of the house.

We go to the field where I usually work out with my men. At this time of day, it's too hot for serious exercise, so the area is largely empty. Still, as we pass by, I see a few of the guards surreptitiously staring at Nora. It makes me want to rip their eyes out. I think they can tell—because they look away as soon as they glance at me. I know it's irrational to be this possessive of her, but I don't care. She belongs to me, and they all need to know that.

"What are we doing first?" she asks as we approach a storage shed in the corner of the training field.

"Shooting." I give her a sideways look. "I want to see how good you are with a gun."

She smiles, her eyes gleaming with eagerness. "I'm not bad," she says, and the confidence in her voice makes me grin. It seems that my pet learned a few things in my absence. I can't wait to see her demonstrate her new skills.

Inside the shed are some weapons and training gear. Going in, I select a few of the most commonly used guns—everything ranging from a 9mm handgun to an M16 assault rifle. I even grab an AK-47, although she might be too small to use it with ease.

Then we go outside to the shooting range.

There are a number of targets set up at different intervals. I have her begin with the closest target: a dozen empty beer cans propped on a wooden table some fifty feet away. Handing her the 9mm, I instruct her on how to use it and then have her aim at the cans.

To my shock, she hits ten of the twelve cans on her first try. "Dammit," she mutters, lowering the weapon. "I can't believe I missed those two."

Surprised and impressed, I have her try out the other guns. She's comfortable with most types of handguns and hunting rifles, hitting most of the targets again, but her arms shake when she tries to aim the AK-47.

"You would have to get stronger to use that one," I tell her, taking the assault rifle from her.

She nods in agreement, reaching for her water bottle. "Yes," she says between sips. "I want to get stronger. I want to be able to handle all these weapons, same as you."

I can't help laughing at that. Despite her generally easygoing nature, Nora has a strong competitive streak. I've noticed it before, when we did that three-mile race on the island.

"Okay," I say, still chuckling. Taking the bottle from her, I drink some water and then return it to her. "I can train you to get stronger as well."

After she practices shooting a few more times, we return the guns to the shed. Then I take her to the indoor training gym, to show her some basic fighting moves.

Lucas is there, sparring with three of the guards. Seeing us enter the room, he stops and respectfully nods at Nora, keeping his eyes fixed firmly on her face.

He knows by now how I feel about her, and is smart enough not to display any interest in her slim, half-naked form. His sparring partners, however, are not that wise, and it takes a murderous glare from me for them to stop gaping at her.

"Hi Lucas," Nora says, ignoring this little interplay. "It's good to see you again."

Lucas gives her a carefully neutral smile. "You too, Mrs. Esguerra."

To my annoyance, Nora visibly flinches at the moniker, and my mild irritation with the guards morphs into sudden anger at her. Her reluctance to marry me earlier is like a festering splinter at the back of my brain, and it doesn't take much to bring back the way I felt at the church.

For all of her supposed love for me, she still refuses to accept our marriage, and I'm no longer inclined to be reasonable and forgiving.

"Out," I bark at Lucas and the guards, jerking my thumb toward the door. "We need this space."

They clear out within seconds, leaving me and Nora alone.

She takes a step back, suddenly looking wary. She knows me well, and I can tell she senses something amiss.

As usual, she can guess what it is. "Julian," she says cautiously, "I didn't mean to react like that. I'm just not used to being called that, that's all . . ."

"Is that right, my pet?" My voice is like brushed silk,

reflecting none of the simmering fury inside. Stepping toward her, I lift my hand and slowly trace my fingers over her jawline. "Would you prefer *not* to be called that? Perhaps you wish I hadn't come back for you at all?"

Her huge eyes grow even larger. "No, of course not! I told you, I want to be here with you——"

"Don't lie to me." The words come out cold and sharp as I drop my hand. It infuriates me that I care about this at all, that I let something as insignificant as Nora's feelings bother me. What does it matter if she loves me? I shouldn't want that from her, shouldn't expect it. And yet I do—it's part of this fucked-up obsession I have with her.

"I'm not lying," she denies vehemently, taking a step back. Her face is pale in the dim light of the room, but her gaze is direct and unwavering as she stares at me. "I shouldn't want to be with you, but I do. Do you think I don't realize how wrong this is? How messed-up? You kidnapped me, Julian . . . You forced me."

The accusation hangs between us, stark and heavy. If I were a different man, a better man, I would look away. I would feel remorse for what I'd done.

But I don't.

I'm not into self-deception. I never have been. When I abducted Nora, I knew that I crossed a line, that I sank to a new low. I did it with the full knowledge of what that makes me: an irredeemable beast, a destroyer of innocence. It's a label I'm willing to live with to have her.

I would do anything to have her.

So instead of looking away, I hold her gaze. "Yes," I say quietly. "I did." My anger is gone, replaced by an emotion I don't want to analyze too closely. Taking a step toward her, I lift my hand again and stroke the plush softness of her lower lip with my thumb. Her lips part at my touch, and the hunger that I've been suppressing all day sharpens, clawing at my insides.

I want her.

I want her, and I'm going to take her.

After this, she will have no doubt that she belongs to me.

CHAPTER TEN

❖ NORA ❖

Staring up at my husband, I fight the urge to back away. I shouldn't have let Julian see my reaction to my new name, but I had been enjoying the shooting session—and Julian's company—so much that I had forgotten the reality of my new situation. Hearing 'Mrs. Esguerra' fall from Lucas's lips startled me, bringing back that disconcerting feeling of lost identity, and, for a moment, I had been unable to hide my dismay.

That moment was all it took to transform Julian from a laughing, teasing companion to the terrifying, unpredictable man who first brought me to his island.

I can feel the rapid beating of my pulse as his thumb caresses my lips, his touch gentle despite the darkness gleaming in his eyes. He doesn't seem upset by my reckless accusations; if anything, he looks calmer now, almost amused. I'm not sure what I thought would happen when I threw the words at him, but I hadn't expected him to admit his crimes so easily, without even a hint of guilt or regret. Most people try to justify their actions to themselves and others, twisting the facts to suit their purposes, but Julian is not most people. He sees things as they are; he's just not bothered by the idea of committing acts most people would cringe at. Instead of a deluded psycho who thinks he's doing the right thing, my new husband is simply a man without a conscience.

A man whom I both love and fear right now.

Without saying another word, Julian lowers his fingers and grips my upper arm, leading me toward one of the wide wrestling mats near the wall. As we walk, I catch a glimpse of the bulge in his shorts, and my breathing speeds up from a combination of anxiety and involuntary desire.

Julian intends to fuck me, right here and now, where anyone can walk in on us.

An uncomfortable mixture of lust and embarrassment makes my skin burn. Logic tells me this is not likely to be one of our more vanilla encounters, but my body doesn't know the difference between a punishment fuck and tender lovemaking. All it knows is Julian, and it's conditioned to crave his touch.

To my surprise, Julian doesn't fall on me right away. Instead he releases my arm and looks at me, his sensuous mouth twisted into a cold, slightly cruel smile. "Why don't you show me what you learned in those self-defense classes of yours, my pet?" he says softly. "Let's see some of the moves they taught you."

I stare at him, my heart climbing into my throat as I realize what Julian wants. He wants me to fight him, to resist—even though it won't change the outcome.

Even though it'll only make me feel helpless and defeated when I lose.

"Why?" I ask in desperation, trying to put off the inevitable. I know Julian is just toying with me, but I don't want to play this game, not after everything that has occurred between us. I want to forget those early days on the island, not relive them in this twisted way.

"Why not?" He begins to circle around me, causing my anxiety to spike. "Isn't that why you took those classes, so you could protect yourself from men like me? Men who want to take you, to abuse you?"

My breathing accelerates further, adrenaline flooding my system as an involuntary fight-or-flight response kicks in. Instinctively I turn, trying to keep him in sight at all times, as if he were a dangerous predator—because he is one right now.

A beautiful, deadly predator who is intent on me as his prey.

"Go ahead, Nora," he murmurs, stopping so that

my back is against the wall. "Fight."

"No." I try not to flinch when he reaches for me, his hand closing around my wrist. "I'm not doing this, Julian. Not like this."

His nostrils flare. He's not used to me denying him anything, and I hold my breath, waiting to see what he will do. My heart is beating painfully in my chest, and a thin trickle of sweat slides down my back as I hold his gaze. By now I know Julian wouldn't truly harm me, but that doesn't mean he won't punish me for my defiance.

"All right," he says softly. "If that's how you want it." And using his grip on my wrist, he twists my arm upwards, forcing me down to my knees. With his free hand, he unzips his shorts, letting his erection spring free. Then he wraps my hair around his fist and pushes my mouth toward his cock. "Suck it," he orders roughly, staring down at me.

Relieved by the simple task, I gladly obey, closing my lips around the thick column of his sex. He tastes like salt and man, the tip of his shaft damp with pre-cum, and some of my anxiety fades, edged out by growing desire. I love pleasuring him like this, and as Julian's grip on my wrist slackens, I use both hands to cup his balls, kneading and massaging them with firm pressure.

He groans, closing his eyes, and I begin to move my mouth back and forth, using a sucking motion to bring him deeper into my throat each time. The way he holds my hair hurts my scalp, but the discomfort only enhances my arousal. Julian was right when he said I have masochistic tendencies. Whether by nature or by nurture, I get off on pain now, my body craving the intensity of these types of sensations.

Looking up at him, I drink in the tortured expression on his face, enjoying the small taste of power he allows me.

Today, though, he doesn't let me set the pace for long. Instead he pushes his hips forward, forcing his cock further into my throat, and I gag, spitting up some saliva. That seems to please him, and he mutters thickly, "Yes, that's it, baby," opening his eyes to watch me as he begins to fuck my face with a hard, relentless rhythm. I choke again, and more saliva dribbles out, coating my chin and his cock with viscous moisture.

He releases me then, but before I can catch my breath, he pushes me down on the mat, face first, causing me to fall onto my hands. Then he gets behind me, and I feel him pulling my shorts and underwear down to my knees. My sex clenches in hungry anticipation . . . but that's not where he wants me today. It's the other opening that holds his attention, and I tense instinctively as I feel the head of his cock pressing between my cheeks.

"Relax, my pet," he murmurs, grasping my hips to hold me in place as he begins to push in. "Just relax . . . Yes, there is a good girl . . ."

I take small, shallow breaths as I try to follow

Julian's advice, fighting the urge to tighten up as he slowly begins to penetrate my ass. I know from experience this will hurt a lot less if I'm not so tense, but my body seems determined to fight this intrusion. After months of abstinence, it's almost as if I'm a virgin there again, and I feel a heavy, burning pressure as my sphincter is forcefully stretched open.

"Julian, please . . ." The words come out in a low, pleading whisper as he ruthlessly pushes deeper, the saliva coating his cock acting as makeshift lube. My insides twist, and sweat breaks out all over my body as the tight ring of muscle finally gives in, letting his massive cock slide all the way in. Now he's throbbing deep inside me, making me feel unbearably full, engulfed and overtaken.

"Please what?" he breathes, sliding one muscular arm under my hips to hold me in place. At the same time, his other hand grabs my hair again, forcing my body to arch backwards. The new angle deepens the penetration, and I cry out, beginning to shake. It's too much, I can't take it, but Julian is not giving me a choice. This is my punishment, being fucked like an animal on a dirty mat, with no care or preparation. It should make me feel sick, killing all traces of desire, but somehow I'm still turned on, my body eager for whatever sensations Julian chooses to dole out. "Please what?" he repeats, his voice low and rough. "Please fuck me? Please give me more?"

"I . . . I don't know . . ." I can hardly speak, my

senses overwhelmed. He stills then, not moving, and I'm grateful for that small mercy, as it gives me a chance to adjust to the brutal hardness lodged within me. I try to steady my breathing, to relax, and the pain gradually begins to lessen, transforming into something else—a sizzling heat that permeates my nerve endings.

He starts to move again, his thrusts slow and deep, and the heat intensifies, centering low in my core. My nipples tighten, and a rush of wetness inundates my sex. Despite the discomfort, there is something perversely erotic about being taken like this, about being possessed in a way that's so dirty and forbidden. Closing my eyes, I begin to get into the primal rhythm of his movements, the thrust and drag that makes my insides churn with agony and pleasure. My clit swells, becoming more sensitive, and I know it will take only a few light touches to make me come, to relieve the tension building within me.

But he doesn't touch my clit. Instead his hand releases my hair and slides down to my neck. Then he grips my throat, forcing me to rise up so that I'm standing on my knees, my back slightly arched. My eyes pop open and my hands automatically fly up, clutching at his strangling fingers, but there's nothing I can do to loosen his hold. In this position, he's even deeper inside me, and I can barely breathe, my heart beginning to pound with a new, unfamiliar fear.

He leans forward then, and I can feel his lips

brushing against my ear. "You are mine for the rest of your life," he whispers harshly, the warmth of his breath making my skin prickle with goosebumps. "Do you understand me, Nora? All of you—your pussy, your asshole, your fucking inner thoughts . . . It's all mine to use and abuse as I will. I own you, inside and out, in every way possible . . ." His sharp teeth sink into my earlobe, causing me to gasp at the sudden pain. "Do you understand me?" There is a dark note in his voice that scares me. This is new—he's never done this to me before—and my pulse soars sky-high as his fingers tighten around my throat, slowly but inexorably cutting off my air supply.

Rising panic sends adrenaline surging through my veins. "Yes . . ." I manage to rasp out, my fingers now clawing at his hand, trying to pry it away. To my horror, I start seeing stars, the room blurring and going dark in front of my eyes. *Surely he doesn't mean to kill me . . . Surely he doesn't mean to kill me . . .* I am terrified, yet for some strange reason, my sex throbs and electric shivers run over my skin as my arousal spirals inexorably higher.

"Good. Now tell me . . . whose wife are you?" His fingers tighten further, and the stars go supernova as my brain struggles to get enough oxygen. My body is on the brink of suffocation, yet it's more alive in this moment than it's ever been, every sensation sharpened and refined. The burning thickness of his cock inside my ass, the heat of his breath on my temple, the pulsing of my engorged clit—it's too much and not enough at the same time. I want to scream and struggle, but I can't move, can't breathe . . . and as if from far away, I hear Julian demanding again, "Whose?"

Right before I pass out, his grip on my throat eases, and I choke out, "Yours" . . . even as my body convulses in a paroxysm of agonized ecstasy, the orgasm sudden and startlingly intense as much-needed oxygen rushes into my lungs.

Frantically gulping in air, I slump against him, trembling all over. I can't believe I came like this, without Julian touching my sex at all.

I can't believe I came while being afraid of dying.

After a moment, I become conscious of his lips grazing my sweat-dampened cheek. "Yes," he murmurs, his hand now gently stroking my throat, "that's right, baby . . ." He's still buried inside me, his hard cock splitting me apart, invading me. "And what's your name?"

"Nora," I gasp out hoarsely, quivering as his fingers trail down from my neck to my breasts. I'm still wearing my sports bra, and his hand burrows under the tight material, cupping my breast.

"Nora what?" he persists, his fingers pinching my nipple. It's erect and sensitive from my orgasm, and his touch sends a fresh ripple of heat down to my core. "Nora what?"

"Nora Esguerra," I whisper, closing my eyes. It's a fact I will never forget now—and as Julian resumes fucking me again, I know that Nora Leston will never exist again.

She is gone for good.

PART II: THE ESTATE

CHAPTER ELEVEN

❖ NORA ❖

Over the next couple of weeks, I slowly acclimate to my new home. The estate is a fascinating place, and I spend much of my time exploring it and meeting its inhabitants.

Besides the guards, there are a few dozen people living here, some by themselves, others with their families. They all work for Julian in one capacity or another, from the oldest generation to the youngest. Some—like Ana and Rosa—take care of the house and the grounds, while others are involved in Julian's business. He may have only recently returned to the compound, but many of his employees have lived here since the time when Juan Esguerra—Julian's father—reigned as one of the most powerful drug lords in the country. To an American like myself, such loyalty to an employer is unfathomable.

"They're well paid, provided with free housing, and your husband even hired a teacher for their children a few years ago," Rosa explains when I ask her about this unusual phenomenon. "He might not have been here much in person, but he's always been good at taking care of his people. They're all free to leave if they want, but they know they're unlikely to find anything better. Besides, here they're protected, but out there, they and their families are fair game for nosy policemen or anyone else seeking information on the Esguerra organization." Giving me a wry smile, she adds, "My mother says that once you're a part of this life, you're always a part of this life. There's no going back."

"So why did they choose this life?" I ask, trying to understand what would make one move to a weapons dealer's isolated compound on the edge of the Amazon rainforest. I don't know many sane people who would do something like that willingly—particularly if they knew there was no easy way to return home.

Rosa shrugs. "Well, everybody has a different story. Some were wanted by the authorities; others made enemies of dangerous people. My parents came here to escape poverty and provide a better life for me and my brothers. They knew they were taking a risk, but they felt they had no other choice. To this day, my mother is convinced that they made the right decision for themselves and their children."

"Even after——?" I start asking, then shut my mouth when I realize that I'm about to bring up painful memories for Rosa again.

"Yes, even after," she says, understanding my half-spoken question. "There are no guarantees in life. They could've died anyway. My father and Eduardo——my oldest brother——were killed doing their jobs, but at least they had jobs. Back at my parents' village, there were no jobs, and the cities were even worse. My parents did whatever they could to keep food on the table, but it wasn't enough. When my mother became pregnant with me, Eduardo, who was twelve at the time, went to Medellín seeking to become a drug mule——just so that our family wouldn't starve. My father went after him to stop him, and that's when the two of them ran into Juan Esguerra, who was in the city for negotiations with the Medellín Cartel. He offered both my father and brother a job in his organization, and the rest is history." She stops and smiles at me before continuing, "So you see, Nora, working for Señor Esguerra was the best alternative for my family. As my mother says, at least I never had to sell myself for food, the way she did in her youth."

Rosa says that last part without any bitterness or self-pity. She's simply stating facts. Rosa genuinely considers herself lucky to have been born on the

Esguerra estate. She's grateful to Julian and his father for providing her family with a good living, and, despite her longing to see America, she doesn't mind living in the middle of nowhere. To her, this compound is home.

I learn all of this during our walks. While Rosa doesn't like jogging, she's more than happy to take a brisk walk with me in the morning, before it gets too hot and muggy. It's something we started doing on my third day here, and it's quickly becoming part of my daily routine. I like spending time with Rosa; she's bright and friendly, reminding me a bit of my friend Leah. And Rosa seems to enjoy my company as well—although I'm sure she would be nice to me regardless, given my position here. Everybody on the estate treats me with respect and politeness.

After all, I'm the Señor's wife.

After the incident at the gym, I have done my best to accept the fact that I'm married to Julian—that the beautiful, amoral man who abducted me is now my husband. It's an idea that still disturbs me on some level, but with each day that passes, I grow more and more accustomed to it. My life changed irrevocably when Julian stole me, and that far-off 'normal' future is a dream I should've given up a long time ago. Clinging to it while falling in love with my kidnapper had been as irrational as developing feelings for him in the first place.

Instead of a house in the suburbs and two-point-five

kids, my future now holds a heavily guarded compound near the Amazon jungle and a man who both excites and terrifies me. It's impossible for me to imagine having children with Julian, and I dread the fact that in a few short months, the three-year birth control implant I got at seventeen will cease to be effective. At some point, I will need to bring up this issue with Julian, but for now I'm trying not to think about it. I'm no more ready to be a mother than I was to be a wife, and the possibility of having that choice forced on me makes me break out in a cold sweat. I love Julian, but raising children with a man who thinks nothing of kidnapping and killing? That's a whole other matter.

My parents and friends back home aren't helping. I spoke once with Leah, telling her about my hasty marriage, and her reaction had been shocked, to say the least.

"You married that arms dealer?" she exclaimed incredulously. "After everything he's done to you and Jake? Are you insane? You're only nineteen—and he should be in jail!" And no matter how much I tried to spin everything in a positive light, I could tell she got off the phone thinking that my abduction left me a few cards short of a full deck.

My parents are even worse. Every time I talk to them, I have to fend off their probing questions about my unexpected marriage and Julian's plans for our future. I don't blame them for adding to my anxiety; I know they're worried sick about me. The last time we had a video call, my mom's eyes were red and swollen, as though she'd been crying. It's obvious that the hastily concocted story I told them at my wedding has done little to alleviate their concerns. My parents know how my relationship with Julian began, and they're having a hard time believing I could be happy with a man they see as pure evil.

And yet I *am* happy, my fretting about the future aside. The icy emptiness inside me is gone, replaced by a dazzling abundance of emotions and sensations. It's as though the black-and-white movie of my life has been redone in technicolor.

When I'm with Julian, I'm complete and content in a way that I don't fully understand and can't quite come to terms with. It's not like I was miserable before I met him. I had great friends, a loving family, and the promise of a good, if unexceptional, life ahead of me. I even had a crush—Jake—who gave me the proverbial butterflies in my stomach. It makes no sense that I somehow needed something as perverse as this relationship with Julian to enrich my life and give me that which I was missing.

Of course, I'm no shrink. Perhaps there is an explanation for my feelings—some childhood trauma that I've repressed, or a chemical imbalance in my brain. Or maybe it's just Julian and the deliberate way he's been molding my physical and emotional responses since those early days on the island. I am cognizant of his conditioning methods, but my recognition of them doesn't alter their effectiveness. It's strange to know that you're being manipulated, and at the same time enjoy the results of that manipulation.

But enjoy them I do. Being with Julian is thrilling—both frightening and exhilarating, like riding a wild tiger. I never know which side of him I will see at any given moment: the charming lover or the cruel master. And as messed-up as it is, I want both—I am addicted to both. The light and the dark, the violence and the tenderness—it all goes together, forming a volatile, dizzying cocktail that plays havoc with my equilibrium and makes me fall even deeper under Julian's spell.

Of course, the fact that I see him now every day doesn't help. On the island, Julian's frequent absences gave me time to recover from the potent effect he has on my mind and body, enabling me to maintain some emotional balance. Here, however, there is no respite from the magnetic pull he exerts on me, no way to shield myself from his intoxicating allure. With each day that passes, I lose a little more of my soul to him, my need for him growing, rather than decreasing with time.

The only thing that keeps me from freaking out is the knowledge that Julian is drawn to me just as strongly. I don't know if it's my resemblance to Maria or just our inexplicable chemistry, but I know the addiction works both ways.

Julian's hunger for me knows no bounds. He takes

me a couple of times every night—and often during the day as well—yet I get the sense he still wants more. It's there in the intensity of his gaze, in the way he always touches me, holds me. He can't keep his hands off me—and that makes me feel better about my own helpless attraction to him.

He also seems to enjoy spending time with me outside of the bedroom. True to his promise, Julian has begun training me, teaching me how to fight and use different weapons. After the initial rocky start, he turned out to be an excellent instructor—knowledgeable, patient, and surprisingly dedicated. We train together nearly every day, and I've already learned more in these couple of weeks than in the prior three months in my self-defense courses. Of course, it would be a misnomer to call what he teaches me self-defense; Julian's lessons have more in common with some kind of assassin bootcamp.

"You aim to kill every time," he instructs during one afternoon session where he makes me throw knives at a small target on the wall. "You don't have the size or the strength, so for you, it's all about speed, reflexes, and ruthlessness. You need to catch your opponents off-guard and eliminate them before they realize how skilled you are. Every strike has to be deadly; every move has to count."

"What if I don't want to kill them?" I ask, looking up at him. "What if I just want to wound them, so I can run away?"

"A wounded man can still hurt you. It doesn't take much strength to squeeze a trigger or stab you with a knife. Unless you have a good reason for wanting your enemy alive, you aim to kill, Nora. Do you understand me?"

I nod and throw a small, sharp knife at the wall. It thuds dully against the target, then falls down, having barely scratched the wood. Not my best attempt, but better than my prior five.

I don't know if I can do what Julian says, but I do know that I never want to feel defenseless again. If it means learning the skills of an assassin, I'm happy to do it. It doesn't mean I will ever use them, but just knowing that I can protect myself makes me feel stronger and more confident, helping me cope with the residual nightmares from my time with the terrorists.

To my relief, those have gotten better as well. It's like my subconscious knows that Julian is here—that I'm safe with him. Of course, it also helps that when I do wake up screaming, he's there to hold me and chase the nightmare away.

The first time it happens is the third night after my arrival at the estate. I dream of Beth's death again, of the ocean of blood that I'm drowning in, but this time, strong arms catch me, save me from the vicious rip current. This time, when I open my eyes, I'm not alone in the darkness. Julian has turned on the bedside lamp and is shaking me awake, a concerned expression on his beautiful face.

"I'm here now," he soothes, pulling me into his lap when I can't stop trembling, tears of remembered horror running down my face. "All is well, I promise . . ." He strokes my hair until my sobbing breaths begin to even out, and then he asks softly, "What's the matter, baby? Did you have a bad dream? You were screaming my name . . ."

I nod, clinging to him with all my strength. I can feel the warmth of his skin, hear the steady beating of his heart, and the nightmare slowly begins to recede, my mind coming back to the present. "It was Beth," I whisper when I can speak without my voice breaking. "He was torturing her . . . killing her."

Julian's arms tighten around me. He doesn't say anything, but I can feel his rage, his burning fury. Beth had been more than a housekeeper to him, though the precise nature of their relationship had always been something of a mystery to me.

Desperate to distract myself from the bloody images still filling my mind, I decide to satisfy the curiosity that had gnawed at me all through my time on the island. "How did you and Beth meet?" I ask, pulling back to look at Julian's face. "How did she come to be on the island with me?"

He looks at me, his eyes dark with memories. Before, whenever I would ask these types of questions, he would brush me off or change the topic, but things are different between us now. Julian seems more willing to talk to me, to let me more fully into his life.

"I was in Tijuana seven years ago for a meeting with one of the cartels," he begins speaking after a moment. "After my business was concluded, I went looking for entertainment in Zona Norte, the red-light district of the city. I was passing by one of the alleys when I saw it . . . a screaming, crying woman huddled over a small figure on the ground."

"Beth," I whisper, remembering what she told me about her daughter.

"Yes, Beth," he confirms. "It wasn't any of my business, but I'd had a couple of drinks and I was curious. So I came closer . . . and that's when I saw that the small figure on the ground was a child. A beautiful baby girl with red curly hair, a tiny replica of the woman crying over her." A savage, furious glint enters his eyes. "The child was lying in a pool of blood, with a gunshot wound in her small chest. She had apparently been killed to punish her mother, who didn't want to let her pimp offer the child to some clients with more *unique* tastes."

Nausea, sharp and strong, rises in my throat. Despite everything I've been through, it still horrifies me to know that there are such monsters out there. Monsters far worse than the man I've fallen in love with.

No wonder Beth saw the world in shades of black; her life had been overtaken by darkness.

"When I heard the full story, I took Beth and her daughter with me," Julian continues in a low, hard voice. "It still wasn't any of my business, but I couldn't let this type of thing slide—at least not after seeing that child's body. We buried the daughter in a cemetery just outside Tijuana. Then I took a couple of my men, and Beth and I came back to look for the pimp." A small, vicious smile appears on his lips as he says softly, "Beth killed him personally. Him and his two thugs—the ones who helped murder her daughter."

I inhale slowly, not wanting to start crying again. "And she came to work for you after that? After you helped her like that?"

Julian nods. "Yes. It wasn't safe for her to stay in Tijuana, so I offered her a job as my personal cook and maid. She accepted, of course—it was far better than being a streetwalker in Mexico—and she traveled with me everywhere after that. It wasn't until I decided to acquire you that I offered her the opportunity to stay permanently on the island and, well, you know the rest of the story."

"Yes, I do," I murmur, pushing against his chest to extricate myself from his embrace—an embrace that suddenly feels suffocating rather than comforting. The 'acquire you' part of the story is an unpleasant reminder of how I came to be here . . . of the fact that the man by my side ruthlessly planned and carried out my abduction. On the spectrum of evil, Julian may not be all the way on the black side, but he's not very far from it.

Still, as days go on, my nightmares slowly ease. As

perverse as it is, now that I'm back with my kidnapper, I'm starting to heal from the ordeal of being stolen from him. Even my art has become more peaceful. I still feel compelled to paint the flames of the explosion, but I have begun to get interested in landscapes again, capturing on canvas the wild beauty of the rainforest that encroaches on the borders of the property.

As before, Julian encourages my hobby. In addition to setting up the studio for me, he retained an art instructor—a thin, elderly man from the south of France who speaks English with a thick accent. Monsieur Bernard had taught in all the best art schools in Europe before retiring in his late seventies. I have no idea how Julian persuaded him to come to the estate, but I'm thankful for his presence. The techniques he teaches me are far more advanced than what I had learned through my instructional videos before, and I'm already starting to see a new level of sophistication in my art—as does Monsieur Bernard.

"You have talent, Señora," he says with his heavy French accent, examining my latest attempt at painting a sunset in the jungle. The trees look dark against the glowing orange and pink of the setting sun, with the edges of the painting blurred out and out of focus. "This has a—how do you say it? An almost *sinister* feel to it?" He glances at me, his faded gaze suddenly sharp with curiosity. "Yes," he continues softly after studying me for a few moments. "You have talent and something more—something inside you that comes out through your art. A darkness I rarely see in one so young."

I don't know how to respond to that, so I simply smile at him. I am not sure whether Monsieur Bernard knows about my husband's profession, but I'm almost certain the elderly instructor has no idea how my relationship with Julian began.

As far as the world is concerned now, I'm the pampered young wife of a handsome, rich man, and that's all there is to it.

* * *

"I've enrolled you for the winter quarter at Stanford," Julian says casually over dinner one night. "They have a new online program. It's still in the experimental stages, but the early feedback is quite good. It's all the same professors; it's just that the lectures are recorded, instead of being live."

My jaw drops. I'm enrolled at *Stanford*? I had no idea college of any kind—much less a top ten university—was even on the table. "What?" I say incredulously, putting down my fork. Ana had prepared a delicious meal for us, but I no longer have any interest in the food on my plate, all my attention focused on Julian.

He smiles at me calmly. "I promised your parents you would get a good education, and I'm delivering on that promise. You don't like Stanford?"

Stunned, I stare at him. I don't have an opinion about Stanford because I had never even entertained the possibility of going there. My grades in school had been good, but my SAT scores weren't sky-high, and my parents couldn't have afforded such an expensive school anyway. Community college followed by a transfer to one of the state colleges was going to be my path to getting a degree, so I never looked at Stanford or any school of its caliber. "How did you get me in?" I finally manage to ask. "Isn't their admission rate in the single digits? Or is the online program less competitive?"

"No, it's even more competitive, I believe," Julian says, filling his plate with a second serving of chicken. "I think they're only taking a hundred students for the program this year, and there were about ten thousand applicants."

"Then how did you—" I begin saying, then shut up as I realize that getting me into an elite school is child's play to someone with Julian's wealth and connections. "So I start in January?" I ask instead, excitement trickling through my veins as the shock begins to wear off. *Stanford. Oh my God, I will be going to Stanford.* I should probably feel guilty that I didn't get in on my own merit—or at least be outraged at Julian's high-handedness—but all I can think about is my parents' reaction when I tell them the news. *I will be going to freaking Stanford!*

Julian nods, reaching for more rice. "Yes, that's

when the winter quarter begins. They should email you an orientation packet in the next couple of days, so you'll be able to order your textbooks once you find out the class requirements. I'll make sure they're delivered to you here in time."

"Wow, okay." I know it's not an appropriate response for something of this magnitude, but I can't think of anything more clever to say. In less than two weeks, I will be a student at one of the most prestigious universities in the world—the last thing I expected when Julian came for me again. Granted, it will be an online program, but it's still far better than anything I could've dreamed of.

A number of questions occur to me. "What about my major? What will I be studying?" I ask, wondering if Julian made that decision for me too. The fact that he took the matter of my college education into his own hands doesn't surprise me; after all, this is the man who abducted me and forced me to marry him. He's not exactly big on giving me choices.

Julian gives me an indulgent smile. "Whatever you want, my pet. I believe there is a common set of subjects you'll need to take, so you won't need to decide your major for a year or two. Do you have some ideas of what you want to study?"

"No, not really." I had been planning to take classes in different areas to figure out what I wanted to do, and I'm glad that Julian left me this option. In high school I had done equally well in most subjects, which made it hard to narrow down my career options.

"Well, you still have time to figure it out," Julian says, sounding for all the world like a guidance counselor. "There is no rush."

"Right, uh-huh." A part of me can't believe we're having this conversation. Less than two hours ago, Julian cornered me by the pool and fucked my brains out on one of the lounge chairs. Less than five hours ago, he taught me how to disable a man by stabbing him in the eye with my fingers. Two nights ago, he tied me to our bed and whipped me with a flogger. And now we're discussing my potential major in college? Trying to wrap my mind around such a strange turn of events, I ask Julian on autopilot, "So what did *you* study in college?"

As soon as the words leave my mouth, I realize that I have no idea if Julian even went to college—that I still know very little about the man I sleep with every night. Frowning, I do some quick mental math. According to Rosa, Julian's parents were killed twelve years ago, at which point he took over his father's business. Given that about twenty months had passed since Beth told me that Julian was twenty-nine, he had to be somewhere around thirty-one today—which meant he took over his father's business at nineteen.

For the first time, it dawns on me that Julian had been right around my age when he took his father's place as the head of an illegal drug operation and transformed it into a cutting-edge—though equally illegal—weapons empire.

To my surprise, Julian says, "I studied electrical engineering."

"What?" I can't hide my shock. "But I thought you took over your father's business really young—"

"I did." Julian gives me an amused look. "I dropped out of Caltech after a year and a half. But while I was there, I studied electrical engineering through an accelerated program."

Caltech? I stare at Julian with newfound respect. I've always known that he's smart, but engineering at Caltech is a whole different level of brilliance. "Is that why you chose to go into arms dealing? Because you had a background in engineering?"

"Yes, partly. And partly because I saw more opportunities there than in the drug trade."

"More opportunities?" Picking up my fork, I twirl it between my fingers as I study Julian, trying to understand what would make one abandon one criminal enterprise for another. Surely someone with his level of intelligence and drive could've chosen to do something better—something less dangerous and immoral. "Why didn't you just get your degree from Caltech and do something legitimate with it?" I ask after a few moments. "I'm sure you could've gotten any job you wanted—or maybe started your own business if you didn't like the corporate world."

He looks at me, his expression unreadable. "I thought about it," he says, shocking me yet again.

"When I left Colombia after Maria's death, I wanted to be done with that world. For the rest of my teenage years, I tried my hardest to forget the lessons my father taught me, to keep the violence within me under control. That's why I enrolled in Caltech—because I thought I could take a different path . . . become someone other than who I was meant to be."

I stare at him, my pulse quickening. This is the first time I've heard Julian admit to ever wanting something different than the life he's currently leading. "So why didn't you? Surely there was nothing tying you to that world once your father was dead . . ."

"You're right." Julian gives me a thin smile. "I could've ignored my father's death and let the other cartel take over his organization. It would've been easy. They had no idea where I was or what name I was using at that point, so I could've started fresh, finishing college and getting a job with one of the Silicon Valley start-ups. And I probably would've done that—if they hadn't also killed my mother."

"Your mother?"

"Yes." His beautiful features twist with hatred. "They gunned her down right here on the estate, along with dozens of others. I couldn't ignore that."

No, of course he couldn't. Not somebody like Julian, who had already killed for revenge. Remembering the story he told me about the men who murdered Maria, I feel a chill rippling over my skin. "So you came back and killed them?"

"Yes. I gathered all of my father's remaining men and hired some new ones. We attacked in the middle of the night, striking at the cartel leaders right in their homes. They weren't expecting such fast retaliation, and we caught them off-guard." His lips curl into a dark smile. "By the time the morning came, there were no survivors—and I knew I had been foolish to think that I could ignore what I am . . . to imagine that I could be something other than the killer I was born to be."

The chill running over my skin transforms into full-on goosebumps. This side of Julian terrifies me, and I clasp my hands together under the table to prevent them from shaking. "You told me you saw a therapist after your parents' death. Because you wanted to kill more."

"Yes, my pet." There is a savage gleam in his blue eyes. "I killed the cartel leaders and their families, and when it was all over, I thirsted for more blood . . . more death. The craving inside me only intensified during the years that I'd been away; leading a so-called 'normal' life made it worse, not better." He pauses, and I shudder at the black shadows I see in his gaze. "Seeing a therapist was a last-ditch attempt to fight against my nature, and it didn't take me long to realize that it was futile—that the only way to move forward was to embrace it and accept my fate."

"And you did that by going into arms dealing." I try to keep my voice steady. "By becoming a criminal."

At that moment, Ana comes into the dining room and begins to clear the dishes off the table. Watching her, I slowly rub my arms, trying to dispel the coldness within me. In a way, it makes it worse, the fact that Julian had a choice and that he consciously chose to embrace the darkest part of himself. It tells me there is no hope for redemption, no chance of making him see the error of his ways. It's not that he never knew there was an alternative to a life of crime; on the contrary, he had experienced such an alternative and decided to reject it.

"Would you like anything else?" Ana asks us, and I shake my head mutely, too disturbed to think about dessert. Julian, however, asks for a cup of hot chocolate, sounding as unruffled as ever.

When Ana exits the room, Julian smiles at me, as though sensing the direction of my thoughts. "I was always a criminal, Nora," he says softly. "I killed for the first time when I was eight, and I knew then that there would be no going back. I tried to bury that knowledge for a while, but it was always there, waiting for me to come to my senses." He leans back in his seat, his posture indolent, yet predatory, like the lazy sprawl of a jungle cat. "The truth of the matter is I need this kind of life, my pet. The danger, the violence—and the power that comes with it all—they suit me in a way that a boring corporate job could never have." He pauses, then adds, his eyes glittering, "They make me feel alive."

* * *

When we get to the bedroom that evening, I go to take a quick shower while Julian responds to a couple of urgent work emails on his iPad. By the time I come out of the bathroom with a towel wrapped around my damp body, he's put the tablet away and is beginning to undress. As he pulls off his shirt, I sense an unusual excitement within him, a pent-up energy in his movements that hadn't been there before.

"What happened?" I ask warily, our earlier conversation fresh in my mind. Things that excite Julian are, more often than not, something that would make me shudder. Pausing by the bed, I adjust the towel, strangely reluctant to bare myself to his gaze quite yet.

He gives me a brilliant smile as he sits down on the bed to take off his socks. "Do you remember when I told you we had some intelligence on two Al-Quadar cells?" When I nod, he says, "Well, we succeeded in destroying them and even captured three terrorists in the process. Lucas is having them brought here for questioning, so they'll be arriving in the morning."

"Oh." I stare at him, my stomach churning with an unsettling mix of emotions. I understand what 'questioning' implies in Julian's world. I should be horrified and disgusted by the idea that my husband will most likely torture those men—and I am—but deep inside, I also feel a kind of sick, vengeful joy. It's an emotion that disturbs me a lot more than the thought of Julian interrogating them tomorrow. I know these men are not the same ones who murdered Beth, but that doesn't change the way I feel about them. There is a part of me that wants them to pay for Beth's death . . . to suffer for what Majid did.

Apparently misinterpreting my reaction, Julian rises to his feet and says softly, "Don't worry, my pet. They won't hurt you—I'll make sure of that." And before I can respond, he pushes down his jeans to reveal a growing erection.

At the sight of his naked body, a wave of desire washes over me, heating me from the inside out despite my mental turmoil. Over the past couple of weeks, Julian has regained some of the muscle he lost during his coma, and he's even more stunning than before, his shoulders impossibly broad and his skin darkly tanned from the hot sun. Raising my eyes to his face, I wonder for the hundredth time how someone so beautiful can carry such evil inside—and whether some of that evil is beginning to rub off on me.

"I know they won't hurt me here," I say quietly as he reaches for me. "I'm not afraid of them."

A sardonic half-smile appears on his lips as he tugs the towel off my body, dropping it carelessly on the floor. "Are you afraid of *me*?" he murmurs, stepping closer to me. Lifting his hands, he cups my breasts in his large palms and squeezes them, his thumbs playing with my nipples. As he gazes down at me, I notice an amused, yet slightly cruel glint in his blue eyes.

"Should I be?" My heartbeat picks up, my core clenching at the feel of his hard cock brushing against my stomach. His hands are hot and rough on the sensitive skin of my bare breasts, and I inhale sharply as my nipples tighten under his touch. "Are you going to hurt me tonight?"

"Is that what you want, my pet?" He pinches my nipples forcefully, then rolls them between his fingers, causing me to bite back a moan of pleasure tinged with pain. His voice deepens, turning dark and seductive. "Do you want me to hurt you . . . to mark your soft skin and make you scream?"

I lick my lips, tremors of heat and anxious excitement running through my body. I should be frightened, particularly after our conversation tonight, but I'm desperately aroused instead. As perverse as it is, I want this too—I want the ferocity of his desire, the cruelty of his affection. I want to lose myself in the twisted rapture of his embrace, to forget about right and wrong and simply feel. "Yes," I whisper, for the first time admitting to my own dark needs—to the aberrant craving he has instilled in me. "Yes, I do . . ."

Heat flares in his eyes, savage and volcanic, and then we're tumbling to the bed in a primal tangle of limbs and flesh. There's no trace of the deceptively gentle lover now, or of the sophisticated sadist who manipulates my mind and body every night. No, this

Julian is pure male lust, untamed and uncontrolled.

His hands roam over my body, and his mouth is on me, licking, sucking, and biting every inch of my flesh. His left hand finds its way between my thighs, and one big finger pushes into me, making me gasp as he ruthlessly drives it in and out of my wet, quivering sex. He's rough, but the heat inside me only intensifies, and I rake my nails down his back, desperate for more as we roll on the bed, going at each other like animals.

I end up on my back, pinned by his muscled body, my arms stretched above my head and my wrists caught in the iron grip of his right hand. It's the position of the conquered, yet my heart pounds with anticipation rather than fear at the look of predatory hunger on his face.

"I'm going to fuck you," he says harshly, his knees wedging between my thighs and spreading them wide. There's no seduction in his voice now, only raw, aggressive need. "I'm going to fuck you until you beg for mercy—and then I'm going to fuck you more. Do you understand me?"

I manage a tiny nod, my chest heaving as I stare up at him. My breathing is coming fast and hard, and my skin burns where his body touches me. For a moment, I can feel the throbbing length of his erection brushing against the inside of my thigh, the broad head smooth and velvety, and then he grasps his cock with his free hand and guides it to my entrance.

I'm wet, but nowhere near ready for the brutal

thrust with which he joins our bodies, and a shock of pain lashes at my nerve endings as he slams into me, nearly splitting me in half. A cry escapes my throat and my inner muscles tighten, resisting the vicious penetration, but he doesn't give me any time to adjust. Instead he sets a hard, bruising pace, claiming me with a violence that leaves me shaken and breathless, helpless to do anything but accept the relentless pounding of my body.

I don't know how long he fucks me like this—or how many times I come from the battering force of his thrusts. All I know is that by the time he reaches his peak, shuddering over me, I'm hoarse from screaming and so sore that it hurts when he pulls out of me, the wetness of his semen stinging my abraded flesh.

I'm also too worn out to move, so he gets up and goes to the bathroom, returning with a cool, wet towel. Pressing it against my swollen sex, he gently cleans me, then goes down on me, his lips and tongue forcing my exhausted body into another orgasm.

And then we sleep, entwined in each other's arms.

CHAPTER TWELVE

❖ JULIAN ❖

The next morning I wake up when the sunlight touches my face. I deliberately left the drapes open last night, wanting to get an early start on the day. Light works better than any alarm with me, and it's far less disruptive to Nora, who's sleeping draped across my chest.

For a few minutes, I just lie there, luxuriating in the feel of her warm skin pressed against mine, in the soft exhalations of her breath and the way her long lashes lie like dark crescents on her cheeks. I had never wanted to sleep with a woman before her, had never understood the appeal of having another person in your bed for anything but fucking. It was only when I acquired my captive that I learned the simple pleasure of drifting off to sleep while holding her sleek little body . . . of feeling her next to me throughout the night.

Taking a deep breath, I gently shift Nora off me. I need to get up, though the temptation to lie there and do nothing is strong. She doesn't wake up when I sit up, just rolls onto her side and continues sleeping, the blanket sliding off her body and leaving her back largely exposed to my gaze. Unable to resist, I lean over to kiss one slender shoulder and notice a few scratches and bruises marring her smooth skin—marks that I must've inflicted on her last night.

It turns me on, seeing them on her. I like the idea of branding her in some way, of leaving signs of my possession on her delicate flesh. She already wears my ring, but it's not enough. I want more. With each passing day, my need for her grows, my obsession with her intensifying rather than lessening with time.

It disturbs me, this development. I had been hoping that seeing Nora every day and having her as my wife would quell this desperate hunger I feel for her all the time, but just the opposite seems to be happening. I resent every minute that I spend away from her, every moment that I'm not touching her. Just like with any addiction, I seem to require larger and larger doses of my chosen drug, my dependence on her increasing until I'm constantly craving my next fix.

I don't know what I would do if I ever lost her. It's a fear that makes me wake up in a cold sweat at night and assaults my mind at random times throughout the day. I know that she's safe here on the estate—nothing short of a direct attack by a full-fledged army can penetrate my security—but I still can't help worrying, can't help fearing that she'll be taken from me somehow. It's insane, but I'm tempted to keep her chained to my side at all times, so I would know she's okay.

Casting one last look at her sleeping form, I get up as quietly as I can and head into the shower, forcing my thoughts away from my obsession. I will see Nora again this evening, but first, there is an overnight delivery that requires my attention. As my mind turns to the upcoming task, I smile with grim anticipation.

My Al-Quadar prisoners are waiting.

* * *

Lucas had them brought to a storage shed on the far edge of the property. The first thing I notice as I walk in is the stench. It's an acrid combination of sweat, blood, urine, and desperation. It tells me that Peter has already been hard at work this morning.

As my eyes adjust to the dim light inside the shed, I see that two of the men are tied to metal chairs, while the third is hanging from a hook in the ceiling, strung up by a rope binding his wrists above his head. All three of them are covered in dirt and blood, making it difficult to tell their age or nationality.

I approach one of the seated ones first. His left eye is swollen shut, and his lips are puffy and encrusted with blood. His right eye, though, is glaring at me with fury and defiance. A young man, I decide, studying him closer. Early twenties or late teens, with a straggly attempt at a beard and close-trimmed black hair. I doubt he's anything more than a foot soldier, but I still intend to question him. Even small fish can occasionally swallow useful bits of information—and then regurgitate them if prompted properly.

"His name is Ahmed," a deep, faintly accented voice says behind me. Turning, I see Peter standing there, his face as expressionless as always. The fact that I didn't spot him right away doesn't surprise me; Peter Sokolov excels at lurking in the shadows. "He was recruited six months ago in Pakistan."

An even smaller fish than I expected, then. I'm disappointed, but not surprised.

"What about this one?" I ask, walking to the other man in a chair. He appears a bit older, closer to thirty, his thin face clean-shaven. Like Ahmed, he's been roughed up a bit, but there is no fury in his gaze as he looks at me. There is only icy hatred.

"John, also known as Yusuf. Born in America to Palestinian immigrants, recruited by Al-Quadar five years ago. That's all I got out of that one thus far,"

Peter says, pointing at the man hanging on the hook. "John himself hasn't talked to me yet."

"Of course." I stare at John, inwardly pleased by this development. If he's trained to withstand a significant amount of pain and torture, then he's at least a mid-level operative. If we manage to crack him, I'm certain we'll be able to get some valuable insights.

"And this one is Abdul." Peter gestures toward the hanging man. "He's Ahmed's cousin. Supposedly, he joined Al-Quadar last week."

Last week? If that's true, the man is all but useless. Frowning, I walk up to him to take a closer look. At my approach, he tenses, and I see that his face is one massive, swollen bruise. He also reeks of urine. As I pause in front of him, he begins to babble in Arabic, his voice filled with fear and desperation.

"He says he told us all he knows." Peter comes to stand next to me. "Claims he only joined his cousin because they promised to give his family two goats. Swears he's not a terrorist, never wanted to hurt anyone in his life, has nothing against America, et cetera, et cetera."

I nod, having gathered that much myself. I don't speak Arabic, but I understand some of it. A cold smile stretches my lips as I take a Swiss army knife out of my back pocket and pull out a small blade. At the sight of the knife, Abdul yanks frantically at the ropes holding him up, and his pleas grow in volume. He's clearly as green as they come—which makes me inclined to believe that he's telling the truth about not knowing anything.

It doesn't matter, though. All I need from him is information, and if he can't provide it, he's a dead man. "Are you sure you don't know anything else?" I ask him, slowly twirling the knife between my fingers. "Perhaps something you might've seen, heard, come across? Any names, faces, anything of that sort?"

Peter translates my question, and Abdul shakes his head, tears and snot running down his battered, bloodied face. He babbles some more, something about knowing only John, Ahmed, and the men who were killed during their capture yesterday. Out of the corner of my eye, I see Ahmed glaring at him, no doubt wishing that his cousin would keep his mouth shut, but John doesn't seem alarmed by Abdul's verbal diarrhea. John's lack of concern only confirms what my instincts are telling me: that Abdul is telling the truth about not knowing anything else.

As though reading my mind, Peter steps next to me. "Do you want to do the honors, or should I?" His tone is casual, like he's offering me a cup of coffee.

"I'll do it," I reply in the same manner. There is no room for softness in my business, no place for sentimentality. Abdul's guilt or innocence doesn't matter; he allied himself with my enemies and, by doing so, signed his own death warrant. The only mercy I will grant him is that of a swift end to the misery of his existence.

Ignoring the man's terrified pleas, I slice my blade across Abdul's throat, then step back, watching as he bleeds out. When it's over, I wipe the knife on the dead man's shirt and turn to the two remaining prisoners.

"All right," I say, giving them a placid smile. "Who's next?"

* * *

To my annoyance, it takes most of the morning to break Ahmed. For a new recruit, he's surprisingly resilient. He ultimately gives in, of course—they all do—and I learn the name of the man who acts as an intermediary between their cell and another one that's run by a more senior leader. I also learn of a plan to blow up a tour bus in Tel-Aviv—information that my contacts in the Israeli government will find quite useful.

I let John watch the whole process, up until the moment Ahmed takes his last breath. Even though John may be trained to withstand torture, I doubt he's psychologically prepared to see his colleague taken apart piece by piece, all the while knowing that he, John, will be next. Few people are capable of maintaining their cool in a situation like that—and I know that John is not one of them when I catch his gaze dropping to the floor during a particularly gruesome moment. Still, I know it will take us at least a few hours to extract anything from him, and I can't neglect my business for the rest of the day. John will have to wait until this afternoon, after I've had lunch and caught up on some work.

"I can start if you'd like," Peter says when I tell him this. "You know I can do this on my own."

I do know that. In the year that he's worked for me, Peter has proven himself more than capable in this area. However, I prefer to be hands-on whenever possible; in my line of work, micromanaging often pays off.

"No, that's okay," I say. "Why don't you take a lunch break as well? We'll resume this at three."

Peter nods, then slips out of the shed, not even bothering to wash the blood off his hands. I'm more fastidious about these matters, so I walk over to a bucket of water sitting by the wall and rinse the worst of the gory residue off my hands and face. At least I don't need to worry about my clothes; I deliberately wore a black T-shirt and shorts today, so the stains wouldn't be visible. This way, if I run into Nora before I have a chance to change, I won't give her nightmares. She knows what I'm capable of, but knowing and seeing are two very different things. My little wife is still innocent in some ways, and I want her to keep as much of that innocence as possible.

I don't see her on my way home, which is probably for the best. I always feel more feral immediately after a kill, edgy and excited at the same time. It used to bother me, this enjoyment I get out of things that would horrify most people, but I no longer worry about it. It's who I am, who I was trained to be. Self-doubt leads to guilt and regret, and I refuse to entertain those useless emotions.

Once inside the house, I take a thorough shower and change into fresh clothes. Then, feeling much cleaner and calmer, I go down to the kitchen to grab a quick lunch.

Ana isn't there when I walk in, so I make myself a sandwich and sit down to eat at the kitchen table. I have my iPad with me, and for the next half hour, I deal with manufacturing issues at my factory in Malaysia, catch up with my Hong Kong-based supplier, and shoot an email to my contact in Israel about the upcoming bombing.

When I'm done with lunch, I still have a number of phone calls to make, so I head to my office, where I have secure lines of communication set up.

I run into Nora on the porch as I exit the house.

She's coming up the stairs, talking and laughing with Rosa. Dressed in a patterned yellow dress, with her hair loose and streaming down her back, she looks like a ray of sunshine, her smile wide and radiant.

Spotting me, she stops in the middle of the stairs, her smile turning a bit shy. I wonder if she's thinking about last night; my own thoughts certainly turned in that direction as soon as I saw her.

"Hi," she says softly, looking at me. Rosa stops too, inclining her head at me respectfully. I give her a curt nod of acknowledgment before focusing on Nora.

"Hello, my pet." The words come out unintentionally husky. Apparently sensing that she's in the way, Rosa mumbles something about needing to help out in the kitchen and escapes into the house, leaving Nora and me alone on the porch.

Nora grins at her friend's prompt departure, then walks up the remaining steps to stand next to me. "I got the orientation packet from Stanford this morning and already registered for all the classes," she says, her voice filled with barely suppressed excitement. "I have to say, they work *fast*."

I smile at her, pleased to see her so happy. "Yes, they do." And they should—given the generous donation one of my shell corporations made to their alumni fund. For three million dollars, I expect the Stanford admissions office to bend over backwards to accommodate my wife.

"I'm going to call my parents tonight." Her eyes are shining. "Oh, they're going to be so surprised . . ."

"Yes, I'm sure," I say dryly, picturing Tony and Gabriela's reaction to this. I've listened to a few more of Nora's conversations with them, and I know they didn't believe me when I said that Nora would get a good education. It will be useful for my new in-laws to learn that I keep my promises—that I'm serious when it comes to taking care of their daughter. It won't change their opinion of me, of course, but at least they'll be a bit calmer about Nora's future.

Nora grins again, likely picturing the same thing, but then her expression turns unexpectedly somber. "So did they already arrive?" she asks, and I hear a trace of hesitation in her voice. "The Al-Quadar men you've captured?"

"Yes." I don't bother to sugarcoat it. I don't want to traumatize her by letting her see that side of my business, but I'm not going to hide its existence from her either. "I've begun interrogating them."

She stares at me, her earlier excitement nowhere in sight. "Oh, I see." Her eyes travel over my body, lingering on my clean clothes, and I'm glad that I took the precaution to shower and change earlier.

When she lifts her eyes to meet my gaze, there is a peculiar look on her face. "So did you learn anything useful?" she asks softly. "By interrogating them, I mean?"

"Yes, I did," I say slowly. It surprises me that she's curious about this, that she's not acting as appalled as I would've expected. I know she hates Al-Quadar for what they did to Beth, but I still would've expected her to cringe at the thought of torture. A smile tugs at my lips as I wonder just how dark my pet is willing to go these days. "Do you want me to tell you about it?"

She surprises me again by nodding. "Yes," she says quietly, holding my gaze. "Tell me, Julian. I want to know."

CHAPTER THIRTEEN

❖ NORA ❖

I don't know what demon prompted me to say that, and I hold my breath, waiting for Julian to laugh at me and refuse. He has never been keen on telling me much about his business, and though he has opened up to me since his return, I get the sense that he's still trying to shield me from the uglier parts of his world.

To my shock, he doesn't refuse or mock me in any way. Instead he offers me his hand. "All right, my pet," he says, an enigmatic smile playing on his lips. "If you'd like to learn, come with me. I have some calls to make."

My heart pounding, I tentatively put my hand in his and let him lead me down the stairs. As we walk toward the small building that serves as Julian's office, I can't help wondering if I'm making a mistake. Am I ready to give up the questionable comfort of ignorance and dive head first into the murky cesspool of Julian's empire? Truthfully, I have no idea.

Yet I don't stop, don't tell Julian that I changed my mind . . . because I haven't. Because deep inside, I know that burying my head in the sand changes nothing. My husband is a dangerous, powerful criminal, and my lack of knowledge about his activities doesn't alter the fact that I'm dirty by association. By willingly going into his arms every night—by loving him despite everything he's done—I am implicitly condoning his actions, and I'm not naïve enough to think otherwise. I might have started off as Julian's victim, but I don't know if I can claim that dubious distinction anymore. Syringe or not, I went with him knowing full well what he was and what kind of life I was signing up for.

Besides, a dark curiosity is riding me now. I want to know what he learned this morning, what kind of information his brutal methods availed him. I want to know what phone calls he's planning to make and to whom he's planning to speak. I want to know everything there is to know about Julian, no matter how much the reality of his life horrifies me.

When we come up to the office building, I see that

the door is made of metal. Just like on the island, Julian opens it by submitting to a retina scan—a security measure that no longer surprises me. Given what I now know about the types of weapons Julian's company produces, his paranoia appears quite justified.

We go inside, and I see that it's all one big room, with a large oval table near the entrance and a wide desk with a bunch of computer screens at the back. Flatscreen TV monitors line the walls, and there are comfortable-looking leather chairs around the table. Everything seems very high-tech and luxurious. To me, Julian's office looks like a cross between an executive conference room and some place I imagine the CIA might meet to strategize.

As I stand there, gaping at everything, Julian places his hands on my shoulders from behind. "Welcome to my lair," he murmurs, his fingers tightening for a brief moment. Then he lets go of me and walks over to sit down behind the desk.

I follow him there, driven by burning curiosity.

There are six computer monitors sitting on the table. Three of them are showing what appears to be a live feed from various surveillance cameras, and two are filled with different charts and blinking numbers. The last computer is the one closest to Julian, and it's displaying some type of unusual-looking email program.

Intrigued, I take a closer look, trying to figure out what I'm seeing. "Are you monitoring your investments?" I ask, peering at the two computers with the blinking numbers. I'm far from a stock guru, but I've seen a couple of movies about Wall Street, and Julian's setup reminds me of the traders' desks they had there.

"You could say that." When I turn to look at him, Julian leans back in his chair and smiles at me. "One of my subsidiaries is a hedge fund of sorts. It dabbles in everything from currencies to oil, with a focus on special situations and geopolitical events. I have some very qualified people running it, but I find that stuff quite interesting and occasionally like to play with it myself."

"Oh, I see . . ." I stare at him, fascinated. This is yet another side of Julian I knew nothing about before. It makes me wonder how many more layers I'm going to uncover with time. "So who are you planning to call?" I ask, remembering the phone calls he mentioned earlier.

Julian's smile widens. "Come here, baby, have a seat," he says, reaching out to grab my wrist. Before I know it, he's got me sitting on his lap, his arms effectively caging me between his chest and the edge of the desk. "Just sit here and be quiet," he whispers in my ear, and quickly types something on his keyboard while I sit there, breathing in his warm scent and feeling his hard body all around me.

I hear a few beeps, then a man's voice comes from the computer. "Esguerra. I was wondering when you would be in touch." The speaker has an American accent and sounds well educated, if a bit stuffy. I immediately picture a middle-aged man in a suit. A bureaucrat of some kind, but a senior one, judging from the confidence in his voice. One of Julian's government contacts, perhaps?

"I assume our Israeli friends filled you in already," Julian says.

Holding my breath, I listen intently, not wanting to miss anything. I don't know why Julian decided to let me learn this way, but I'm not about to quibble.

"I don't have much to add," Julian continues. "As you already know, the operation was a success, and I now have a couple of detainees that I'm milking for information."

"Yes, so we've heard." There is silence for a second, then the man says, "We would appreciate hearing this kind of news first next time. It would've been nice if the Israelis had heard about the bus from us, rather than the other way around."

"Oh, Frank . . ." Julian sighs, wrapping his arm around my waist and shifting me slightly to the left. Feeling off-balance, I clutch at Julian's arm, trying not to make any sounds as he settles me more comfortably on his leg. "You know how these things work. If you'd like to be the one spoon-feeding the Israelis, I need a little something to sweeten the deal."

"We already wiped away all traces of your misadventure with the girl," Frank says evenly, and I tense, realizing he's referring to my abduction.

A misadventure? Really? For a second, irrational fury spikes through me, but then I take a calming breath and remind myself that I don't actually want Julian punished for what he did to me—not if it means being separated from him again. Still, it would've been nice if they had at least acknowledged that Julian committed a crime instead of calling it a fucking 'misadventure.' It's stupid, but I feel disrespected somehow—like I don't even matter.

Oblivious to my stewing over his word choice, Frank continues, "There's nothing more we can give you at this point—"

"Actually, you can," Julian interrupts. Still holding me tightly, he strokes my arm in a proprietary, soothing gesture. As usual, his touch warms me from within, takes away some of my tension. He probably understands why I'm upset; no matter how you slice it, it's insulting to have your kidnapping talked about so casually.

"How about a little tit for tat?" Julian continues softly, addressing Frank. "I let you be the heroes next time, and you let me in on some back-channel action with Syria. I'm sure there are a few tidbits you'd like to leak . . . and I'd love to be the one to help you out."

There is another moment of silence, then Frank says gruffly, "Fine. Consider it done."

"Excellent. Until next time then," Julian says and, reaching forward, clicks on the corner of the screen to disconnect the call.

As soon as he's done, I twist around in Julian's arms to look at him. "Who was that man?"

"Frank is one of my contacts at the CIA," Julian replies, confirming my earlier supposition. "A paper pusher, but one who's quite good at his job."

"Ah, I thought so." Beginning to feel restless, I push at Julian's chest, needing to get up. He releases me, watching with a faint smile as I back up a couple of steps, then prop my hip against the desk and give him a questioning look. "What was that about Israelis and the bus? And Syria?"

"According to one of my Al-Quadar guests, there is an attack planned on a tour bus in Tel-Aviv," Julian explains, leaning back in his chair. "I notified the Mossad—the Israeli intelligence agency—about it earlier today."

"Oh." I frown. "So why did Frank object to that?"

"Because the Americans have a savior complex—or would like the Israelis to think they do. They want this information to be coming from them instead of me, so that the Mossad owes *them* a favor."

"Ah, I see." And I do. I'm beginning to understand how this game works. In the shadowy world of intelligence agencies and off-the-record politics, favors are like currency—and my husband is rich in more ways than one. Rich enough to ensure that he would never be prosecuted for petty crimes like kidnapping or illegal arms dealing. "And you want Frank to give you some info to leak to Syria, so they owe *you* a favor, right?"

Julian grins at me, white teeth flashing. "Yes, indeed. You're a quick study, my pet."

"Why did you decide to let me listen in today?" I ask, eyeing him curiously. "Why today of all days?"

Instead of responding, he rises to his feet and comes toward me. Stopping next to me, he bends forward and places his hands on the desk on both sides of my body, trapping me again. "Why do you think, Nora?" he murmurs, leaning closer. His breath is warm against my cheek, and his arms are like steel beams surrounding me. It makes me feel like a small animal caught in a hunter's snare—an unsettling sensation that nonetheless turns me on.

"Because we're married?" I guess in an uneven voice. His face is mere inches from mine, and my lower belly tightens with a strong surge of arousal as he nudges his hips forward, letting me feel his hardening erection.

"Yes, baby, because we're married," he says huskily, his eyes darkening with lust as my peaked nipples brush against his chest, "and because I think you're no longer as fragile as you seem . . ."

And lowering his head, he captures my mouth in a hungry, possessive kiss, his hands sliding up my thighs with familiar intent.

* * *

Over the next few days, I learn more about Julian's dark empire, and I begin to understand how little most people know about what goes on behind the scenes. None of what I hear in Julian's office ever shows up on the news . . . because if it did, heads would roll, and some very important people would end up in jail.

Amused by my continued interest, Julian lets me listen in on more conversations. Once I even get to watch a video conference from the back of the room, where I can't be seen by the camera. To my shock, I recognize one of the men on the video feed. It's a prominent US general—someone I've seen a couple of times on popular talk shows. He wants Julian to move his manufacturing operations from Thailand out of fear that political instability in the region could derail the next shipment of the new explosive—the shipment that's supposed to go to the US government.

My former captor hadn't been lying when he said he has connections; if anything, he'd understated the extent of his reach.

Of course, politicians, military leaders, and others of their ilk are but a small fraction of the people Julian deals with on a daily basis. The majority of his interactions are with clients, suppliers, and various intermediaries—shady and usually frightening individuals from all over the world. His acquaintances range from Russian mafia and Libyan rebels to dictators in obscure African countries. When it comes to selling weapons, my husband is very egalitarian. Terrorists, drug lords, legitimate governments—he does business with them all.

It turns my stomach, but I can't bring myself to stay out of Julian's office. Every day I follow him there, driven by morbid curiosity. It's like watching some kind of undercover exposé; the things I learn are both fascinating and disturbing.

It takes Julian three days, but he manages to break the last Al-Quadar prisoner. How, he doesn't tell me and I don't ask. I know it's through torture, but I don't know the particulars. I just know that the information he extracts results in Julian locating two more Al-Quadar cells—and the CIA owing him another favor.

Now that Julian has decided to let me into that portion of his life, we spend even more time together. He likes having me in his office. Not only is it convenient for when he wants sex—which is at least once during the day—but he also seems to enjoy the speed with which I'm learning. I'm sharp, he says. Intuitive. I see things as they are instead of as I want them to be—a rare gift, according to Julian.

"Most people wear blinders," he tells me over lunch one day, "but not you, my pet. You face reality head-on . . . and that's what lets you see beneath the surface."

I thank him for the compliment, but inwardly I wonder if it's necessarily a good thing, seeing beneath the surface like that. If I could pretend to myself that at the core, Julian is a good man—that he is simply misunderstood and can ultimately be reformed—it would be so much easier for me. If I were blind to my husband's nature, I wouldn't feel so conflicted about my feelings for him.

I wouldn't worry that I'm in love with the devil.

But I do see him for what he is—a demon in a handsome man's disguise, a monster wearing a beautiful mask. And I wonder if that means that I'm a monster too . . . that I'm evil for loving him.

I wish I had Beth to talk to about this. I know she wasn't exactly an expert on normal, but I still miss her unorthodox views on things, the way she could turn everything on its head and have it make some kind of twisted sense. I'm pretty sure I know what she would say in regard to my situation. She would tell me I'm lucky to have someone like Julian—that we are meant to be together and everything else is bullshit.

And she would probably be right. When I think back to those lonely, empty months before Julian's return—when I had my freedom and normal life, but didn't have *him*—all my doubts fade away. No matter what he is or what he does, I would sooner die than go through that soul-crushing misery again.

For better or worse, I'm no longer complete without Julian, and no amount of self-flagellation can alter that fact.

* * *

A week after Julian's conversation with Frank, I knock on the heavy metal door and wait for him to let me in. I had spent the morning walking with Rosa and preparing for my upcoming classes, while Julian went in without me to do some paperwork for his offshore accounts. Apparently, even crime lords have to deal with taxes and legal matters; it appears to be a universal evil that no one can avoid.

When the door swings open, I'm surprised to see a tall, dark-haired man sitting across the large oval table from Julian. He looks to be in his mid-thirties, just a few years older than my husband. I have seen him walking around the estate before, but I've never had an occasion to interact with him in person. From a distance, he'd reminded me of a sleek, dark predator— an impression that's only strengthened by the way he's looking at me now, his gray eyes tracking my every move with a peculiar mix of watchfulness and indifference.

"Come in, Nora," Julian says, gesturing for me to join them. "This is Peter Sokolov, our security consultant."

"Oh, hi. It's very nice to meet you." Walking over to the table, I give Peter a cautious smile as I sit down next to Julian. Peter is a good-looking man, with a strong jaw and high, exotically slanted cheekbones, but for some reason, he makes the fine hair at the back of my neck stand up. It's not what he says or does—he nods at me politely while sitting there, his pose deceptively calm and relaxed—it's what I see in his steel-colored eyes.

Rage. Pure, undiluted rage. I sense it within Peter, feel it emanating from his pores. It's not anger or a momentary flare-up of temper. No, this emotion goes deeper than that. It's a part of him, like his hard-muscled body or the white scar that bisects his left eyebrow.

For all his cold, carefully controlled demeanor, the man is a deadly volcano waiting to explode.

"We were just finishing up," Julian says, and I catch a note of displeasure in his voice. Tearing my eyes away from Peter, I see a tiny muscle flexing in Julian's jaw. I must've stared at Peter for too long without realizing it, and my husband misinterpreted my involuntary fascination as interest.

Shit. A jealous Julian is never a good thing. In fact, it's a very, very bad thing.

As I rack my brain trying to figure out how to diffuse the situation, Peter rises to his feet. "We can resume this tomorrow if you'd like," he says calmly, addressing Julian. I can't help noticing that unlike most on the estate, Peter doesn't defer to my husband. Instead he speaks to Julian as an equal, his demeanor respectful, yet utterly self-assured. I catch a faint Eastern European accent in his speech, and I wonder where he's from. Poland? Russia? Ukraine?

"Yes," Julian says, getting up as well. His expression is still dark, but his voice is now smooth and even. "I'll see you tomorrow."

Peter disappears, leaving us alone, and I slowly rise to my feet, my palms beginning to sweat. I didn't do anything wrong, but convincing Julian of that won't be easy. His possessiveness borders on the obsessive; sometimes I'm surprised he doesn't keep me locked away in his bedroom, so that other men will never see me.

Sure enough, as soon as the door closes behind Peter, Julian steps toward me. "Did you like Peter, my pet?" he says softly, crowding me with his powerful body until I'm forced to back up against the table. "Do you have a thing for Russian men?"

"No." I shake my head, holding Julian's gaze. I'm hoping he can see the truth on my face. Peter might be handsome, but he's also scary—and the only scary man I want is the one glaring at me right now. "Not even a little bit. That's not why I was looking at him."

"No?" Julian's eyes narrow as he grasps my chin. "Why then?"

"He frightened me," I admit, figuring that honesty is the best policy here. "There's something about him that I found disturbing."

Julian studies me intently for a second, then releases my chin and steps back, causing me to let out a relieved breath. *Storm averted.*

"As insightful as always," he murmurs, his voice holding a note of rueful amusement. "Yes, you're right, Nora. There is indeed something disturbing about

Peter."

"What is his deal?" I ask, my curiosity reawakening now that Julian is no longer angry with me. I know Julian doesn't employ choirboys, but what I sensed in Peter is different, more volatile. "Who is he?"

Julian gives me a small, grim smile and walks over to sit down behind his desk. "He's former Spetsnaz— Russian Special Forces. He was one of the best until his wife and son were killed. Now he wants revenge, and he came to me hoping that I can help him."

I feel a flicker of pity. It's not only rage then; Peter is also filled with grief and pain.

"Help him how?" I ask, leaning back against the table. Julian's security consultant didn't strike me as someone who'd need help with many things.

"By using my connections to get him a list of names. Apparently, there were some NATO soldiers involved, and the cover-up is a mile deep."

"Oh." I stare at Julian, feeling uneasy. I can only imagine what Peter intends to do with those soldiers. "So did you give him this list?"

"Not yet. I'm working on it. A lot of this information seems to be classified, so it's not easy."

"Can't you ask your contact at the CIA to help you?"

"I did ask him. Frank is dragging his feet because there are some Americans on that list." Julian looks annoyed for a brief second. "He'll come through eventually, though. He always does. I just need to have something the CIA wants badly enough."

"Right, of course," I murmur. "A favor for a favor . . . Is that why Peter is working for you? Because you promised him this list?"

"Yes, that's our deal." Julian smiles sharply. "Three years of loyal service in exchange for getting him those names at the end. I also pay him, of course—but Peter doesn't care about money."

"What about Lucas?" I ask, my thoughts turning to Julian's right-hand man. "Does he also have a story?"

"Everybody has a story," Julian says, but he sounds distracted now, his attention straying to the computer screen. "Even you, my pet."

And before I can pry further, he busies himself with emails, putting an end to our discussion for the day.

CHAPTER FOURTEEN

❖ JULIAN ❖

The next few weeks come as close to domestic bliss as I have ever experienced. Other than one day trip to Mexico for a negotiation with the Juarez cartel, I spend all my time on the estate with Nora.

With her classes having started, Nora's days are filled with textbooks, papers, and tests. She's so busy that she often studies late into the evening—a practice that I dislike, but don't put a stop to. She seems determined to prove that she can hold her own with the students who got into the Stanford program on their own merit, and I don't want to discourage her. I know she's doing this partly for her parents—who continue to worry about her future with me—and partly because she's enjoying the challenge. Despite the added stress, my pet seems to be thriving these days, her eyes bright with excitement and her movements filled with purposeful energy.

I like that development. I like seeing her happy and confident, content with her life with me. Though the monster inside me still gets off on her pain and fear, her growing strength and resilience appeal to me. I never wanted to break her, only to make her mine— and it pleases me to see her becoming my match in more ways than one.

Although schoolwork consumes much of her time, Nora continues her tutelage with Monsieur Bernard, saying that she finds it relaxing to draw and paint. She also insists that I continue giving her self-defense and shooting lessons twice a week—a request that I'm more than happy to fulfill, as it gives us more time together. As the training progresses, I see that she's better with guns than with knives, though she's surprisingly decent with both. She's also becoming quite good at certain fighting moves, her small body slowly but surely turning into a lethal weapon. She even manages to bloody my nose one time, her sharp elbow connecting with my face before I have a chance to block her lightning-fast strike.

It's an achievement she should be proud of, but, of course, being the good girl that she is, Nora is immediately horrified and remorseful.

"Oh my God, I'm so sorry!" She rushes to me, grabbing a towel to stop the bleeding. She appears so distraught that I burst out laughing, though my nose throbs like a son of a bitch. This is what I get for being distracted during training. She'd managed to catch me off-guard at a moment when I was looking at her breasts and fantasizing about pulling up her sports bra.

"Julian! Why are you laughing?" Nora's voice rises in pitch as she presses the towel to my face. "You should see a doctor! It could be broken——"

"It's fine, baby," I reassure her between bouts of laughter, taking the towel from her shaking hands. "I can promise you I've had worse. If it were broken, I'd know it." My voice sounds nasal due to the towel pressed against my nose, but I can feel the cartilage with my fingers, and it's straight, undamaged. I'll have a black eye, but that's about it. If I hadn't deflected to the right at the last second, though, her move could've crushed my nose completely, forcing fragments of bone into my brain and killing me on the spot.

"It's not fine!" Nora steps away, still looking extremely upset. "I could've seriously hurt you!"

"Wouldn't I have deserved it?" I say, only half-teasing. I know there is a part of her that still resents me for the way I took her—that will always resent me for that. If I were her, I wouldn't apologize for causing me pain. I'd look for opportunities to kick my ass any chance I got.

She glares at me, but I see that she's beginning to calm down now that the immediate shock is over. "Probably," she says in a more level tone of voice. "But that doesn't mean I want you to suffer. I'm stupid and irrational like that, you see."

I grin at her, lowering the towel. The bleeding is almost over; as I had suspected, it was only a mild hit. "You're not stupid," I say softly, stepping closer to her. Though my nose still hurts, there is a new, growing ache in a much lower region of my body. "You're exactly as I want you to be."

"Brainwashed and in love with my kidnapper?" she asks drily as I reach for her, dropping the bloodied towel on the floor.

"Yes, exactly," I murmur, pulling off her sports bra to bare her small, perfectly shaped breasts. "And very, very fuckable . . ."

And as I tug her down to the mat, my injury is the last thing on my mind.

* * *

As Nora's semester progresses, we develop a routine. I usually wake up before her and go for a training session with my men. When I return, she's awake, so we eat breakfast, and then I head into the office while Nora goes for a walk with Rosa and listens to the online lectures. After a few hours, I come back to the house, and we have lunch together. Then I go back to my office, and Nora either meets Monsieur Bernard for her art lesson or joins me in the office, where she studies quietly while I work or conduct meetings. Even though she appears not to be paying attention at those times, I know that she does—because she often asks me follow-up questions about the business at dinner.

I don't mind her curiosity, even though I know she silently condemns what I do. The idea that I supply weapons to criminals and the often-brutal methods I use to maintain control over the business are anathema to Nora. She doesn't understand that if I didn't do this, someone else would, and the world would not necessarily be safer or better. Drug lords and dictators would get their weapons one way or another. The only question is who would profit from it—and I would prefer that person to be me.

I know Nora doesn't agree with that reasoning, but it doesn't matter. I don't need her approval—all I need is her.

And I have her. She's with me so much that I'm beginning to forget what it feels like not to have her by my side. We're rarely apart for more than a few hours at a time, and when we are, I miss her so intensely, it's like a physical ache in my chest. I have no idea how I had been able to leave her alone on the island for days or even weeks at a time. Now I don't even like to see Nora go for a run without me, so I do my best to accompany her when she sprints around the estate in late afternoon.

I do that because I want my wife's company, but also to make sure that she's safe. Though my enemies can't steal her here, there are snakes, spiders, and poisonous frogs in the area. And in the nearby rainforest, there are jaguars and other jungle predators. The chances of her getting stung or seriously hurt by a wild animal are small, but I'm not willing to risk it. I can't bear the thought of any harm coming to her. When Nora had her appendicitis attack, I'd nearly gone out of my mind with panic—and that was before my addiction to her reached this new, utterly insane level.

My fear of losing her is starting to border on the pathological. I recognize that, but I don't know how to control it. It's a sickness that seems to have no cure. I worry about Nora constantly, obsessively. I want to know where she is at every moment of every day. She's rarely out of my sight, but when she is, I can't concentrate, my mind conjuring up deadly accidents that could befall her and other frightening scenarios.

"I want you to put two guards on Nora," I tell Lucas one morning. "I want them to tail her whenever she walks around the estate, so they can make sure nothing happens to her."

"All right." Lucas doesn't blink at my unusual request. "I'll work with Peter to free up two of our best men."

"Good. And I want them to text me a report on her every hour on the dot."

"Consider it done."

The guards' hourly reports keep my fears at bay for a couple of weeks—until I get an email that turns my world upside down.

* * *

"Majid is alive," I tell Nora at dinner, carefully watching her reaction. "I just heard from one of Peter's contacts in Moscow. He's been spotted in Tajikistan."

Her eyes widen in shock and dismay. "What? But he died in the explosion!"

"No, unfortunately he didn't." I do my best to keep my rage under control. The fact that Beth's murderer is alive makes my blood boil with pure acid. "It turns out he and four others left the warehouse two hours before I got there. You didn't see him there when I came for you, right?"

"No, I didn't." Nora frowns. "I assumed he was outside, guarding the building or something . . ."

"That's what I thought, too. But he wasn't. He was nowhere near the warehouse when the explosion occurred."

"How do you know this?"

"The Russians captured one of the four men who left with Majid that night. They caught him in Moscow, plotting to blow up the subway." Despite my best efforts, fury seeps into my voice, and I can see the corresponding tension in Nora. If there's any topic that can move my pet to anger, it's that of Beth's murderers.

"They interrogated him and learned that he's been in hiding in Eastern Europe and Central Asia for the past few months, along with Majid and the three others."

Before Nora can respond, Ana walks into the dining room.

"Would you like some dessert?" the housekeeper asks us, and Nora shakes her head, her soft mouth drawn in a tight line.

"None for me, thanks," I say curtly, and Ana disappears, leaving us alone once again.

"So what now?" Nora asks. "Are you going to track him down?"

"Yes." And when I do, I'm going to take him apart, one piece of flesh and bone at a time—but I don't tell Nora that. Instead I explain, "His cohort admitted to last seeing Majid in Tajikistan, so that's where we'll start our search. Apparently, he's managed to gather a sizable group of new followers in the last few months, injecting fresh blood into Al-Quadar."

That last tidbit worries me quite a bit. Though we've done serious damage to the terrorist group over the past couple of months, the Al-Quadar organization is so spread out that there could still be a dozen functional cells throughout the world. Combined with the new recruits, these cells could be just powerful enough to be dangerous—and, according to the intelligence Peter got from his contacts, Majid is getting ready for something big . . . something in Latin America.

He's preparing to strike back at me.

He won't penetrate the security of the estate, of course, but just the possibility of these motherfuckers coming within a hundred miles of Nora makes me livid with rage and awakens the fear that I can't quite shake.

The stark, irrational fear of losing her.

There are two-hundred-plus highly trained men guarding the compound and dozens of military-grade drones sweeping the area. Nobody can touch her here, but that doesn't change the way I feel, doesn't quell the primitive panic gnawing at my insides. All I want to do is grab Nora and carry her as far away as possible, to a place where no one will ever find her . . . where she will be mine and mine alone.

But there is no place like that anymore. My enemies know about her, and they know that she's important to me. I've proven that by coming after her before. If they still want the explosive—and I am certain that they do—they will try to get her, again and again, until they are completely wiped out.

Overkill or not, given this new information, I need to take additional precautions to ensure Nora's safety.

I need to make sure I always have a connection to her.

"What are you thinking?" Nora asks, a concerned expression on her face, and I realize that I've been staring at her for a couple of minutes without saying anything.

I force myself to smile. "Nothing much, my pet. I

just want to make sure you're safe, that's all."

"Why wouldn't I be safe?" She looks more puzzled than worried.

"Because there is a rumor Majid may be planning something in Latin America," I explain as calmly as I can. I don't want to frighten her, but I do want her to understand why I have to take these precautions.

Why I have to do what I'm about to do to her.

"You think they're coming here?" Her face pales a bit, but her voice remains steady. "You think they're going to try to attack the estate?"

"They might. It doesn't mean they will succeed, but they will most likely try." Reaching across the table, I close my fingers around her delicate hand, wanting to reassure her with my touch. Her skin is chilled, betraying her agitation, and I massage her palm lightly to warm it up. "That's why I want to make sure that I can always find you, baby—that I can always know where you are."

She frowns, and I feel her hand growing even colder before she pulls it out of my grasp. "What do you mean?" Her voice is even, but I can see the pulse at the base of her throat beginning to quicken. As I had anticipated, she's not overjoyed with the idea.

"I want to put some trackers on you," I explain, holding her gaze. "They will be embedded in a couple of places on your body, so if you're ever stolen from me, I would be able to locate you right away."

"Trackers? You mean ... like GPS chips or

something? Like something you would use to tag cattle?"

My lips tighten. She's going to be difficult about this, I can already tell. "No, not like that," I say evenly. "These trackers are currently classified and intended specifically for human use. They will have GPS chips, yes, but they will also have sensors that measure your heart rate and body temperature. This way I will always know if you're alive."

"And you will always know where I am," she says quietly, her eyes dark in her pale face.

"Yes. I will always know where you are." The thought fills me with immense relief and satisfaction. I should've done this weeks ago, as soon as I retrieved her from Illinois. "It's for your own safety, Nora," I add, wanting to emphasize that point. "If you had these trackers when you and Beth were taken, I would've found you right away."

And Beth would still be alive. I don't say that last part, but I don't need to. At my words, Nora flinches, like I just struck her a blow, and pain flashes across her face.

She recovers her composure a second later, however. "So let me get this straight . . ." She leans forward, placing her forearms on the table, and I see that her fingers are tightly laced together, her knuckles white with tension. "You want to implant some chips *inside my body* that will tell you where I am *all the time*—just so I'll be safe on a remote compound that has more security than the White House?"

Her tone is heavy with sarcasm, and I feel my temper rising in response. I indulge her in many things, but I will not take risks with her safety. It would've been easier if she'd chosen to cooperate, but I'm not about to let her reluctance deter me from doing the right thing.

"Why, yes, my pet, that's right," I say silkily, getting up from my chair. "That's exactly what I want. You're getting these trackers today. Now, in fact."

CHAPTER FIFTEEN

❖ NORA ❖

Stunned, I stare at Julian, my heartbeat roaring in my ears. A part of me can't believe he's going to do this to me against my will—tag me like some dumb animal, depriving me of any semblance of privacy and freedom—while the rest of me is screaming that I'm an idiot, that I should've known that a tiger doesn't change his stripes.

It's just that the last few weeks had been so different from anything we've had together before. I'd begun to imagine that Julian was opening up to me, that he was truly letting me into his life. Despite his dominance in the bedroom and the control he exerts over all aspects of my life, I'd started to feel less like his sex toy and more like his partner. I let myself believe that we were becoming something like a normal couple, that he was beginning to genuinely care for me . . . to respect me.

Like a fool, I bought into the delusion of a happy life with my kidnapper—with a man utterly lacking in conscience or morals.

How stupid, how gullible of me. I want to kick myself and cry at the same time. I've always known what kind of man Julian is, but I still let myself get taken in by his charm, by the way he seemed to want me, need me.

I allowed myself to think I could be something more than a possession to him.

Realizing that I'm still sitting there, reeling from the painful disillusionment, I push back my chair and get up to face Julian from across the table. The kicked-in-the-stomach sensation is still there, but now so is anger. Pure and intense, it's spreading through my body, sweeping out the remnants of shock and hurt.

These trackers have nothing to do with my safety. I know the extent of the security measures on the estate, and I know that the chances of anyone being able to take me again are beyond minuscule. No, the renewed terrorist threat is just a pretext, a convenient excuse for Julian to do what he's probably been planning to do all along. It gives him a reason to increase his control over me, to bind me to him so tightly that I will never so much as take a breath without his knowledge.

The trackers will make me his prisoner for the rest of my life . . . and as much as I love Julian, that is not a fate I'm willing to accept.

"No," I say, and I'm surprised at how calm and steady my voice sounds. "I'm not getting these implants."

Julian raises his eyebrows. "Oh?" His eyes glint with anger and a faint hint of amusement. "And how would you prevent it, my pet?"

I lift my chin, my heartbeat accelerating further. Despite all the hours of training in the gym, I'm still no match for Julian in a fight. He can subdue me in thirty seconds flat—not to mention he has all these guards under his command. If he's set on forcing these trackers on me, I won't be able to stop him.

But that doesn't mean I won't try.

"Fuck you," I say, clearly enunciating each word. "Fuck you and these chips of yours." And operating on pure adrenaline-driven instinct, I shove the dinner plates across the table at Julian and bolt for the door.

The plates crash to the floor with a shattering noise, and I hear Julian cursing as he jumps back to avoid getting splattered with food. He's distracted for a moment, and that's all the time I need as I sprint to the door and out into the foyer. I don't know where I'm going, nor do I have anything resembling a plan. All I know is that I can't stay there and meekly go along with this new violation.

I can't be Julian's submissive little victim again.

I hear him chasing after me as I run through the house, and I have a sudden flashback to my first day on the island. I ran then too, trying to escape from the man who would become my entire life. I remember how terrified I felt, how woozy from the drugs he'd given me. That was the day Julian had first introduced me to the devastating pleasure-pain of his touch, the day I first realized I was no longer in charge of my life.

I don't know why I let this tracker thing surprise me. Julian has never once expressed regret over taking away any of my choices, has never apologized for kidnapping me or forcing me to marry him. He treats me well because he wants to, not because there are any adverse consequences to doing otherwise. There's no one to stop him from doing anything he wants with me, no safe word that I can use to enforce my limits.

I may be his wife, but I'm still his captive in every way that counts.

I'm at the front door now, and I grab the handle, pulling it open. Out of the corner of my eye, I see Ana standing near the wall, gaping at me as I fly out the door with Julian hot on my heels. I'm running so fast that I feel only a flash of embarrassment at the notion of her seeing us like this. I think our housekeeper suspects the BDSM-y nature of our relationship—my summer clothes don't always hide the marks Julian leaves on my skin—and I hope she chalks this up to nothing more than a kinky game.

I have no idea where I'm heading as I sprint down

the front steps, but that doesn't matter. All I want is to evade Julian for a few moments, to buy myself some time. I don't know what it will gain me, but I know that I need this—that I need to feel like I did *something* to defy him, that I didn't bow down to the inevitable without a fight.

I'm halfway across the wide green lawn when I feel Julian gaining on me. I can hear his harsh breathing—he must be going at his top speed as well—and then his hand closes around my left upper arm, spinning me around and yanking me into his hard body.

The impact stuns me for a moment, knocking the breath out of my lungs, but my body reacts on autopilot, my self-defense training kicking in. Instead of attempting to pull away, I drop down like a stone, trying to pull Julian off-balance. At the same time, my knee comes up, aiming for his balls, and my right fist flies straight at his chin.

Anticipating my move, he twists at the last moment, turning so that my fist misses his face and my knee connects with his thigh instead. Before I get a chance to try anything else, he drops me, letting my back hit the grass, and immediately pins me down with his full weight, using his legs to control mine and catching my wrists to stretch my arms up above my head.

I'm now completely incapacitated, as helpless as ever, and Julian knows it.

A soft chuckle escapes his throat as he meets my furious gaze. "Dangerous little thing, aren't you?" he murmurs, settling more comfortably on top of me. To my annoyance, his breathing is already beginning to return to normal, and his blue eyes are glowing with unconcealed amusement and delight. "You know, if I hadn't been the one to teach you that move, my pet, it might've actually worked."

My chest heaving, I glare up at him, seething with an urge to do something violent to him. The fact that he's enjoying this only intensifies my fury, and I buck upward with all my strength, trying to throw him off me. It's futile, of course; he's more than twice my size, every inch of his powerful body packed with steely muscle. All I succeed in doing is amusing him further.

Well, that, and arousing him—as evidenced by the hardening bulge against my leg.

"Let go of me," I hiss between clenched teeth, sharply cognizant of my body's automatic response to that hardness—to his body pressing against me this way. Being held down like this is something I associate with sex these days, and I hate that I'm turned on right now, my core pulsing with heated need despite my anger and resentment. It's yet another thing I have no control over; my body is conditioned to respond to Julian's dominance no matter what.

His sensuous lips curl into a satisfied half-smile. The bastard is undoubtedly aware of my involuntary arousal. "Or what, my pet?" he breathes, staring at me as he pries my tense legs apart with his knees. "What are you going to do?"

I glare at him defiantly, doing my best to ignore the threat of his rock-hard erection pressing against my entrance. Only his jeans and my flimsy underwear separate us now, and I know Julian can get rid of these barriers in a heartbeat. The only obstacle to him fucking me right now—and the one I'm counting on—is the fact that we're in full view of all the guards and whoever else happens to be strolling by the house at this particular moment. Exhibitionism is not Julian's thing—he's too possessive for that—and I feel reasonably certain he won't take me out in the open like this.

He may do other things to me, but I'm safe from sexual punishment for now.

That fact and my anger spur my reckless reply. "Actually, the real question is what are *you* going to do, Julian?" I say, my voice low and bitter. "Are you going to drag me kicking and screaming to get these trackers put in? Because that's what you'll have to do, you know—I'm not going to go along with this like some good little captive. I'm done playing that role."

His smile disappears, replaced by a look of ruthless determination. "I'm going to do whatever it takes to keep you safe, Nora," he says harshly and rises to his feet, hauling me up with him.

I struggle, but it's pointless; within a second, he has me lifted up in his arms, one of his hands restraining my wrists and the other arm tightly hooked under my knees, essentially immobilizing my legs. Incensed, I arch my spine, trying to break his grip, but he's holding me too securely for that. All I succeed in doing is tiring myself out, and after a couple of minutes, I stop, panting in frustrated exhaustion as Julian begins walking back toward the house, carrying me like a helpless child.

"You can scream if you want," he informs me as we approach the porch steps. His voice is calm and detached, and his face is empty of all emotion as he glances down at me. "It won't change anything, but you're welcome to try."

I know he's probably using reverse psychology on me, but I remain silent as he pushes open the front door with his back and enters the house. My earlier anger is fading, a kind of weary resignation taking its place. I've always known that fighting Julian is pointless, and what happened today only confirms that fact. I can resist all I want, but it will avail me nothing.

As Julian carries me into the foyer, I see Ana still standing there, staring at us in shock and fascination. She must've stayed to watch the conclusion of the chase through the window, and I can feel her gaze following us as Julian walks past her without a word.

Now that the immediate rush of adrenaline has passed, I am aware of a deep flush of embarrassment. It's one thing for Ana to notice a few faint bruises on my thighs, but it's another thing entirely for her to see us like this. I'm sure she's seen worse—after all, she works for a crime lord—but I still can't help feeling uncomfortably exposed. I don't want people on the estate to know the truth about my relationship with Julian; I don't want them to look at me with pity in their eyes. I had plenty of that back home in Oak Lawn, and I'm not eager to repeat the experience.

"Are you just going to shove the trackers in?" I ask Julian as he brings me into our bedroom. "With no anesthesia or anything?" My tone is deeply sarcastic, but I am genuinely wondering about that. I know my husband enjoys inflicting pain on me sometimes, so it's not entirely out of the question that this will be some type of a sexual thing for him.

Julian's jaw flexes as he lowers me to my feet. "No," he says curtly, releasing me and stepping back. My eyes immediately stray to the door, but Julian is between me and the exit as he walks over to a small commode and rummages through the drawers. "I'll make sure you don't feel a thing." And as I watch, he pulls out a small, very familiar-looking syringe.

My insides grow cold. I recognize that syringe—it's the one he had in his pocket when he came back for me, the one he would've used on me if I hadn't gone with him of my own volition.

"Is that how you drugged me when you stole me from the park?" My voice is even, betraying little of the fact that I'm crumbling inside. "What kind of drug is that?"

Julian sighs, looking inexplicably weary as he comes toward me. "It has a long, complicated name that I don't remember off the top of my head—and yes, it's what I used to bring you to the island. It's one of the best drugs of its kind, with very few side effects."

"Few side effects? How lovely." Taking a step back, I cast a frantic glance around the room, looking for something I can use to defend myself. There's nothing, though. Other than a jar of hand creme and a box of tissues on the bed stand, the room is immaculately neat, free of clutter. I keep backing away until my knees hit the bed, and then I know I have nowhere else to go.

I'm trapped.

"Nora . . ." Julian is less than a foot from me now, the syringe in his right hand. "Don't make this harder than it has to be."

Harder than it has to be? Is he fucking serious? A fresh spurt of fury gives me renewed strength. I throw myself on the bed and roll across it, hoping to make it to the other side so I can dash for the door. Before I get to the edge, however, Julian is on top of me, his muscular body pressing me into the mattress. With my face buried in the fluffy blanket, I can hardly breathe, but before I get a chance to panic, Julian shifts most of his weight off me, enabling me to turn my head to the side. As I suck in air, I feel him moving—he's uncapping the syringe, I realize with an icy shudder— and I know I have only seconds before he drugs me again.

"Don't do this, Julian." The words come out in a desperate, broken plea. I know begging him is futile, but there is nothing else I can do at this point. My heart pounds heavily in my chest as I play my last card. "Please, if you care for me at all—*if you love me*—please don't do this . . ."

I can hear his breath catching, and for a moment, I feel a spark of hope—a spark that's immediately extinguished as he gently moves my tangled hair off my neck, exposing my skin. "It's really not going to be that bad, baby," he murmurs, and then I feel a sharp prick in the side of my neck.

Immediately my limbs grow heavy, my vision dimming as the drug kicks in. "I hate you," I manage to whisper, and then the darkness claims me again.

CHAPTER SIXTEEN

❖ JULIAN ❖

I hate you . . . If you love me, don't do this . . .

As I pick up her unconscious body, Nora's words echo in my mind, repeating over and over like a glitchy record. I know it shouldn't hurt this much, but it does. With just a couple of sentences, she somehow managed to flay me open, to break through the wall that has encased me since Maria's death—the wall that has enabled me to keep a distance from everyone and everything except her.

She doesn't truly hate me. I know that. She wants me. She loves me or, at the very least, thinks she does.

Once all of this is over, we're going to go back to the life we've had for the past couple of months, except I will feel better, more secure.

Less afraid of losing her.

If you love me, don't do this . . .

Fuck. I don't know why I care that she said that. I certainly don't love her. I can't. Love is for those who are noble and selfless, for people who still have some semblance of a heart.

That's not me. It's never been me. What I feel for Nora is nothing like the soft, flowery emotion depicted in all the books and movies. It's deeper, far more visceral than that. I need her with a violence that twists my guts, with a longing that both demolishes and uplifts me. I need her like I need air, and I would do whatever it takes to keep her with me.

I would die for her, but I would never let her go.

Cradling her small, limp body in my arms, I carry her out of the bedroom to the living room. David Goldberg, our resident doctor, is already there, waiting with his medical bag and supplies on the couch. I'd asked him to stop by earlier today, so he can do the procedure as soon as possible after dinner, and I'm glad that he's on time. I only gave Nora a quarter of the drug that was in the syringe, and I want to make sure everything is done before she wakes up.

"She's already under?" Goldberg asks, getting up to greet us. A short, balding man in his forties, he's one of the most talented surgeons I've ever met. I pay him an arm and a leg to treat minor injuries, but I consider it worth it. In my line of work, one never knows when a good doctor will come in handy.

"Yes." I carefully put Nora down on the couch. Her left arm hangs off the edge, so I gently arrange her in a more comfortable pose, making sure that her dress covers her slim thighs. Goldberg won't care either way—he's far more likely to get a hard-on for me than for my wife—but I still don't like the idea of exposing her unnecessarily, even to a man who's openly gay.

"You know, I could've just numbed the area," he says, pulling out the tools he needs. All of his movements are practiced and efficient; he's a master at what he does. "It's a simple procedure—nothing that requires the patient to be unconscious."

"It's better this way." I don't explain further, but I think Goldberg gets it, because he doesn't say anything else. Instead he puts on his gloves, takes out a large syringe with a thick hypodermic needle, and approaches Nora.

I step back to give him some room.

"How many trackers would you like? One or more?" he asks, glancing in my direction.

"Three." I've thought about this before, and that's what makes the most sense to me. If she's ever stolen, my enemies might think to look for a locator chip on her body, but they're unlikely to look for three of them.

"Okay. I will put one in her upper arm, one in her hip, and one in her inner thigh."

"That should work." The trackers are tiny, about the size of a grain of rice, so Nora won't even feel them there after a few days. I'm also planning to have her wear a special wristband as a decoy; it will have a fourth tracker in it. This way, if her abductors find the wristband tracker, they might be foolish enough to get rid of it and not look for any on her body.

"Then that's what I'll do," Goldberg says and, swabbing Nora's upper arm with a disinfecting solution, presses the needle to her skin. A small droplet of blood wells up as the needle goes in, depositing the tracker; then he disinfects the area again and tapes a small bandage over it.

The implant in her hip is next, followed by one in her inner thigh. It takes less than six minutes between the start and the end of the procedure, and Nora sleeps peacefully through it all.

"All done," Goldberg says, pulling off his gloves and packing up his bag. "You can take off the bandages in an hour, once the bleeding stops, and put on regular Band-Aids. Those areas might be tender for a couple of days, but there shouldn't be any scarring, particularly if you keep the insertion points clean in the meantime. If anything, call me, but I don't anticipate any problems."

"Excellent, thank you."

"My pleasure." And with that, Goldberg packs up his bag and exits the room.

* * *

Nora regains consciousness around three in the morning.

I'm sleeping lightly, so I wake up as soon as she begins to stir. I know she'll have a headache and some nausea from the drug, and I have a water bottle prepared in case she's thirsty. I expect the side effects to be mild, since I gave her a small dose. When I took her from the park, I had to give her a lot more to make sure she stayed under for the full twenty-hour-plus trip to the island, so she should recover much faster today.

I hate you.

Fuck, not again. I push away the memory of her small, accusing whisper and focus on the present. I can feel her stirring next to me, a small sound of discomfort escaping her throat as the mattress rubs against the tender spot in her upper arm. That sound does something to me, gets under my skin for some reason. I don't want Nora in pain—not from this, at least—and I reach for her, pulling her closer to me so I can hug her from the back.

She stiffens at my touch, rigid tension spreading through her body, and I know that she's awake now, that she remembers what happened.

"How are you feeling?" I ask, keeping my voice low and soothing as I stroke the smooth curve of her outer thigh with my hand. "Do you want some water or anything?"

She doesn't say anything, but I feel her head moving

slightly, and I interpret that as a nod.

"All right then." Reaching back with my hand, I grab the water bottle, fumbling a bit in the dark. Propping myself up on one elbow, I turn on the bedside lamp, so I can see, and hand the bottle to Nora.

She blinks a few times, squinting at the light, and takes the water from me, her slender fingers curving around the bottle as she sits up. The movement causes the blanket to slide down, exposing her upper body. I undressed her before putting her in bed, so she's naked now, with only her thick hair hiding her pretty, pink-tipped breasts from my gaze. Familiar lust stirs within me, but I push it down, wanting to make sure she's okay first.

I let her take a few sips of the water before asking again, "How are you feeling?"

She shrugs, her eyes not meeting mine. "Fine, I guess." Her hand lifts across her body to her upper arm, touching the Band-Aid there, and I see her shiver slightly, as though she's cold. "I have to use the bathroom," she says suddenly and, not waiting for my response, climbs out of bed. I catch a brief glimpse of her rounded little ass before she disappears through the bathroom door, and my dick jumps, ignoring my mind's directive to be still for once.

Sighing, I lie back on the pillow to wait for her. Who am I kidding? My pet always has that effect on me. I can no more ignore seeing her naked than I can stop breathing. Almost involuntarily, my hand slips under the blanket, my fingers curling around my hard shaft as I close my eyes and imagine her hot, velvety inner walls gripping my cock, her pussy wet and deliciously tight . . .

I hate you.

Fuck. My eyes fly open, some of the heat inside me cooling. I'm still hard, but now the lust is intermixed with a strange heaviness in my chest. I don't know where this is coming from. I should feel happier now that the trackers are in, but I don't. Instead I feel like I lost something . . . something I didn't even know I had.

Annoyed, I close my eyes again, this time purposefully focusing on the growing ache in my balls as I pump my fist up and down my dick, letting the hunger build. Even if she does hate me, so what? She probably *should* hate me, given everything I've done to her. I've never let such concerns stop me from doing what I wanted, and I'm not about to start now. Nora will get used to the trackers just as she got used to being mine, and if the compound security is ever breached, she'll thank her lucky stars for my foresight.

Hearing the door open, I open my eyes and see her emerging from the bathroom. She still doesn't look at me directly. Instead she keeps her eyes on the floor as she scurries to the bed and climbs under the covers, pulling the blanket up to her chin. Then she stares blankly at the ceiling, as if I don't even exist.

She might as well have slapped my face with her indifference.

The lust inside me turns sharper, darker. I won't stand for this kind of behavior, and she knows it. The urge to punish her is strong, nearly irresistible, and it's only the knowledge that she's already hurt that prevents me from tying her up and giving in to my sadistic inclinations.

Still, I'm not going to let her get away with this. Not tonight, not ever.

Throwing off my blanket, I sit up and command sharply, "Come here."

She doesn't move for a moment, but then her eyes lift to my face. There's no fear in her gaze, no emotion of any kind, in fact. Her huge dark eyes are lifeless, like those of a beautiful doll.

The heaviness in my chest region grows. "Come here," I repeat, the harshness of my tone masking the intensifying turmoil within me. "Now."

She obeys, her conditioning finally kicking in. Pushing away her blanket, she comes to me on all fours, crawling across the bed with her back arched and her ass slightly raised. It's exactly the way I like her to move in the bedroom, and my breathing quickens, my cock swelling to an almost painful thickness. I've trained her well; even distressed, my pet knows how to please me.

"Good girl," I murmur, reaching for her as soon as she's within my grasp. Sliding my left hand into her hair, I wrap my right arm around her waist and pull her into my lap, gathering her against me. Then I slant my mouth across hers, kissing her with a hunger that seems to emanate from the very core of my being.

She tastes like minty toothpaste and herself, her lips soft and receptive as I plunder the silky depths of her mouth. As the kiss goes on, her eyes close, and her hands come up to rest tentatively at my sides. I can feel her nipples pebbling against my chest, and the realization that she's responding the same as always sends a wave of relief through me, alleviating much of my uncharacteristic unease.

Whatever strange mood she's in, she's still mine in all the ways that matter.

Still kissing her, I lean forward until we're both lying flat on the bed, with me covering her. I'm careful to handle her gently, so I don't put any pressure on the Band-Aid-covered areas. The monster inside me may crave her pain and tears, but that desire pales in comparison to my overwhelming need to comfort her, to take away that lifeless look in her eyes.

Reining in my own lust, I set about caring for her the only way I know how. I kiss her all over, tasting her soft, warm skin as I make my way from the delicate curve of her ear down to her little toes. I massage her hands, arms, feet, legs, and back, enjoying her quiet moans of pleasure as I rub out all stiffness in her muscles. Then I bring her to orgasm with my mouth and my fingers, delaying my own release until my balls almost turn blue.

When I finally enter her body, it's like coming

home. Her hot, slick sheath welcomes me, squeezes me so tightly that I nearly explode on the spot. As I begin to move inside her, her arms close around my back, embracing me, holding me close—and then we detonate together at the end, our bodies straining together in violent, mind-shattering bliss.

CHAPTER SEVENTEEN

❖ NORA ❖

I wake up later than usual, my head and mouth feeling like they've been stuffed with cotton. For a moment, I struggle to remember what happened—*did I somehow have too much to drink?*—but then memories of last night seep into my mind, twisting my stomach into knots and flooding me with confused despair.

Julian made love to me last night. He made love to me after violating me—after drugging me and forcing the trackers on me against my will—and I let him. No, I didn't just let him; I reveled in his touch, allowing the blazing heat of his caresses to burn away the frozen hurt inside me, to make me forget, if only for a moment, about the ragged wound he inflicted on my heart.

I don't know why this, out of all the horrible things Julian has done, affects me so strongly. In the grand scheme of things, putting the trackers under my skin—allegedly to keep me safe—is nothing compared to kidnapping me, beating up Jake, or blackmailing me into marriage. These trackers are not even necessarily forever. Theoretically, if I ever make it off the estate, I can go to a doctor and have the implants removed, so I may not even be stuck with them for the rest of my life. My fear yesterday definitely had an irrational component to it; I was reacting on instinct and not thinking things through.

Nonetheless, it felt like a part of me died last evening—like the prick of that syringe killed something inside me. Maybe it's because I had begun to feel that Julian and I were growing closer, that we were becoming more like a regular couple. Or maybe because my Stockholm Syndrome—or whatever psychological issue I have—made me imagine rainbows and unicorns where there were none. Whatever the reason, Julian's actions felt like the most agonizing betrayal. When I regained consciousness last night, I felt so devastated that I wanted to crawl into a hole and disappear.

But Julian didn't let me. He made love to me. He made love to me when I thought he would whip me—

when I expected him to punish me for not being his compliant little pet. He gave me tenderness when I expected cruelty; instead of taking me apart, he made me feel whole again, even if it was only for a few hours.

And now . . . now I miss him. Without him by my side, the coldness within me is beginning to creep back, the pain slowly returning to choke me from the inside. The fact that Julian did this to me against my objections—that he did this even though I *begged him not to*—is almost more than I can handle. It tells me that he doesn't love me—that he may never love me.

It tells me that the man I'm married to may never be anything more than my captor.

* * *

At breakfast Julian is not there, a fact that contributes to my growing depression. I've gotten so used to having most of my meals with him that his absence feels like a rejection—though how I can still crave his company after everything is beyond my comprehension.

"Señor Esguerra grabbed a quick snack earlier," Ana explains, serving me eggs mixed with refried beans and avocado. "He received some news that he had to deal with right away, so he's not able to join you this morning. He apologized for that and told me that you can come to the office whenever you're ready." Her voice is unusually warm and kind, and there is sympathy on her face as she looks at me. I don't know if she knows all the details about what happened last night, but I have a feeling she overheard the gist of it.

Embarrassed, I lower my gaze to my plate. "Okay, thank you, Ana," I murmur, staring at the food. It looks as delicious as usual, but I have no appetite this morning. I know I'm not sick, but I feel that way, with my stomach churning and my chest aching. The fresh implants in my thigh, hip, and upper arm throb with a nagging pain. All I want to do is crawl under the covers and sleep the day away, but unfortunately, that's not an option. I have a paper to do for my English Literature class, and I'm two lectures behind for my Calculus class. I did cancel my morning walk with Rosa, though; I have no desire to see my friend while I'm feeling this way.

"Would you like some hot chocolate or anything? Maybe coffee or tea?" Ana asks, still hovering by the table. Normally, when Julian and I are eating together, she makes herself scarce, but for some reason, she seems reluctant to leave me alone this morning.

I look up from my plate and force myself to give her a smile. "No, I'm okay, Ana, thanks." Picking up my fork, I spear some eggs and bring them to my mouth, determined to eat something to alleviate the concern I see on the housekeeper's softly rounded face.

As I chew, I see Ana hesitating for a moment, as though she wants to say something else, but then she disappears into the kitchen, leaving me to my breakfast.

For the next few minutes, I make a serious attempt to eat, but everything tastes like sand and I finally give up.

Getting up, I head to the porch, wanting to feel the sun on my skin. The coldness inside me seems to be spreading with each moment, my depression deepening as the morning wears on.

Stepping out the front door, I walk over to the edge of the porch and lean on the railing, breathing in the hot, humid air. As I gaze out onto the wide green lawn and the guards in the distance, I feel my vision blurring, hot tears welling up and beginning to slide down my cheeks.

I don't know why I'm crying. Nobody died; nothing truly terrible has happened. I've been through so much worse in the past two years, and I've coped with it— I've adjusted and survived. This relatively minor thing shouldn't make me feel like my heart has been ripped out.

My growing conviction that Julian is not capable of love shouldn't destroy me like this.

A hand gently touches my shoulder, startling me out of my misery. Swiftly wiping my cheeks with the back of my hand, I turn around and am surprised to see Ana standing there, an uncertain expression on her face.

"Señora Esguerra . . . I mean, Nora . . ." She stumbles over my name, her accent thicker than usual. "I'm sorry to interrupt, but I was wondering if you had a minute to talk?"

Taken aback by the unusual request, I nod. "Of course, what is it?" Ana and I are not particularly close; she's always been somewhat reserved around me, polite but not overly friendly. Rosa told me that Ana is like that because that's what Julian's father demanded of his staff, and the habit is difficult for her to break.

Looking relieved by my response, Ana smiles and walks up to join me at the railing, placing her forearms on the painted white wood. I give her a questioning look, wondering what she wants to discuss, but she seems content to just stand there for a moment, her gaze trained on the jungle in the distance.

When she finally turns her head to look at me and speaks, her words catch me off-guard. "I don't know if you know this, Nora, but your husband lost everybody he's ever cared about," she says softly, no trace of her customary reserve in sight. "Maria, his parents . . . Not to mention many others he knew both here on the estate and out in the cities."

"Yes, he told me," I say slowly, eyeing her with some caution. I don't know why she's suddenly decided to talk to me about Julian, but I'm more than happy to listen. Maybe if I understand my husband better, it will be easier for me to maintain my emotional distance from him.

Maybe if he's not such a puzzle, I won't be drawn to him as strongly.

"Good," Ana says quietly. "Then I hope you understand that Julian didn't mean to hurt you last night . . . that whatever he did was because he cares for you."

"Cares for me?" The laugh that escapes my throat is sharp and bitter. I don't know why I'm talking about this with Ana, but now that the floodgates have been opened, I can't seem to close them again. "Julian doesn't care about anyone but himself."

"No." She shakes her head. "You're wrong, Nora. He does. He cares about you very much. I can see it. He's different with you than with others. Very different."

I stare at her. "What do you mean?"

She sighs, then turns to face me fully. "Your husband was always a dark child," she says, and I see a deep sadness in her gaze. "A beautiful boy, with his mother's eyes and her features, but so hard inside . . . It was his father's fault, I think. The older Señor never treated him like a child. From the time Julian was old enough to walk, his father would push him, make him do things that no child should do . . ."

I listen raptly, hardly daring to breathe as she continues.

"When Julian was little, he was afraid of spiders. We have big ones here, very scary ones. Some poisonous ones. When Juan Esguerra found out, he led his five-year-old son into the forest and made him catch a dozen large spiders with his bare hands. Then he made the boy kill them slowly with his fingers, so Julian would see what it's like to conquer his fears and make his enemies suffer." She pauses, her mouth tight-lipped with anger. "Julian didn't sleep for two nights after that. When his mother found out, she cried, but there was nothing she could do. Señor's word here was law, and everyone had to obey."

I swallow the bile rising in my throat and look away. What I just learned only adds to my despair. How can I expect Julian to love someone after being raised that way? The fact that my husband is a stone-cold killer with sadistic tendencies is not surprising; the only wonder is that he's not even worse.

It's hopeless. Utterly hopeless.

Sensing my distress, Ana lays her hand on my arm, her touch warm and comforting, like that of my mom.

"For the longest time, I thought Julian would grow up to be just like his father," she says when I turn to look at her. "Cruel and uncaring, incapable of any softer emotion. I thought that until I saw him with a kitten one day when he was twelve. It was a tiny creature, all fluffy white fur and big eyes, barely old enough to eat on its own. Something happened to its mother, and Julian found the kitten outside and brought it in. When I saw him, he was trying to coax it to drink milk, and the expression on his face——" She blinks, her eyes looking suspiciously wet. "It was so . . . so tender. He was so patient with the kitten, so gentle. And I knew then that his father hadn't succeeded in breaking Julian completely, that the boy could still feel."

"What happened to that kitten?" I ask, bracing myself. I'm prepared to hear another horror story, but Ana just shrugs in response.

"It grew up in the house," she says, gently squeezing my arm before taking her hand away. "Julian kept it as his pet, named it Lola. He and his father had a fight about that—the older Señor hated animals—but by then Julian was old enough, and tough enough, to stand up to his father. Nobody dared to touch the little creature for as long as it was under Julian's protection. When he left for America, he took the cat with him. As far as I know, it lived a nice long life and passed away from old age."

"Oh." Some of my tension fades. "That's good. Not good that Julian lost his pet, I mean, but that it lived for a long time."

"Yes. It's good indeed. And you know, Nora, the way he looked at that kitten . . ." She trails off, gazing at me with a strange smile.

"What?" I ask warily.

"He looks at you like that sometimes. With that same kind of tenderness. He might not always show it, but he treasures you, Nora. In his own way, he loves you. I truly believe that."

I press my lips together, trying to hold back the tears that threaten to flood my eyes again. "Why are you telling me this, Ana?" I ask when I'm certain I can speak without breaking down. "Why did you come out here?"

"Because Julian is the closest thing I have to a son," she says softly. "And because I want him to be happy. I want both of you to be happy. I don't know if this changes anything for you, but I thought you should know a little more about your husband." Reaching out, she squeezes my hand and then walks back inside the house, leaving me standing by the railing, even more confused and heartsick than before.

* * *

I don't join Julian in the office that afternoon. Instead I lock myself in the library and work on the paper, trying not to think about my husband and how much I want to be sitting by his side. I know that just being near him would make me feel better, that his presence alone would help with my hurt and anger, but some masochistic impulse keeps me away. I don't know what I'm trying to prove to myself, but I'm determined to keep my distance for at least a few hours.

Of course, there's no avoiding him at dinner.

"You didn't come today," he observes, watching me as Ana ladles us some mushroom soup for an appetizer. "Why not?"

I shrug, ignoring the imploring look Ana gives me before going back to the kitchen. "I wasn't feeling well."

Julian frowns. "You're sick?"

"No, just a bit under the weather. Plus I had a paper

to finish and some lectures to catch up on."

"Is that right?" He stares at me, his eyebrows drawn together. Leaning forward, he asks softly, "Are you sulking, my pet?"

"No, Julian," I reply as sweetly as I can, dipping my spoon in the soup. "Sulking would imply that I'm mad at something you did. But I don't get to be mad, do I? You can do whatever you want to me, and I'm supposed to just accept it, right?" And taking a sip of the richly flavored soup, I give him a saccharine smile, enjoying the way his eyes narrow at my response. I know I'm tugging on a tiger's tail, but I don't want a sweet, gentle Julian tonight. It's too misleading, too unsettling for my peace of mind.

To my frustration, he doesn't take the bait. Whatever anger I managed to provoke is short-lived, and in the next moment, he leans back, a slow, sexy smile teasing at the corners of his lips. "Are you trying to guilt me, baby? Surely you know by now that I'm beyond that kind of emotion."

"Of course you are." I meant the words to sound bitter, but they come out breathless instead. Even now, he has the power to make my senses whirl and spin with nothing more than a smile.

He grins, knowing full well how he affects me, and dips his own spoon into the soup. "Just eat, Nora. You can show me how mad you are in the bedroom, I promise." And with that tantalizing threat, he begins consuming his soup, leaving me no choice but to follow his lead.

As we eat, Julian peppers me with questions about my classes and how my online program is going so far. He seems genuinely interested in what I have to say, and I soon find myself talking to him about my difficulties with Calculus—*has a more boring subject ever been invented?*—and discussing the pros and cons of taking a Humanities course next semester. I'm sure he must find my concerns amusing—after all, it's just school—but if he does, he doesn't show it. Instead he makes me feel like I'm talking to a friend, or maybe a trusted advisor.

That's one of the things that make Julian so irresistible: his ability to listen, to make me feel important to him. I don't know if he does it on purpose, but there are few things more seductive than having someone's undivided attention—and I always have that with Julian. I've had it since day one. Evil kidnapper or not, he's always made me feel wanted and desired, like I'm the center of his world.

Like I genuinely matter.

As the dinner continues, Ana's story plays over and over in my mind, making me viciously glad that Juan Esguerra is dead. How could a father do that to his son? What kind of monster would purposefully try to mold his child into a killer? I picture twelve-year-old Julian standing up to that brute for a defenseless kitten, and I feel an unwitting flash of pride at my husband's courage. I have a feeling keeping that pet against his father's wishes had been far from easy.

I'm still nowhere near ready to forgive Julian, but as we make our way through the second course, I consider the possibility that something other than Julian's stalker tendencies was behind his desire to implant those trackers in me. Could it be that instead of not caring for me, he cares too much? Could his love be that dark and obsessive? That twisted? I'd known, of course, about Maria's death and that of his parents, but I never put the two events together, never thought of it as Julian losing everyone he's ever cared about. If Ana is right—if I truly am that special to Julian—then it's not particularly surprising that he'd go to such lengths to ensure my safety, especially since he almost lost me once.

It's insane and scary, but not particularly surprising.

"So what was so urgent this morning?" I ask, finishing my second serving of the baked salmon dish Ana prepared as the main course. My appetite is back with a vengeance, all traces of my earlier malaise gone. It's amazing what even a little bit of Julian's company does to me; his proximity is better than any mood-boosting drug on the market. "When you couldn't join me for breakfast, I mean?"

"Oh, yes, I've been meaning to tell you about that," Julian says, and I see a gleam of dark excitement in his eyes. "Peter's contacts in Moscow got us permission to move in with an operation to extract Majid and the rest of the Al-Quadar fighters from Tajikistan. As soon as we're ready—hopefully in a week or so—we'll be making our move."

"Oh, wow." I stare at him, both excited and disturbed by the news. "When you say 'we,' you mean your men, right?"

"Well, yes." Julian appears puzzled by my question. "I'm going to take a group of about fifty of our best soldiers and leave the rest to guard the compound."

"You're going to go on this operation yourself?" My heart skips a beat as I wait anxiously for his answer.

"Of course." He looks surprised that I would think otherwise. "I always go on these types of missions myself if I can. Besides, I have some business in Ukraine that's best handled in person, so I'll deal with that on the way back."

"Julian . . ." I feel sick all of a sudden, all the food I've eaten sitting in my stomach like a rock. "This sounds really dangerous . . . Why do you have to go?"

"Dangerous?" He laughs softly. "Are you worried about me, my pet? I can assure you, there's no need. The enemy is going to be outnumbered and outgunned. They don't stand a chance, believe me."

"You don't know that! What if they set off a bomb or something?" My voice rises as I remember the horror of the warehouse explosion. "What if they trick you in some way? You know they want to kill you—"

"Well, technically, they want to force me to give them the explosive," he corrects me, a dark smile curving his lips, "and *then* they want to kill me. But you have nothing to worry about, baby. We'll scan their quarters for any signs of bombs before we go in, and we'll all be wearing full-body armor that can withstand all but a rocket blast."

I push my plate away, not the least bit reassured. "So let me get this straight . . . You're forcing me to wear trackers here, where nobody can touch a single hair on my head, and you're planning to traipse off to Tajikistan to play 'capture the terrorist'?"

Julian's smile disappears, his expression hardening. "I'm not playing, Nora. Al-Quadar represents a very real threat, and it's one that I need to eliminate as quickly as possible. We need to strike at them before they come after us, and this is the perfect opportunity to do that."

I glare at him, the sheer unfairness of the whole thing making my blood pressure rise. "But why do you have to go in person? You have all these soldiers and mercenaries at your command—surely they don't need you there—"

"Nora . . ." His voice is gentle, but his eyes are hard and cold, like icicles. "This is not up for debate. The day I start fearing my own shadow is the day I need to leave this business for good—because it will mean that I have grown soft. Soft and lazy, like the man whose factory I took when I was first starting out . . ." He smiles again at my look of shock. "Oh, yes, my pet, how do you think I switched from drugs to weapons? I took over someone's existing operation and built on it. My predecessor also had soldiers and mercenaries at his command, but he was little more than a glorified paper pusher and everyone knew it. He didn't keep tight reins on his organization, and it was a simple matter to bribe a few people and overthrow him, taking his rocket factory for my own." Julian pauses to let me digest that for a second, then adds, "I'm not going to be that man, Nora. This mission is important to me, and I have every intention of overseeing it myself. Majid will not survive this time—I will make sure of that."

CHAPTER EIGHTEEN

❖ JULIAN ❖

After dinner is over, I lead Nora to our bedroom, my hand resting on the small of her back as we walk up the stairs. She's quiet, like she's been ever since I explained to her about the upcoming mission, and I know that she's still upset with me, both about the trackers and the trip itself.

I find her concern touching, even sweet, but I have no intention of passing up this opportunity to lay my hands on Majid. My pet doesn't understand the dark thrill of being in the middle of action, of feeling the jolt of adrenaline and hearing the whizzing of bullets. She doesn't realize that to someone like me the sight of blood and the sound of my enemies' screams are a turn-on, that I crave them almost as much as sex. This trait of mine is why one shrink thought I might be borderline sociopathic . . . well, this and my general lack of remorse. It's a label that's never particularly bothered me—at least not once I got past my youthful delusion that I could someday lead a 'normal' life.

As we enter the bedroom, the hunger that I've been restraining since yesterday intensifies, the monster inside me demanding his due. The distance I'm sensing from Nora only makes it worse. I can feel the barriers she's trying to erect between us, the way she's trying to shut me out of her thoughts, and it maddens me, feeding the sadistic yearning coiling within.

I am going to smash those barriers tonight. I am going to tear them down until she has no defenses left—until I own her mind fully again.

She excuses herself to go take a quick shower, and I let her, walking over to the bed to wait for her return. I am already semi-hard, my cock stirring in anticipation of what I'm going to do to her, and my pants are starting to feel uncomfortably tight. Hearing the water turn on, I undress, then reach into the bedside drawer and pull out an assortment of tools I plan to use on her tonight.

True to her word, Nora doesn't take long. Five minutes, and she's coming out of the bathroom, a plush white towel wrapped around her petite body. Her hair is piled on top of her head in a messy bun, and her golden skin is damp, droplets of water still clinging to her neck and shoulders. She must've taken off the Band-Aids in order to shower, because I can see a tiny scab and some bruising on her arm where the tracker went in. The sight of it fills me with an odd mixture of emotions—relief that I can now always keep an eye on her and something that tastes strangely like regret.

Her gaze flicks toward the bed, and she stops dead in her tracks, her eyes widening as she takes in the objects I laid out.

I smile, enjoying the startled expression on her face. We haven't played with toys in a while—at least not to this extent. "Drop the towel and get on the bed," I command, getting up and reaching for the blindfold.

She looks up at me, her lips parted and her skin softly flushed, and I know that she's excited by this too—that her needs now mirror mine. There's only a hint of hesitation in her movements as she unwraps the towel and lets it fall to the floor, leaving her standing there fully naked.

As I feast my eyes on her slim, shapely body, my balls tighten and my heartbeat picks up. Rationally I know there must be women more beautiful than Nora out there, but if there are, I can't think of any. From the top of her head down to her dainty toes, she fits my preferences to a tee. My body craves her with an intensity that seems to be growing stronger every day, with a desperation that almost consumes me.

She climbs onto the bed, getting into a kneeling position with her feet tucked underneath her tight, round ass. Her movements are fluid and graceful, like those of a sleek little cat.

Getting on my knees behind her, I move her hair off her shoulder and gently kiss her neck, enjoying the way her breathing changes in response. She smells like warm female skin and flower-scented body wash, a mixture that makes my head spin and my dick throb with need. Some nights this is all I want from her—the sweetness of her response, the feel of her in my arms. Some nights I want to treat her like the fragile, breakable creature she is.

Tonight, however, I want something different.

Pulling back, I tie the blindfold around her eyes, making sure she can't see anything. I want her to focus solely on the sensations she'll be experiencing, to feel everything as acutely as possible. Next, I pick up a pair of padded handcuffs and snap them around her wrists, securing her hands behind her back.

"Um, Julian . . ." Her tongue comes out to moisten her lower lip. "What are you going to do to me?"

I smile, the tiny hint of fear in her voice turning me on even more. "What do you think I'm going to do to you, my pet?"

"Flog me?" she guesses, her voice low and a bit husky. I can see her nipples growing taut as she speaks, and I know the idea is not exactly repellent to her.

"No, baby," I murmur, reaching for one of the other

items I have prepared—a pair of nipple clamps connected by a thin metal chain. "You're not healed enough for that yet. I have other things in mind for you today." And picking up the clamps, I wrap my arms around her from the back and pinch her left nipple between my fingers. Then I apply one of the clamps to the hard bud, tightening the screw until her breath hisses out between her teeth.

"How does it feel?" I ask softly, leaning down to kiss the top of her ear as I reach for her right nipple. Her bound hands, curled tightly into fists, press into my stomach, reminding me of her helplessness. "I want to hear you describe it . . ."

She draws in a shuddering breath, her chest heaving. "It hurts—" she begins to say, then cries out sharply as I apply the second clamp to her nipple and tighten it the same way.

"Good . . ." I lightly bite her earlobe. My erection brushes against her lower back, the contact sending vibrations of pleasure down to my balls. "And now?"

"It—it hurts even more . . ." Her words come out in a ragged whisper. Her back is tense against me, and I know that she's telling the truth, that her sensitive nipples are likely in agony from the vicious bite of the toy. I've used nipple clamps on her before, on the island, but those were a gentler version, capable of applying only light pressure. These are much more hardcore, and I smile darkly as I imagine how much they'll hurt when they come off.

Cupping the undersides of her breasts with my hands, I squeeze them lightly, molding the soft flesh with my fingers. "Yes, it hurts, doesn't it?" I murmur as she jerks in pain, the movement of my hands pulling on the chain between her nipples. "My poor baby, so sweet, yet so abused . . ."

Releasing her breasts, I run my hand down her smooth, flat stomach until I reach the soft folds between her legs. As I had suspected, despite the pain—or more likely, because of it—she's soaking wet, her pussy already liquid with need. My cock throbs in response. The sight of her restrained, with her delicate nipples clamped and hurting, appeals to me in a way that my old shrink would've undoubtedly found disturbing. Doing my best to control my hunger, I touch her small clit with my thumb, pressing on it lightly, and she moans, leaning back against my chest, her hips lifting up in a silent plea for more.

"Tell me what you're feeling now." I deliberately keep the pressure on her clit feather-light. "Tell me, Nora."

"I . . . I don't know . . ."

"Tell me how those little nipples feel. I want to hear you say it." I accompany the demand with a firm pinch of her clit, causing her to cry out and buck against me from the sudden pain.

"They—they still hurt," she gasps when she recovers, "but it's different now, less sharp and more like a steady throb . . ."

"Good girl . . ." I stroke her swollen clit gently as a reward. "And what does it feel like when I touch you like this?"

Her small pink tongue comes out again, flicking over her bottom lip. "It feels good," she whispers, "really good . . . Please, Julian . . ."

"Please what?" I prod, wanting to hear her beg. She has the perfect voice for begging, sweet and innocently sexy. Her pleading affects me in a way that's just the opposite of what she intends—it makes me want to torment her more.

"Please touch me . . ." She lifts her hips again, trying to intensify the pressure on her sex.

"Touch you where?" I move my hand, depriving her of my touch altogether. "Tell me exactly where you want me to touch you, my pet."

"My . . . my clit . . ." The words come out on a breathless moan. I can see the sheen of sweat on her forehead, and I know that my torture is having an effect on her, that the sensations she's feeling are as intense as I intended.

"All right, baby." I touch her again, pressing my fingers into her slick folds to stimulate the bundle of nerves with light, even strokes. "Like that?"

"Yes." She's breathing faster now, her chest rising and falling as her orgasm approaches. "Yes, just like that . . ." Her voice trails off, her body tightening like a string, and then she cries out, jerking in my arms as she reaches her peak. I hold her through it, keeping the pressure on her clit steady until her contractions abate, and then I reach for another item I have prepared.

It's a dildo this time, one that's roughly the size of my own dick. Made of a special blend of silicone and plastic, it's designed to imitate the feel of human flesh, right down to the skin-like texture on the outside. It's as close as I will let Nora get to experiencing another man's cock.

Holding her against me with one arm, I bring the dildo to her sex and position the broad head at her slick, quivering opening. "Tell me what you're feeling now," I order her, and begin to push the object in.

She gasps, her breathing quickening again, and I feel her squirming as the large toy slowly enters her pussy. Her fingers clench and unclench against my stomach in an agitated tempo, her nails scratching my skin. "I—I don't . . ."

"You don't what?" My tone sharpens as her sentence trails off. "Tell me how it feels to you."

"It feels . . . thick and hard." The tremor in her voice stiffens my cock further, making it pulse with hungry need.

"And?" I prompt, pushing the object deeper. The dildo looks almost too big for her delicate body to accept, and the sight of her tight sheath gradually engulfing it is almost painfully erotic.

"And"—she exhales sharply, her head falling back against my shoulder—"and it feels like it's stretching me and filling me . . ."

"Yes, baby, that's right." By now the dildo is all the way inside her, with only the end sticking out. I reward her for her honesty by rubbing her clit with my fingers, spreading wetness from her dripping opening all around her soft folds. When she's panting again, her hips undulating against my hand, I stop before she can come and release her from my hold, moving back a bit. Then I push her forward, pressing her face against the mattress, and pull her legs out from underneath her, making her lie flat on her belly.

As much as I want to continue playing with her, I can no longer wait to fuck her.

Deprived of my touch and with her clamped nipples rubbing painfully against the sheets, she whimpers, trying to roll over onto her side. I don't let her, holding her down with one hand as I shove a pillow under her hips with another. Then I grab lube and squirt it directly on the small, puckered opening between her ass cheeks, right above where the edge of the dildo is protruding from her stretched, glistening pussy.

She tenses, now realizing my intentions, and I slap her ass with one hand, quelling any protest she might've been trying to make. "Easy now. You need to tell me how it feels, do you understand me, my pet?"

She whimpers as I straddle her and press the tip of my cock to her tight little asshole, but I feel her trying to relax underneath me, just like I taught her. Anal sex is something she's still not entirely comfortable with, and her reluctance pleases me in some perverse way. It shows me both how far I've come with her training and how far I still have to go.

"Do you understand?" I repeat in a harsher tone when she remains silent, breathing heavily into the mattress, her bound hands tightly clenched behind her back. I desperately want to shove my cock in all the way, but I settle for just nudging her with it, smearing the lube all around her back opening. Tonight I want to get inside her mind just as much as I want to get inside her body, and I won't settle for anything less.

"Yes . . ." Her words are muffled by the blanket as I press forward and begin to penetrate her ass, ignoring her attempts to squirm away. "It feels . . . oh God . . . I can't . . . Julian, please, it's too much—"

"Tell me," I order, continuing to press in, pushing past the resistance of her sphincter. With her pussy already filled with the dildo, her ass is so tight around my cock that I'm shaking from the effort it's taking to control myself. My voice is thick with lust when I rasp out, "I want to hear everything."

"It—it burns . . ." She's panting, and I can see droplets of sweat gathering between her shoulder blades, strands of her long hair sticking to her damp skin. "Oh fuck . . . I'm too full . . . It's too intense . . ."

"Yes, that's good . . . Continue talking . . ." I'm now almost all the way in, and I can feel my dick rubbing against the dildo as only a thin wall separates it from the toy. She's trembling underneath me now, her body overwhelmed by the sensations, and I stroke her back in a soothing motion as I press forward one last inch, bottoming out deep within her body.

She makes an incoherent noise, her shoulders beginning to shake, and her muscles tighten around my cock in a futile effort to push me out. The movement shifts the dildo within her, and she cries out, her shaking intensifying. "I can't . . . Julian, please, I can't . . ."

I groan, explosive pleasure zinging through my balls as her ass squeezes my dick. My control dissolving, I withdraw from her halfway and then plunge back in, reveling in the feel of her body's resistance, in the almost agonizing tightness of her hot, smooth passage around my shaft.

She screams into the blanket as I begin to drive into her in earnest, a mix of sobs and gasping pleas escaping her throat as I set a hard, rhythmic pace. Leaning forward, I brace myself over her with one hand and slide the other under her hips, finding her sex. Now every thrust of my hips presses her clit against my fingers, and her screams take on a different note, that of unwilling pleasure, of ecstasy mixed with pain. I can feel the dildo shifting and moving as I fuck her, and my orgasm boils up with sudden intensity, my spine tightening as my balls draw up flush against my body. Just as I'm about to erupt, her ass clamps down on me, and I realize with dark pleasure that she's coming too, that her muscles are spasming around my cock as she cries out underneath me. And then the orgasm hits me, a shockwave of pleasure ripping through my body as jets of my seed spurt out into her hot depths, leaving me stunned and breathless from the force of my release.

When my heart no longer feels like it's about to explode, I carefully withdraw from her ass and pull the dildo from her pussy. She lies there limp and pliant, small sobs still shaking her frame as I unlock the handcuffs and massage her delicate wrists. Next, I untie the blindfold, sliding it out from under her. The silky piece of cloth is drenched from Nora's tears, and as I gently turn her over, I see wet streaks on her blanket-creased cheeks. She blinks at me, squinting against the bright light, and I reach for her nipples, releasing first one, then the other from the clamps. She doesn't react for a moment, but then her entire body jolts as blood rushes back to the abused buds. A moan escapes her throat, and fresh tears well up in her eyes as her hands go up to cover her breasts, cradling them protectively against the pain.

"Shh," I soothe, leaning down to kiss her. Her lips taste salty from her tears, and a tiny flame of arousal reignites within me. My cock, now flaccid, twitches, her pain and tears turning me on despite my extreme satiation. I'm not up for round two quite yet, though, and instead of deepening the kiss, I reluctantly lift my head and gaze down at her.

She stares up at me, her eyes slightly unfocused, and I know she's still recovering from the intensity of the experience I put her through. In this moment, she's utterly defenseless, both mind and body unshielded, and I use her weakened state to press my advantage. "Tell me how you feel now," I murmur, raising one hand to tenderly caress her jaw. "Tell me, baby."

She closes her eyes, and I see a single tear roll down her cheek. "I feel . . . empty and full at the same time, destroyed, yet replenished," she whispers, her words barely audible. "I feel like you shredded me into pieces and then remade those pieces into something else, something that's no longer me . . . something that belongs to you . . ."

"Yes." I absorb her words hungrily. "And what else?"

She opens her eyes, meeting my gaze, and I see a strange sort of hopelessness etched into her face. "And I love you," she says quietly. "I love you even though I see you for what you are—even though I know what you're doing to me. I love you because I'm no longer capable of *not* loving you . . . because you're now part of me, for better or for worse."

I hold her gaze, the dark empty corners of my soul sucking in her words like a desert plant takes in water. Her love may not be freely given, but it's mine. It will always be mine. "And you are part of *me*, Nora," I admit, my voice low and unusually hoarse. This is the closest I can come to telling her how much she means to me, how deep my longing for her runs. "I hope you know that, my pet."

And before she can respond, I kiss her again, then slide my arms under her body, pick her up, and carry her to the bathroom to wash up.

CHAPTER NINETEEN

❖ NORA ❖

The week before Julian's departure is bittersweet. I still have not entirely forgiven him for the forced tracker implants—or for the bracelet embedded with yet another tracker he made me start wearing a couple of days later. Nevertheless, ever since Julian's words that evening, I've been feeling infinitely better.

I know what he said is not exactly a declaration of undying love, but from a man like Julian, it might as well be. Ana is right: Julian lost everyone who has ever mattered to him. Everyone except me, that is. The fact that he clings to me with such brutal possessiveness may be overwhelming at times, but it's also an indication of his feelings.

His love for me is wrong and perverse in many ways, but it's no less real because of that.

Of course, knowing this makes my fear for Julian's safety on the upcoming trip even more intense. As his departure time approaches, my joy over his confession fades, and anxiety takes its place.

I don't want Julian to leave. Every time I think of him going on this mission, I'm gripped by a suffocating sense of dread. I know there is an irrational component to my fear, but that doesn't lessen it in any way. Aside from the very real danger Julian will face, I'm simply afraid to be alone. We've spent so little time apart in the past couple of months that the thought of being without him for even a few days makes me feel deeply stressed and uneasy.

It doesn't help that I have exams and papers galore, or that my parents have been steadily pressuring me to come for a visit—something that Julian won't allow until the Al-Quadar threat is fully contained.

"You can't leave the estate, but they can come visit us here if you'd like," he tells me during shooting practice one afternoon. "I would advise against it, though. Right now your parents are more or less off the radar, but the more contact I appear to have with your family, the more danger they'll be in. It's up to you, though. Just say the word, and I'll send a plane for them."

"No, that's okay," I say hastily. "I don't want to draw any unnecessary attention to them." And raising my gun, I start shooting at the beer cans on the far edge of the field, letting the now-familiar jolt of the weapon take away some of my frustration.

I realized that my parents are in danger a couple of days after we came to the estate. To my relief, Julian told me that he'd already put a discreet security detail on them—highly trained bodyguards whose job is to protect my family while letting them go about their lives. The alternative, he explained, is to bring them to the estate with us—a solution that my parents rejected as soon as I brought it up.

"What? We're not moving to Colombia to live with an illegal arms dealer!" my dad exclaimed when I told him about the potential danger. "Who does that bastard think he is? I just got a new job—not to mention, we can't leave all of our friends and relatives!"

And that was as far as that got. I can't say I blame my parents for not wanting to move halfway across the world to be with me in my abductor's compound. They're still young, both in their early forties, and they've always led active, busy lives. My dad plays lacrosse nearly every weekend, and my mom has a group of girlfriends who get together for wine and gossip on a regular basis. My parents are also still very much in love with each other, with my dad constantly surprising my mom with little gifts of flowers, chocolate, or a dinner out. Growing up, I had no doubt that they both loved me, but I also knew that I wasn't the absolute epicenter of their lives.

No, if what Julian says is true—and I'm inclined to trust him on this—it's best if my parents don't appear to have too close of a connection to the Esguerra organization.

Their ability to lead a normal life depends on it.

* * *

On the night before Julian is scheduled to leave, I ask Ana to prepare a special dinner for us. I recently discovered that Julian has a weakness for tiramisu, so that is our dessert for tonight. For the main course, Ana makes lasagna the same way that Julian's mother used to make it. The housekeeper told me it was his favorite dish when he was a boy.

I don't know why I'm doing this. It's not like a good meal will suddenly convince Julian to forego the cruel pleasure of getting his hands on Majid. I know my husband well enough to understand that nothing can dissuade him from that. Julian is used to danger. I think he even craves it to some extent. I'm not foolish enough to think that I can domesticate him with one dinner.

Still, I want this evening to be special. I need it to be special. I don't want to think about terrorists and torture, abduction and mind fuckery. For just one night, I want to pretend that we're a regular couple, that I'm simply a wife who wants to do something nice for her husband.

Before dinner, I take a shower and blow-dry my long brown hair until it's smooth and shiny. I even apply a little eyeshadow and lipgloss. I don't normally put this much effort into my appearance, since Julian is already insatiable as is, but tonight I want to look extra pretty for him. My dress for the evening is a strapless little number, ivory with a black trim at the waist, and my shoes are sexy black peep-toe pumps. Underneath, I'm wearing a black strapless pushup bra and a matching thong, the most wicked lingerie set I have in my wardrobe.

I'm going to seduce Julian tonight, for no other reason other than because I want to.

He gets delayed by some last-minute logistics, so I end up waiting for him at the candle-lit dinner table for a few minutes, anxiety and excitement battling for supremacy in my chest. Anxiety because I feel sick thinking about tomorrow, and excitement because I can't wait to spend time with Julian.

When he finally walks into the room, I stand up to greet him, and his gaze fastens on me with breathtaking intensity. Stopping a few feet away, he runs his eyes over my body. When he lifts his eyes back to my face, the fire that burns in the blue depths sends an electric tingle straight to my core. A slow, sensual smile curls his lips as he says softly, "You look gorgeous, my pet . . . Absolutely gorgeous."

A flush of pleasure warms my skin at the compliment. "Thank you," I whisper, my eyes glued to his face. He changed for dinner as well, putting on a light blue polo shirt and a pair of gray khaki pants that fit his tall, broad-shouldered body like they were made for him. With his dark, lustrous hair back to its former length, Julian can easily pass for a model or a movie star vacationing on a golf resort. My voice sounds breathless as I say, "You look pretty amazing yourself."

His smile widens as he approaches the table and stops in front of me. "Thank you, baby," he murmurs, his strong fingers curving around my bare shoulders as he lowers his head and captures my mouth in a deep, yet incredibly tender kiss. I melt on the spot, my neck arching back under the hungry pressure of his lips, and it's not until Ana pointedly clears her throat behind us that I regain my senses enough to realize that we're not in our own bedroom. Embarrassed, I push him away, and Julian lets me, releasing me and stepping back with a smile.

"Dinner first, I guess," he says wryly and, walking around the table, takes a seat across from me.

Ana, her cheeks slightly red, serves us lasagna, pours us each a glass of wine, and disappears before I have a chance to do more than say a quick thank-you.

"Lasagna . . ." Julian sniffs appreciatively at the food. "I can't remember the last time I had this."

"Ana told me your mother used to make it for you

when you were little," I say softly, watching as he takes the first bite. "I hope you still like it."

His eyes lift from his plate, his gaze locking on mine as he chews the food. "You arranged this?" he asks after he swallows, and there is a strange note in his voice. He gestures toward the wine and the candles burning on the outer edges of the table. "It wasn't Ana who set all of this up?"

"Well, she did all the work," I admit. "I merely asked her for a few things. I hope you don't mind."

"Mind? No, of course not." His voice still sounds a bit odd, but he doesn't question me further. Instead he begins to eat in earnest, and the conversation turns to my upcoming exams.

After we're done with the lasagna, Ana brings out the dessert. It looks as rich and scrumptious as any I've seen in an Italian restaurant, and I watch Julian's reaction as Ana places it on the table in front of him.

If he's surprised, he doesn't show it. Instead he gives Ana a warm smile and thanks her for the efforts. It's not until she leaves the room that he turns to look at me. "A tiramisu?" he says softly, his eyes reflecting the dancing light from the candles. "Why, Nora?"

I shrug. "Why not?"

He studies me for a moment, his gaze unusually thoughtful as it lingers on my face, and I wait for him to press further. But he doesn't. Instead he picks up his fork. "Why not indeed," he murmurs and turns his attention to the mouthwatering dessert.

I follow his lead, and soon our plates are all but licked clean.

* * *

When we get upstairs, Julian leads me to the bed. Instead of undressing me right away, however, he captures my face between his palms. "Thank you for a wonderful evening, baby," he whispers, his eyes dark with some indefinable emotion.

I smile up at him, my hands coming up to rest on his waist. "Of course . . ." My heart feels like it's about to overflow with happiness. "It's my pleasure."

He looks as though he's about to say something else, but then he just slants his mouth across mine and begins to kiss me with deep, almost desperate passion. My eyes drift shut as pleasure spirals through me. His lips are unbelievably soft, his tongue skillfully caressing mine, and the rich, dark taste of him makes my head spin. As we kiss, his hands slide around my back, pressing me closer to him. The hardness of his erection against my belly sends a spear of heat straight to the center of my sex, and I clutch at his sides, my knees weakening as his lips wander from my mouth to my earlobe and then down to my neck.

"You are so fucking hot," he mutters thickly. His breath almost burns my sensitive skin, and I moan, my head falling back as he arches me over his arm to nibble at the tender area just above my collarbone. My nipples tighten, and my sex begins to ache with the familiar pulsing tension as Julian licks my skin, then blows cool air over the wet spot, sending erotic chills all over my body.

Before I can recover, he tugs me upright, spinning me around so that I'm standing with my back to him. Then his hands are on the back of my dress, pulling down the zipper. The little dress falls to the floor, leaving me wearing nothing but my black heels, push-up bra, and thong.

Julian sucks in an audible breath, and I turn around, giving him a slow, teasing smile. "You like?" I murmur, taking a couple of steps back to give him a better view. The expression on his face makes my pulse quicken with excitement. He's looking at me like a starving man looks at a piece of cake, with agonized longing and naked lust. His eyes say that he wants to devour me and savor me at the same time . . . that I'm the hottest woman he's ever seen in his life.

Instead of answering, he steps toward me and reaches behind my back to unhook my bra. As soon as my breasts are free, he covers them with his warm palms, his thumbs rasping across my hardened nipples. "You are fucking exquisite," he whispers roughly, staring down at me, and I draw in a shaky breath, his words and the touch of his hands making my insides quiver. "You're all I can think about, Nora . . . all I can focus on . . ."

His confession turns my bones to jelly. The

knowledge that I have this effect on him—that this powerful, dangerous man is just as consumed by me as I am by him—makes my heart pound in a wild, erratic rhythm. Regardless of how it all began, Julian is now mine, and I want him as much as he wants me.

Emboldened, I wrap my arms around his neck and pull his head down toward me. As our lips meet, I put everything I have into that kiss, letting him feel how much I need him, how much I love him. My hands slide into his thick, silky hair as his arms close around my back, pressing me against him, and my peaked nipples rub against the ribbed cotton of his shirt, reminding me of the tantalizing contrast between my near-nakedness and his clothed state. His hard erection pushes into my belly, and the heat within me spikes as our mouths mesh in a symphony of lust, coming together with explosive yearning.

I'm not sure how we end up on the bed, but I find myself there, my hands frantically tearing at Julian's clothes as he rains hot kisses on my chest and stomach. His hand closes around my thong, ripping it off with a single motion, and then his fingers push into my opening, two big fingers penetrating me with a roughness that makes me gasp and arch against him. "You're so fucking wet," he growls, thrusting his fingers deeper into me before pulling them out and bringing them to my face. "Taste how much you want me."

Unbearably aroused, I close my lips around his

fingers, sucking them into my mouth. They're coated with my moisture, but the taste doesn't repel me. If anything, it turns me on, makes me burn even hotter. Julian groans as I suck on his fingers, swirling my tongue around them as if they were his cock, and then he pulls his hand away. Rearing up, he pulls his shirt over his head with a single motion, exposing the rippling muscles underneath. His pants are next, and I catch a brief glimpse of his erection before he climbs on top of me, his powerful hands grabbing my wrists and pinning them next to my shoulders. Then his eyes lock on mine, and he pushes my thighs apart with his knees, pressing the head of his cock against my opening.

My heart thrumming with anticipation, I hold his gaze. His face is taut with lust, his jaw clenched tight as he slowly penetrates me. I expected him to take me roughly, but he's careful tonight, working his thick cock into me with a deliberateness that's both arousing and frustrating. There's no pain as my body stretches to accept him, only pleasurable fullness, but some sick part of me now wants the roughness, the violence.

"Julian . . ." I run my tongue over my lips. "I want you to fuck me. *Really* fuck me." To emphasize my request, I wrap my legs around his hips, pulling him all the way into me. We both groan at the intense sensation, and I see his pupils dilating until only a thin rim of blue remains around the black circle.

"You want me to fuck you?" His voice is guttural, so filled with hunger that I can barely make out the words.

His hands tighten on my wrists, almost cutting off my circulation. "To really fuck you?"

I nod, my pulse somewhere in the stratosphere. It still feels wrong to admit this about myself, to acknowledge that I need something I once dreaded.

To know that I'm *asking* my kidnapper to abuse me.

Julian inhales sharply, and I can feel the dam of his control cracking. His mouth descends on mine, his lips and tongue now savage, almost vicious. This kiss devours me, steals my breath and soul. At the same time, his cock withdraws from me nearly all the way and then slams back in with a hard, brutal thrust that splits me in half—and sets my nerve endings on fire.

I cry out into his mouth, my legs wrapping tighter around his firm, muscled ass as he begins to fuck me without restraint. It's a possession as violent as any rape, but I revel in it, my body loving the ferocious assault. It's what I want now, what I need. I may have bruises tomorrow, but for the moment, all I can feel is the massive tension gathering within me, the pressure coiling deep within my sex. Each ruthless thrust winds me tighter and tighter, until I feel like I will shatter . . . and then I do, an explosion of pleasure rocketing through my body as I fly apart in Julian's arms, utterly swamped by the dark bliss.

He comes then too, his head thrown back in pained ecstasy, each muscle in his neck tightly corded as he grinds his cock deeper into me with a harsh cry. The pressure of his groin against my clit prolongs my contractions, wringing every drop of sensation from my body, leaching all remnants of strength from my muscles.

In the aftermath, he rolls off me and gathers me against him, cradling me from behind. And as our breathing begins to slow, we drift off into a deep and dreamless sleep.

CHAPTER TWENTY

❖ JULIAN ❖

The next morning I wake up before Nora, as usual. She's sleeping in her favorite position: draped across my chest, one of her legs resting on top of mine. Quietly extricating myself from her, I head into the shower, trying not to think of the temptation of her sexy little body lying there, all soft and warm from sleep. It's unfortunate, but I don't have time to sate myself with her this morning; the plane is already waiting for me on the landing strip.

She managed to surprise me last night. All week long I'd sensed a slight, almost imperceptible distance from her. I may have broken through her barriers that night, but she rebuilt them to a small degree. She hadn't been pouting or giving me the silent treatment, but I could tell that she hadn't fully forgiven me either.

Until last evening.

I thought I didn't need her forgiveness, but the light, almost euphoric feeling in my chest today says otherwise.

My shower takes less than five minutes. Once I'm dressed and ready to go, I walk over to the bed to give Nora a kiss before I leave. Leaning over her, I brush my lips against her cheek, and in that moment, her eyes flutter open.

Her lips curve upward in a sleepy smile. "Hi . . ."

"Hi yourself," I say huskily, reaching over with my hand to brush a tangled strand of hair off her face. Fuck, she does things to me. Things that no small girl should be able to do. I'm about to finally get revenge on the man who killed Beth and stole Nora from me, and all I can think about is climbing back into bed with her.

She blinks a few times, and I see her smile fading as she remembers that today is not just any morning. All traces of sleepiness disappear from her face as she sits up and stares at me, heedless of the blanket falling down and exposing her naked torso.

"You're leaving already?"

"Yes, baby." Trying to keep my eyes off her round, perky breasts, I sit down on the bed next to her and clasp her hand between both of my palms, rubbing it softly. "The plane is already fueled up and waiting for me."

She swallows. "When are you going to be back?"

"If all goes well, in about a week. I have to meet with a couple of officials in Russia first, so I won't get to Tajikistan right away."

"Russia? Why?" A small frown bisects her forehead. "I thought you were going to take care of some business in Ukraine on your way back."

"I was, but things changed. Yesterday afternoon I received a call from one of Peter's contacts in Moscow. They want me to meet with them first, or else they won't let us get to Tajikistan."

"Oh." Nora looks even more concerned now, her frown deepening. "Do you know why?"

I have some suspicions, but none that I want to share with her at the moment. She's far too worried as is. Russians have always been unpredictable, and the increasingly volatile situation in that region doesn't help matters.

"I've had some interactions with them in the past," I say noncommittally, and get up before she has a chance to question me further. "I have to go now, baby, but I'll see you in a few days. Good luck with your tests, okay?"

She nods, her eyes suspiciously bright as she looks at me, and unable to resist, I bend down and kiss her one last time before walking out of the room.

* * *

Moscow in March is colder than a witch's tit. The cold seeps through my thick layers of clothing and settles deep within my bones, making me feel as if I'll never get warm again. I have never particularly liked Russia, and this visit only solidifies my negative opinion of the place.

Freezing. Dirty. Corrupt.

I can deal with the last two, but all three combined is too much. No wonder Peter was glad to remain behind to watch the compound. The bastard knew exactly what I would be getting into. I could see the smirk on his face as he watched the plane take off. After the tropical heat of the jungle, the bone-chilling temperatures of Moscow in the last grip of winter feel downright painful—as do my negotiations with the Russian government.

It takes nearly an hour, ten different appetizers, and half a bottle of vodka before Buschekov gets to the point of the meeting. The only reason I tolerate this is because it takes about this long for my feet to defrost from the sub-zero chill outside. The traffic on the way to the restaurant was so bad that Lucas and I ended up getting out of the car and walking eight blocks, freezing our asses off in the process.

Now, however, I'm finally able to move my toes— and Buschekov seems ready to talk business. He's one of the unofficial officials here: a person who wields significant influence in the Kremlin, but whose name never comes up on the news.

"I have a delicate matter I'd like to discuss with you," Buschekov says after the waiter clears off some of the empty platters. Or, rather, our interpreter says that after Buschekov says something in Russian. Since neither Lucas nor I understand more than a few words of the language, Buschekov hired a young woman to translate for us. Pretty, blond, and blue-eyed, Yulia Tzakova looks to be only a couple of years older than my Nora, but the Russian official assured me that the girl knows how to be discreet.

"Go on," I say in response to Buschekov's statement. Lucas sits next to me, silently consuming his second serving of caviar-stuffed blinis. He's the only one I brought with me to this meeting. The rest of my men are stationed nearby in case of any difficulties. I doubt the Russians will try anything at the moment, but one can never be too cautious.

Buschekov gives me a thin-lipped smile and responds in Russian.

"I'm sure you are aware of the difficulties in our region," Yulia translates. "We would like you to assist us in resolving this matter."

"Assist you how?" I have a good idea of what the Russians want, but I still want to hear him lay it all out.

"There are certain parts of Ukraine that need our help," Yulia says in English after Buschekov answers. "But, world opinion being what it is right now, it would be problematic if we went in and actually gave that help."

"So you would like me to do it instead."

He nods, his colorless eyes trained on my face as Yulia translates my statement. "Yes," he says, "we would like a sizable shipment of weapons and other supplies to reach the freedom fighters in Donetsk. It cannot be traced back to us. In return, you would be paid your usual fee and granted safe passage to Tajikistan."

I smile at him blandly. "Is that all?"

"We would also prefer it if you avoided any dealings with Ukraine at this time," he says without blinking. "Two chairs and one ass and all that."

I assume that last statement makes more sense in Russian, but I understand the gist of what he's saying. Buschekov is not the first client to demand this from me, and he won't be the last. "I'm afraid I will require additional compensation for that," I say calmly. "As you know, I don't usually take sides in these types of conflicts."

"Yes, so we've heard." Buschekov picks up a piece of salted fish with his fork and chews it slowly as he looks at me. "Perhaps you might reconsider that position in our case. The Soviet Union may be gone, but our influence in this region is still quite substantial."

"Yes, I'm aware. Why do you think I'm here right now?" The smile that I give him now has a sharper edge. "But neutrality is an expensive commodity to give up. I'm sure you understand."

Something icy flickers in Buschekov's gaze. "I do. I'm authorized to offer you twenty percent more than the usual payment for your cooperation in this matter."

"Twenty percent? When you're cutting my potential profits in half?" I laugh softly. "I don't think so."

He pours himself another shot of vodka and swirls it around the glass, regarding me thoughtfully. "Twenty percent more and the captured Al-Quadar terrorist remitted into your custody," he says after a few moments. "This is our final offer."

I study him while I pour myself some vodka as well. Truthfully, this is better than I had been hoping to get out of him, and I know better than to push too far with the Russians. "We have a deal then," I say and, lifting my glass in an ironic toast, knock back the shot.

* * *

My car is waiting for us on the street when we exit the restaurant. The driver finally made it through the traffic, which means we won't freeze on our way to the hotel.

"Would you mind giving me a lift to the nearest subway?" Yulia asks as Lucas and I approach the car. I can see her already beginning to shiver. "It should be about ten blocks from here."

I give her a considering look, then motion Lucas

over with a short gesture. "Frisk her."

Lucas walks over and pats her down. "She's clean."

"Okay, then," I say, opening the car door for her. "Hop in."

She climbs in and settles next to me in the back, while Lucas joins the driver in the front. "Thank you," she says with a pretty smile. "I really appreciate it. This is one of the worst winters in recent years."

"No problem." I'm not in the mood to make small talk, so I pull out my phone and begin answering emails. There's one from Nora, which makes me grin. She wants to know if I landed safely. *Yes*, I write back. *Now just trying not to get frostbite in Moscow.*

"Are you staying here for long?" Yulia's soft voice interrupts me as I'm about to pull up a report detailing Nora's movements around the estate in my absence. When I glance up at her, the Russian girl smiles and crosses her long legs. "I could show you around town if you'd like."

Her invitation couldn't be more blatant if she'd palmed my cock right then and there. I can see the hungry gleam in her eyes as she looks at me, and I realize that she's one of those: a woman turned on by power and danger. She wants me because of what I represent—because of the thrill it gives her to play with fire. I have no doubt that she would let me do whatever I want to her, no matter how sadistic or depraved, and then she would beg for more.

She's exactly the type of woman I would've gladly

fucked before meeting Nora. Unfortunately for Yulia, her pale beauty does nothing for me now. The only woman I want in my bed is the dark-haired girl who's currently several thousand miles away.

"Thanks for the invitation," I say, giving Yulia a cool smile. "But we'll be leaving soon, and I'm afraid I'm too exhausted to do your town justice tonight."

"Of course." Yulia smiles back, unfazed by my rejection. She clearly has enough self-confidence not to be offended. "If you change your mind, you know where to find me." And as the car rolls to a halt in front of the subway stop, she gracefully climbs out, leaving behind a faint trail of expensive perfume.

As the car begins moving again, Lucas turns around to face me. "If you don't want her, I'd be happy to entertain her tonight," he offers casually. "If that's all right with you, of course."

I grin. Hot blondes have always been Lucas's weakness. "Why not," I say. "She's all yours if you want her." We don't fly out until tomorrow morning, and I have plenty of security in place. If Lucas wants to spend the night fucking our interpreter, I'm not about to deny him that pleasure.

As for me, I plan to use my fist in the shower while thinking of Nora, and then get a good night's rest.

Tomorrow is going to be an eventful day.

* * *

The flight to Tajikistan from Moscow is supposed to take a little over six hours in my Boeing C-17. It's one of the three military airplanes that I own, and it's big enough for this mission, easily fitting in all of my men and our equipment.

Everyone, myself included, is dressed in the latest combat gear. Our suits are bulletproof and flame-retardant, and we're fully armed with assault rifles, grenades, and explosives. It may be overkill, but I'm not taking chances with my men's lives. I enjoy danger, but I'm not suicidal, and all the risks I take in my business are carefully calculated. Nora's rescue in Thailand was probably the most perilous operation I've been involved with in recent years, and I wouldn't have done it for anyone else.

Only for her.

I spend the majority of the flight going through the manufacturing specifications for a new factory in Malaysia. If all goes well, I may shift missile production there from its current location in Indonesia. The local officials in the latter region are getting too greedy, demanding higher bribes each month, and I'm not inclined to indulge them for much longer. I also answer a few questions from my Chicago-based portfolio manager; he's working on setting up a fund-of-funds through one of my subsidiaries and needs me to give him some investment parameters.

We're flying over Uzbekistan, just a few hundred miles from our destination, when I decide to check in with Lucas, who's piloting the plane.

He turns toward me as soon as I enter the cabin. "We're on track to get there in about an hour and a half," he says without my asking. "There is some ice on the landing strip, so they're de-icing it for us right now. The helicopters are already fueled up and ready to go."

"Excellent." The plan calls for us to land about a dozen miles from the suspected terrorist hideout in the Pamir Mountains and fly by helicopters the rest of the way. "Any unusual activities in that area?"

He shakes his head. "No, everything is quiet."

"Good." Entering the cabin, I sit down next to Lucas in the copilot's seat and strap myself in. "How was the Russian girl last night?"

A rare smile flashes across his stony face. "Quite satisfying. You missed out."

"Yes, I'm sure," I say, though I don't feel even the slightest flicker of regret. There's no way some one-night stand can approximate the intensity of my connection with Nora, and I have no desire to settle for anything less than that.

Lucas grins—an expression that's even more uncommon on his hard features. "I have to say, I never expected to see you as a happily married man."

I raise my eyebrows. "Is that right?" This is probably the most personal observation he's ever made to me. In all the years he's been with my organization, Lucas has never before bridged the distance from loyal employee to friend—not that I've encouraged him to do so. Trust has never come easy to me, and there have been only a handful of individuals I've been able to call 'friend.'

He shrugs, his face smoothing out into his usual impassive mask, though a hint of amusement still lurks in his eyes. "Sure. People like us aren't generally considered good husband material."

An involuntary chuckle escapes my throat. "Well, I don't know if, strictly speaking, Nora considers me 'good husband material.'" A monster who abducted her and fucked with her head, sure. But a good husband? Somehow I doubt it.

"Well, if she doesn't, then she should," Lucas says, turning his attention back to the controls. "You don't cheat, you take good care of her, and you've risked your life to save her before. If that's not being a good husband, then I don't know what is." As he speaks, I see a small frown appearing on his face as he peers at something on the radar screen.

"What is it?" I ask sharply, all of my instincts suddenly on alert.

"I'm not sure," Lucas begins saying, and at that moment, the plane bucks so violently that I'm nearly thrown out of my seat. It's only the seatbelt I'd strapped on out of habit that prevents me from hitting the ceiling as the plane takes a sudden nosedive.

Lucas grabs the controls, a steady stream of obscenities coming out of his mouth as he frantically tries to correct our course. "Shit, fuck, shit, shit, motherfucking shit——"

"What hit us?" My voice is steady, my mind strangely calm as I assess the situation. There is a grinding, sputtering noise coming from the engines. I can smell smoke and hear screams in the back, so I know there's a fire. It had to be an explosion. That means someone either shot at us from another plane or a surface-to-air missile exploded in close vicinity, damaging one or more of the engines. It couldn't have been a direct missile hit because the Boeing is equipped with an anti-missile defense that's designed to repel all but the most advanced weapons—and because we are still alive and not blown into pieces.

"I'm not sure," Lucas manages to say as he wrestles with the controls. The plane evens out for a brief second and then nosedives again. "Does it fucking matter?"

I'm not sure, to be honest. The analytical part of me wants to know what—or who—is going to be responsible for my death. I doubt it's Al-Quadar; according to my sources, they don't have weapons this sophisticated. That leaves the possibility of error by some trigger-happy Uzbekistani soldier or an intentional strike by someone else. The Russians, perhaps, though why they would do this is anyone's guess.

Still, Lucas is right. I don't know why I care. Knowing the truth won't change the outcome. I can see the snowy peaks of Pamir in the distance, and I know we're not going to make it there.

Lucas resumes his cursing as he fights with the controls, and I grip the edge of my seat, my eyes trained on the ground rushing toward us at a terrifyingly rapid pace. There is a roaring sound in my ears, and I realize that it's my own heartbeat—that I can actually hear the blood coursing through my veins as surging adrenaline sharpens all of my senses.

The plane makes a few more attempts to come out of the nosedive, each one slowing our fall by a few seconds, but nothing seems able to arrest the lethal descent.

As I watch us plummeting to our deaths, I have only one regret.

I will never get to hold Nora again.

PART III: THE CAPTIVE

CHAPTER TWENTY-ONE

❖ NORA ❖

Two days without Julian.

I can't believe it's been two entire days without Julian. I've been going about my usual routine, but without him here, everything feels different.

Emptier. Darker.

It's like the sun has hidden behind a cloud, leaving my world in shadow.

It's crazy. Utterly insane. I've been without Julian before. When I was on the island, he would leave on these trips all the time. In fact, he spent more time *off* the island than *on* it, and somehow I still managed to function. This time around, however, I have to constantly fight off a horrible feeling of unease, of anxiety that seems to worsen with every hour.

"I really don't know what's wrong with me," I tell Rosa during our morning walk. "I lived for eighteen years without him, and now all of a sudden, I can't go for two days?"

She grins at me. "Well, of course. The two of you are all but inseparable, so this doesn't surprise me in the least. I've never seen a couple this much in love before."

I sigh, ruefully shaking my head. For all her seeming practicality, Rosa has a romantic streak as wide as the sea. A couple of weeks ago, I finally confided in her, telling her how Julian and I met and about my time on the island. She had been shocked, but not nearly as much as I would've been in her place. In fact, she seemed to think the whole thing was rather poetic.

"He stole you because he couldn't live without you," she said dreamily when I tried to explain to her why I still have reservations about Julian. "It's like the kind of thing you read about in books or see in movies . . ." And when I stared at her, hardly able to believe my ears, she added wistfully, "I wish someone wanted *me* enough to steal me away."

So yes, Rosa is definitely not the person to knock some sense into me. She thinks my withering away without Julian is a natural result of our grand love affair, instead of something that likely requires psychiatric help.

Of course, Ana is not much better either.

"It's normal to miss your husband," the housekeeper tells me when I can barely force myself to eat at dinner. "I'm sure Julian misses you just as much."

"I don't know, Ana," I say doubtfully, pushing the rice around on my plate. "I haven't heard from him all day. He responded to my email yesterday, but I sent him two emails today—and nothing." This, more than anything, is what upsets me, I think. Julian either doesn't care about the fact that I'm worried—or he's not in a position to respond to me, being knee-deep in fighting terrorists.

Either possibility makes me queasy.

"He could be flying somewhere," Ana says reasonably, taking my plate away. "Or be someplace with no signal. Truly, you shouldn't worry. I know Julian, and he can take care of himself."

"Yes, I'm sure he can, but he's still human." He can still be killed by a stray bullet or an untimely bomb.

"I know, Nora," Ana says soothingly, patting my arm, and I see the same worry reflected in the depths of her brown eyes. "I know, but you can't let yourself think bad thoughts. I'm sure you'll hear from him in a few hours. He'll contact you by morning at the latest."

* * *

I sleep fitfully, waking up every couple of hours to check my email and phone. By morning, there's still no word from Julian, and I stumble wearily out of bed, bleary-eyed but determined.

If Julian isn't contacting me, I'm going to take matters into my own hands.

The first thing I do is hunt down Peter Sokolov. He's talking with a few guards on the far edge of the estate when I find him, and he seems surprised when I approach him and ask to speak to him privately. Nevertheless, he accommodates my request right away.

As soon as we're out of earshot of the others, I ask, "Have you heard from Julian?" I still find the Russian man intimidating, but he's the only one I know who may have answers.

"No," he responds in his accented voice. "Not since their plane took off from Moscow yesterday." There is a hint of tension around his eyes as he speaks, and my anxiety triples as I realize that Peter is concerned too.

"They were supposed to check in, weren't they?" I say, staring up at his exotically handsome features. My chest feels like I can't get enough air. "Something went wrong, didn't it?"

"We can't assume that yet." His tone is carefully neutral. "It's possible they're not responding to our calls because of security reasons—because they don't want anyone to intercept their communications."

"You don't really believe that."

"It's unlikely," Peter admits, his gray eyes cool on

my face. "This is not the usual procedure in these types of cases."

"Right, of course." Doing my best to battle the nauseating fear spreading through me, I ask evenly, "So what's Plan B? Are you going to send in a rescue team? Do you have more men standing by that can act as backup?"

Peter shakes his head. "There's nothing to be done until we know more," he explains. "I've already put out feelers in Russia and Tajikistan, so we should have a better idea of what happened soon. So far, all we know is that their plane took off from Moscow without any problems."

"When do you think you'll hear back from your sources?" I'm trying to contain my panic, but some of it seeps through in my voice. "Today? Tomorrow?"

"I don't know, Mrs. Esguerra," he says, and I see a hint of pity in those merciless gray eyes. "It could be at any time. I will let you know as soon as I hear something."

"Thanks, Peter," I say and, not knowing what else to do, walk back to the house.

* * *

The next six hours go by at a crawl. I pace around the house, going from room to room, unable to focus on any specific activity. Whenever I sit down to study or try to paint, a dozen different scenarios, each one more horrible than the next, start playing in my head. I want to believe that everything will be okay, that Julian's plane disappeared off the grid for some innocuous reason, but I know better than that.

There are no fairy tales in the world Julian and I live in, only savage reality.

I haven't been able to eat anything all day, though Ana has tried tempting me with everything from steak to dessert. To pacify her, I eat a few bites of papaya around lunchtime and resume my aimless pacing around the house.

By early afternoon, I'm literally sick from anxiety. My head is pounding, and my stomach feels like it's eating itself, the acid burning a hole in my insides.

"Let's go for a swim," Rosa offers when she finds me in the library. I can see the concern on her face, and I know Ana probably sent her to distract me. Rosa is usually too busy with her duties to take off in the middle of the day, but she's obviously making an exception today.

The last thing I feel like doing is swimming, but I agree. Rosa's company is better than driving myself insane with worry.

As we exit the library together, I see Peter walking in our direction, a grave expression on his face.

My heart stops for a moment, then begins slamming furiously against my ribcage.

"What is it?" My tongue can barely form the words. "Did you hear anything?"

"The plane went down in Uzbekistan, a couple of hundred miles from the Tajikistan border," he says quietly, stopping in front of me. "It looks like there was a miscommunication, and the Uzbekistani military shot them down."

Blackness creeps in at the edges of my vision. "Shot them down?" My voice sounds like it's coming from a distance, like the words belong to someone else. I am vaguely aware of Rosa placing a supportive arm around my back, but her touch does nothing to arrest the iciness spreading through me.

"We're looking for the wreckage right now," Peter says, almost gently. "I'm sorry, Mrs. Esguerra, but I doubt they could've survived."

CHAPTER TWENTY-TWO

❖ NORA ❖

I'm not sure how I get to the bedroom, but I find myself there, curled up in a ball of silent agony on the bed that Julian and I shared.

I can feel soft hands on my hair, hear voices murmuring in Spanish, and I know both Ana and Rosa are there with me. The housekeeper sounds like she's crying. I want to cry too, but I can't. The pain is too raw, too deep to allow the comfort of tears.

I thought I knew what it feels like to have your heart ripped out. When I mistakenly thought that Julian was dead, I had been devastated, destroyed. Those months without him had been the worst ones of my life. I thought I knew what it was like to feel loss, to know that I would never see his smile again or feel the warmth of his embrace.

It's only now that I realize that there are degrees of agony. That pain can range from devastating to soul-shattering. When I lost Julian before, he had been the center of my world. Now, however, he is my entire world, and I don't know how to exist without him.

"Oh, Nora . . ." Ana's voice is thick with tears as she strokes my hair. "I'm sorry, child . . . I'm so sorry . . ."

I want to tell her that I'm sorry too, that I know Julian mattered to her as well, but I can't. I can't speak. Even breathing seems to require exorbitant effort, as though my lungs have forgotten how to function. One tiny breath in, one tiny breath out—that's all I seem capable of doing at the moment.

Just breathing. Just not dying.

After a while, the quiet murmurs and soothing touches stop, and I realize that I'm alone. They must've covered me with a blanket before they left, because I can feel its soft fluffy weight on top of me. It should make me feel warm, but it doesn't.

All I feel is a frozen, aching void where my heart used to be.

* * *

"Nora, child . . . Come, drink something . . ."

Ana and Rosa are back, their soft hands pulling me to a sitting position. A cup of hot chocolate is offered to me, and I accept it on autopilot, cradling it between my cold palms.

"Just a sip," Ana urges. "You haven't eaten all day. Julian wouldn't want this, you know that."

The jolt of agony at the mention of his name is so strong that the cup almost slips out of my grip. Rosa grabs for it, steadying my hands, and gently, but inexorably pushes the cup toward my lips. "Come on, Nora," she whispers, her gaze filled with sympathy. "Just drink some."

I force myself to take a few sips. The rich, warm liquid trickles down my throat, the combined rush of sugar and caffeine chasing away some of my numb exhaustion. Feeling a fraction more alive, I glance at the window and realize with shock that it's already dark—that I must've lain there for a few hours without registering the passage of time.

"Any word from Peter?" I ask, looking back at Ana and Rosa. "Did they find the wreckage?"

Rosa looks relieved that I'm talking again. "We haven't seen him since the afternoon," she says, and Ana nods, her eyes red-rimmed and swollen.

"Okay." I take a few more sips of the hot chocolate and then hand the cup back to Ana. "Thank you."

"Can I get you something to eat?" Ana asks hopefully. "A sandwich perhaps, or some fruit?"

My stomach roils at the thought of food, but I know

that I need to eat something. I can't die alongside Julian, no matter how appealing that option seems at the moment. "Yes, please." My voice sounds strained. "Just a piece of toast with cheese, if you don't mind."

Jumping off the bed, Rosa gives me a huge, approving smile. "There we go. See, Ana, I told you she's a fighter." And before I can change my mind about the meal, she runs out of the room to grab the food.

"I'm going to shower," I tell Ana, getting up as well. All of a sudden, I have a strong urge to be alone—to be away from the smothering concern I see on Ana's face. My body feels cold and brittle, like an icicle that might shatter at any moment, and my eyes are burning with unshed tears.

Just focus on breathing. Just one tiny breath after another.

"Of course, child." Ana gives me a kind, weary smile. "You go right ahead. The food will be waiting for you when you come out."

And as I make my escape into the bathroom, I see her quietly slipping out of the room.

* * *

"Nora! Oh my God, Nora!"

Rosa's screams and frantic knocking on the bathroom door startle me out of my numb, almost catatonic state. I have no idea how long I've been standing under the hot spray, but I immediately jump out. Then, wrapping a towel around myself, I race to the door, my wet feet sliding on cold tiles.

My heart hammering in my throat, I yank open the door. "What is it?"

"He's alive!" Rosa's scream nearly deafens me with its high-pitched volume. "Nora, Julian is alive!"

"Alive?" For a moment, I can't process what she's saying, my brain sluggish from hunger and grief. "Julian is alive?"

"Yes!" she squeals, grabbing my hands and jumping up and down. "Peter just got word that they found him and a few of his men alive. They're being taken to the hospital as we speak!"

My knees buckle, and I sway on my feet. "To the hospital?" My voice is barely above a whisper. "He's really alive?"

"Yes!" Rosa pulls me into a bone-crushing hug, then releases me, stepping back with a giant grin on her face. "Isn't that amazing?"

"Yes, of course . . ." My head is spinning with joy and disbelief, my pulse racing a mile a minute. "You said he's being taken to a hospital?"

"Yes, that's what Peter said." Rosa's expression sobers a bit. "He's talking to Ana downstairs. I didn't stay to listen—I wanted to give you the news as soon as possible."

"Of course, thank you!" I'm electrified all of a sudden, all traces of my mental fog and despair falling away. *Julian is alive and being taken to a hospital!*

Running to the closet, I pull out the first dress I find and throw it on, dropping the towel on the floor. Then I dash to the door and fly down the stairs, with Rosa hurrying after me.

Peter is in the kitchen next to Ana. The housekeeper's eyes widen as she sees me barreling toward them, my feet bare and my hair dripping-wet from the shower. I probably look like a crazy woman, but I don't give a damn. All I care about is finding out more about Julian.

"How is he?" I pant, skidding to a stop a foot away from the two of them. "What kind of condition is he in?"

An expression shockingly similar to a smile flickers across Peter's hard face as he looks at me. "They're going to run some tests at the hospital, but right now it looks like your husband survived a plane crash with nothing worse than a broken arm, a couple of cracked ribs, and a nasty gash on his forehead. He's unconscious, but that appears to be mostly due to blood loss from his head wound."

And as I stare at Peter in open-mouthed incredulity, he explains, "The plane fell in a heavily wooded area, so the trees cushioned much of the impact. The pilot's cabin—where Esguerra and Kent were sitting—got ripped off by the force of the impact, and that seems to have saved their lives." The smile disappears then, and his metallic eyes darken. "Most of the others died, though. The fuel was in the back, and it exploded, destroying that portion of the plane. Only three of the soldiers back there survived, and they're badly burned. If it weren't for the combat gear they were all wearing, they would not have survived either."

"Oh my God." A wave of horror washes over me. Julian is alive, but nearly fifty of his men perished. I've had minimal interaction with most of the guards, but I've seen many of them around the estate. I know them, if only by sight. They were all strong, seemingly indestructible men. And now they're dead. Gone—just as Julian would've been if he hadn't been up front.

"What about Lucas?" I ask, starting to shake with delayed reaction. It's beginning to hit me that Julian was in a plane crash and *survived*. That, like a cat with nine lives, he beat the odds yet again.

"Kent has a broken leg and a severe concussion. He was also unconscious when they were found."

Relief spirals through me, and my eyes, burning with dryness before, fill with sudden tears. Tears of gratitude, of joy so intense that it's impossible to contain. I want to laugh and sob at the same time.

Julian is alive, and so is the man who once saved his life.

"Oh, Nora, child . . ." Ana's plump arms close around me as my tears overflow. "It will be all right now . . . Everything will be all right . . ."

Shaking with repressed sobs, I let her hold me for a moment in a motherly embrace. Then I pull away, smiling through the tears. For the first time, I believe that it *will* be all right. That the worst is now over.

"How soon can we fly out?" I ask Peter, wiping at the wetness on my cheeks. "Can the plane be ready in an hour?"

"Fly out?" He gives me a strange look. "We can't fly out, Mrs. Esguerra. I'm under strict orders to remain on the estate and make sure that you are safe here."

"What?" I stare at him incredulously. "But Julian is hurt! He's in the hospital, and I'm his wife—"

"Yes, I understand." Peter's expression doesn't change, his eyes cool and veiled as he looks at me. "But I'm afraid Esguerra will quite literally murder me if I allow you to be in danger."

"Are you telling me that I can't go see my husband who was just in a plane crash?" My voice rises as a wave of sudden fury sweeps through me. "That I'm supposed to sit here and do nothing while Julian is lying injured half a world away?"

Peter doesn't appear impressed with my outburst. "I will do my best to arrange a secure phone call and perhaps a video connection for you," he says calmly. "I will also keep you informed of any developments in regards to his health. Beyond that, I'm afraid there is nothing I can do at the moment. I am currently working to tighten security around the hospital where Esguerra and the others are being taken, so hopefully he will return here safe and sound, and you will see him shortly."

I want to scream, yell, and argue, but I know it won't do any good. I have about as much leverage over Peter as I do over Julian—which is none at all. "Fine," I say, taking a deep breath to calm myself. "You do that—and I want to know as soon as he regains consciousness."

Peter inclines his head. "Of course, Mrs. Esguerra. You will be informed right away."

CHAPTER TWENTY-THREE

❖ JULIAN ❖

I first become aware of the noises. Low feminine murmurs intermingled with rhythmic beeping. A hum of electricity in the background. All of this overlaid with a throbbing pain in the front of my skull and a strong antiseptic odor in my nostrils.

A hospital. I'm in a hospital of some kind.

My body hurts, the pain seemingly everywhere. My first instinct is to open my eyes and seek answers, but I lie still, letting the recollections come to me.

Nora. The mission. Flying to Tajikistan. I relive it all, the remembered sensations sharp and vivid. I see myself talking to Lucas in the cabin, feel the plane bucking underneath us. I hear the sputtering whine of the engines and experience the gut-churning sensation of falling from the sky. I endure the paralysis of fear in those last few moments as Lucas tries to level out the plane above the tree line to buy us precious seconds— and then I feel the bone-jarring impact of the crash.

Beyond that, there is nothing else, just darkness.

It should've been the permanent darkness of death, yet I'm alive. The pain in my battered body tells me so.

Continuing to lie still, I assess my new situation. The voices around me—they're speaking in a foreign language. It sounds like a mixture of Russian and Turkish. Likely Uzbek, given where we were flying at the time of the crash.

It's two women speaking, their tone casual, almost gossipy. Logic tells me they are probably nurses at this hospital. I can hear them moving about as they chat with one another, and I carefully crack open one eye to look at my surroundings.

I'm in a drab room with pale green walls and a small window on the far wall. Fluorescent lights on the ceiling emit a low buzzing sound—the hum of electricity I'd noticed earlier. A monitor is hooked up to me, with an IV line connected to my wrist. I can see the nurses on the other side of the room. They're changing the sheets on an empty bed that's standing there. A thin curtain separates my area from that bed, but it's drawn open, enabling me to see the room fully.

Other than the two nurses, I'm alone. There's no sign of any of my men. My pulse jumps at the realization, and I do my best to steady my breathing before they notice. I want them to continue thinking that I'm unconscious. There doesn't seem to be any overt threat, but until I know what happened to the plane and how I ended up here, I don't dare drop my guard.

Cautiously flexing my fingers and toes, I close my eyes and take mental stock of my injuries. I feel weak, like I lost a lot of blood. My head throbs, and I can feel a heavy bandage over my forehead. My left arm—which aches mercilessly—is immobilized, as if it's in a cast. My right one seems fine, however. It hurts to breathe, so I assume my ribs are damaged in some way. Beyond that, I can feel all of my appendages, and the pain in the rest of my body feels more like scrapes and bruises than broken bones.

After a few minutes, one of the nurses leaves while the other one walks over to my bed. I remain still and quiet, feigning unconsciousness. She adjusts the sheet covering me, then checks the bandage on my head. I can hear her humming softly under her breath as she turns to leave as well, and at that moment, heavier footsteps enter the room.

A man's voice, deep and authoritative, asks a question in Uzbek.

I crack open my eyes again to steal a glance at the doorway. The new arrival is a lean middle-aged man wearing a military officer's uniform. Judging by the insignia on his chest, he must be fairly high up.

The nurse answers him, her voice soft and uncertain, and then the man approaches my bed. I tense, prepared to defend myself if necessary despite the weakness in my muscles. However, the man doesn't reach for a weapon or make any threatening moves. Instead he studies me, his expression oddly curious.

Going on instinct, I open my eyes fully and look at him, my body still coiled for a potential strike. "Who are you?" I ask bluntly, figuring that the direct approach is best at this point. "Where is this place?"

He looks startled, but recovers his composure almost right away. "I'm Colonel Sharipov, and you are in Tashkent, Uzbekistan," he answers, taking half a step back. "Your airplane crashed, and you were brought here." He has a thick accent, but his English is surprisingly good. "The Russian embassy has been in contact about you. Your people are sending another plane to pick you up."

He knows who I am then. "Where are my men? What happened to my plane?"

"We're still investigating the cause of the crash," Sharipov says, his eyes shifting slightly to the side. "It's unclear at this point—"

"Bullshit." My voice is deadly quiet. I can tell when someone is lying, and this fucker is definitely trying to blow smoke up my ass. "You know what happened."

He hesitates. "I'm not authorized to discuss the

investigation—"

"Did your military fire a missile at us?" I use my right arm to prop myself up into a sitting position. My ribs protest the movement, but I ignore the pain. I may feel as weak as an infant, but it's never a good idea to seem that way in front of an enemy. "You might as well tell me now because I will learn the truth one way or another."

His face tightens at my implied threat. "No, it was not us. Right now, it appears that one of our missile launchers was used, but nobody issued the order to shoot down your plane. We received word from Russia that you would be passing through our airspace, and we were told to let you through."

"You have an idea of who is responsible, though," I observe coldly. Now that I'm sitting up, I don't feel quite as vulnerable—though I would feel even better if I had a gun or a knife. "You know who used the launcher."

Sharipov hesitates again, then reluctantly admits, "It's possible that one of our officers may have been bribed by the Ukrainian government. We're looking into that possibility now."

"I see." It all finally makes sense. Somehow Ukraine got word of my cooperation with the Russians and decided to eliminate me before I became a threat. *Those fucking bastards.* This is why I try not to take sides in these petty conflicts—it's too costly, in more ways than one.

"We have stationed a few soldiers on this floor," Sharipov says, changing the topic. "You will be safe here until the Russian envoy arrives to bring you to Moscow."

"Where are my men?" I repeat my earlier question, my eyes narrowing as I see Sharipov's gaze slide away again. "Are they here?"

"Four of them," he admits quietly, looking back at me. "I am afraid the rest didn't make it."

I keep my expression impassive, though it feels like a sharp blade is twisting in my insides. I should be used to it by now—to people dying around me—but somehow it still weighs on me. "Who are the survivors?" I ask, keeping my voice level. "Do you have their names?"

He nods and rattles off a list of names. To my relief, Lucas Kent is among them. "He regained consciousness briefly," Sharipov explains, "and helped identify the others. Besides you, he's the only one who wasn't burned by the explosion."

"I see." My relief is replaced by slowly building rage. Nearly fifty of my best men are dead. Men I've trained with. Men I've gotten to know. As I process that fact, it occurs to me that there is only one way the Ukrainian government would've known about my negotiations with the Russians.

The pretty Russian interpreter. She was the only outsider privy to that conversation.

"I need a phone," I tell Sharipov, swinging my feet

to the floor and standing up. My knees shake a bit, but my legs are able to hold my weight. This is good. It means I'm capable of walking out of here under my own steam.

"I need it right now," I add when he just gapes at me as I pull the IV needle out of my arm with my teeth and peel the monitor sensors off my chest. My hospital gown and bare feet undoubtedly look ridiculous, but I don't give a fuck. I have a traitor to deal with.

"Of course," he says, recovering from his shock. Reaching into his pocket, he pulls out a cell phone and hands it to me. "Peter Sokolov wanted to talk to you as soon you woke up."

"Good. Thanks." Placing the phone in my left hand, which protrudes from the cast, I begin to punch in numbers with my right. It's a secure line that moves through so many relays, it would take a world-class hacker to trace it to its destination. As I hear the familiar clicks and beeps of the connection, I reclaim the phone with my right hand and tell Sharipov, "Please ask one of the nurses to get me some regular clothes. I'm tired of wearing this."

The colonel nods and walks out of the room. A second after he leaves, Peter's voice comes on the line: "Esguerra?"

"Yes, it's me." My grip on the phone tightens. "I assume you heard the news."

"Yes, I heard." A pause on the line. "I had Yulia Tzakova detained in Moscow. It seems like she's got some connections that our Kremlin friends overlooked."

So Peter is already on top of this. "Yes, it seems like it." My voice is even, though anger boils within me. "Needless to say, we're scrapping the mission. When are we getting picked up?"

"The plane is on its way. It should be there in a few hours. I sent Goldberg along in case you could use a doctor."

"Good thinking. We'll be waiting. How is Nora?"

There is a brief moment of silence. "She's better now that she knows you're alive. She wanted to fly out there as soon as she heard."

"You didn't let her, though." It's a statement, not a question. Peter knows better than to fuck up like that.

"No, of course not. Do you wish to see her? I may be able to set up a video connection with the hospital."

"Yes, please set it up." What I really want is to see her and hold her in person, but the video will have to do for now. "In the meantime, I'm going to check on Lucas and the others."

* * *

Because of the bulky cast on my arm, it's a struggle to put on the clothes the nurse brings me. The pants go on without any issues, but I end up having to rip out the left sleeve to get the cast through the armhole. My ribs hurt like hell, and every movement requires tremendous effort as my body wants nothing more than to lie back down on the bed and rest. I persist, though, and after a few tries, finally succeed in clothing myself.

Thankfully, walking is easier. I can maintain a regular stride. As I exit the room, I see the soldiers Sharipov mentioned earlier. There are five of them, all dressed in army fatigues and toting Uzis. Seeing me emerge into the hallway, they silently fall into step behind me, following me as I head over to the Intensive Care Unit. Their expressionless faces make me wonder if they're there to protect me or to protect others *from* me. I can't imagine the Uzbekistani government is thrilled to have an illegal arms dealer in their civilian hospital.

Lucas is not there, so I check on the others first. As Sharipov told me, they are all badly burned, with bandages covering most of their bodies. They're also heavily sedated. I make a mental note to transfer a huge bonus into each of their bank accounts to compensate them for this, and to have them seen by the best plastic surgeons. These men knew the risks when they came to work for me, but I still want to make sure they're taken care of.

"Where is the fourth man?" I ask one of the soldiers accompanying me, and he directs me to another room.

When I get there, I see that Lucas is asleep. He doesn't look nearly as bad as the others, which is a relief. He'll be able to return with me to Colombia once the plane arrives, whereas the burned men will have to stay here for at least a few more days.

Coming back to my room, I find Sharipov there, placing a laptop on the bed. "I was asked to give this to you," he explains, handing me the computer.

"Excellent, thank you." Taking the laptop from him with my right hand, I sit down on the bed. Or, more appropriately, collapse on the bed, my legs shaking from the strain of walking all over the hospital. Thankfully, Sharipov doesn't see my ungainly maneuver, as he's already heading out the door.

As soon as he's gone, I go on the internet and download a program designed to conceal my online activities. Then I go to a special website and put in my code. That brings up a video chat window, and I put in yet another code there, connecting to a computer back at the compound.

Peter's image appears first. "Finally, there you are," he says, and I see the living room of my house in the background. "Nora is coming down."

A moment later, Nora's small face shows up on the screen. "Julian! Oh my God, I thought I would never see you again!" Her voice is filled with barely contained tears, and there are wet tracks on her cheeks. Her smile, however, radiates pure joy.

I grin at her, all my anger and physical discomfort forgotten in a sudden surge of happiness. "Hi baby, how are you?"

She gapes at me. "How am *I*? What kind of question

is that? You're the one who was just in a plane crash! How are *you*? Is that a cast on your arm?"

"It appears to be." I lift my right shoulder in a brief shrug. "It's my left arm, though, and I'm right-handed, so it's not a big deal."

"What about your head?"

"Oh, this?" I touch the thick bandage around my forehead. "I'm not sure, but since I'm walking and talking, I assume it's something minor."

She shakes her head, staring at me with disbelief, and my grin broadens. Nora probably thinks I'm trying to be all macho in front of her. My pet doesn't realize that these kinds of injuries truly are minor for me; I've had worse from my father's fists as a child.

"When are you coming home?" she asks, bringing her face closer to the camera. Her eyes look enormous this way, her long lashes spiky with residual wetness. "You *are* coming home now, right?"

"Yes, of course. I can't exactly go after Al-Quadar like this." I wave my right hand toward the cast. "The plane is already on its way to get me and Lucas, so I'll be seeing you very soon."

"I can't wait," she says softly, and my chest tightens at the raw emotion I see on her face. A feeling very much like tenderness winds through me, intensifying my longing for her until I ache with it.

"Nora—" I begin saying, only to be interrupted by a sharp *crack* outside. It's followed by several more, a rapid-fire burst of noise that I recognize right away.

Gunshots. The guns are using silencers, but nothing can quiet the deafening bang of a machine gun going off.

Immediately, there are screams and answering gunfire. Un-silenced this time. The soldiers stationed on the floor must be responding to whatever threat is out there.

In a millisecond, I'm off the bed, the laptop sliding to the floor. Adrenaline rockets through me, speeding up everything and at the same time slowing my perception of time. It feels like things are happening in slow motion, but I know that it's just an illusion—that it's my brain's attempt to deal with intense danger.

I operate on instinct honed by a lifetime of training. In an instant, I assess the room and see that there's no place to hide. The window on the opposite wall is too small for me to fit through, even if I were inclined to risk falling from the third floor. That leaves only the door and the hallway—which is where the gunshots are coming from.

I don't bother trying to figure out who's attacking. It's immaterial at the moment. The only thing that matters is survival.

More gunfire, followed by a scream right outside. I hear the heavy *thump* of a body falling nearby, and I choose that moment to make my move.

Pushing open the door, I dive in the direction of the thumping sound, using the momentum of the dive to slide on the linoleum floor. My cast knocks against the wall as I bump into the dead soldier, but I don't even register the pain. Instead I pull him over me, using his body as a shield as bullets begin flying all around me. Spotting his weapon on the floor, I grasp it with my right hand and begin firing shots into the other end of the hallway, where I see masked men with guns crouched behind a hospital gurney.

Too many. I can already see that. There are too fucking many of them and not enough bullets in my gun. I can see the bodies littering the hallway—the five Uzbekistani soldiers have been mowed down, as well as a few of the masked attackers—and I know it's futile. They will get me too. In fact, it's surprising that I'm not already riddled with holes, human shield or not.

They don't want to kill me.

I realize that fact just as my gun bucks one last time, discharging the last round of bullets. The floor and walls around me are destroyed from their bullets, but I'm unscathed. Since I don't believe in miracles, that means the attackers are not aiming *at* me.

They're aiming all around me, to keep me contained in one spot.

Rolling the dead man off me, I slowly get to my feet, keeping my gaze trained on the armed figures at the far end of the hallway. The gunfire stops as I begin to move, the silence deafening after all the noise.

"What do you want?" I raise my voice just enough to be heard on the other end of the hallway. "Why are you here?"

A man rises up from behind the gurney, his weapon trained on me as he begins to walk in my direction. He's masked like all the others, but something about him seems familiar. As he stops a few feet away, I see the dark glitter of his eyes above the mask, and recognition spears through me.

Majid.

Al-Quadar must've heard that I'm here, within their reach.

I move without thinking. I'm still holding the now-empty machine gun, and I lunge at him, swinging the gun as I would a bat, arching it deceptively high before jabbing it low. Even with my injuries, my reflexes are excellent, and the butt of the weapon makes contact with Majid's ribs before I'm thrown back against the wall, my left shoulder exploding in agony. My ears are ringing from the blast as I slide down the wall, and I realize that I've been shot—that he managed to fire his weapon before I could inflict real damage.

I can hear yelling in Arabic, and then rough hands grab me, dragging me along the floor. I struggle with all of my remaining strength, but I can feel my body beginning to shut down, my heart laboring to pump its dwindling supply of blood. Something presses down on my shoulder, exacerbating the fiery pain, and black spots cover my vision.

My last thought before I lose consciousness is that death will likely be preferable to what awaits me if I survive.

CHAPTER TWENTY-FOUR

❖ NORA ❖

I don't realize that I'm screaming until a hand slaps over my mouth, muffling my hysterical shrieks.

"Nora. Nora, stop it." Peter's steady voice pulls me out of the vortex of horror, dragging me back to reality. "Calm down and tell me exactly what you saw. Can you calm down enough to talk?"

I manage a small nod, and he releases me, stepping back. Out of the corner of my eye, I see Rosa and Ana standing a few feet away. Ana's hands are clamped over her mouth, tears running down her cheeks again, and Rosa looks scared and distraught.

"I didn't"—I can barely force the words through my swollen throat—"I didn't *see* anything. I just heard it. We were talking, and then all of a sudden, there were gunshots and—and screaming, and then more gunshots. Julian—" My voice breaks as I speak his name. "Julian must've dropped the computer because everything went topsy-turvy on the screen, and then all I could see was the wall, but I heard it—the gunfire, the screams, more gunfire..." I am not conscious of sobbing uncontrollably until Peter's hands close around my shoulders and gently guide me toward the couch.

He forces me to sit down as I begin to shake, the terror of what I just witnessed combining with memories from a few months earlier, when I had been taken by Al-Quadar in the Philippines. For a few horrifying moments, the past and the present merge, and I'm again in that clinic, hearing those gunshots and feeling fear so intense that my mind can't register it. Only now it's not Beth and I who are in danger.

It's Julian.

They came for him—and I know exactly who *they* are.

"It's Al-Quadar." My voice is hoarse as I get up, ignoring the tremors that continue to rack my body. "Peter—it's Al-Quadar."

He nods in agreement, and I see that he's already on his phone. "Da. Da, eto ya," he says, and I realize that he's speaking Russian. "V gospitale problema. Da, seychas-zhe." Lowering the phone, he tells me, "I just notified the Uzbekistani police of the events in the hospital. They're on their way, as are more soldiers. They'll be there within minutes."

"It will be too late." I don't know where my certainty comes from, but I can feel it deep within my bones. "They have him, Peter. If he's not dead yet, he will be very shortly."

He looks at me, and I can see that he knows it too—that he knows how hopeless the whole thing is. We're dealing with one of the most dangerous terrorist organizations in the world, and they have the man who's been hunting them down and decimating their ranks.

"We're going to track them down, Nora," Peter says quietly. "If they haven't killed him yet, there's a chance we may be able to retrieve him."

"You don't really believe that." I can see it on his face. He's just saying it to placate me. Majid's people have been able to evade detection for months, and it's only the lucky capture of that terrorist in Moscow that led to the discovery of their whereabouts. They will disappear again, hiding somewhere else now that they know their location in Tajikistan has been compromised.

They will disappear, and so will Julian.

Peter gives me an indecipherable look. "It doesn't matter what I believe. The fact is that they want something from your husband: the explosive. They wanted it before, and I'm certain that they want it now. It would be very foolish of them to kill him right away."

"You think they're going to torture him first." Bile rises in my throat as I remember Beth's screams, the blood spreading everywhere as Majid systematically cut off bits and pieces of her body. "Oh my God, you think they're going to torture him until he breaks and gives them this explosive."

"Yes," Peter says, his gray eyes steady on my face as Ana begins to sob quietly into Rosa's shoulder. "I do. And that gives us time to find them."

"Not enough time." I stare at him, sick with terror. "Not nearly enough time. Peter, they're going to torture him and kill him while we look for them."

"We don't know that for sure," he says, pulling out his phone again. "I'm going to throw all of our resources at this. If Al-Quadar so much as blips on the radar someplace, we'll know it."

"But that could take weeks—even months!" My voice rises as hysteria grabs hold of me again. I can feel my grip on sanity slipping as the roller coaster of grief, joy, and terror I've been riding for the past couple of days plunges me into a bottomless pit of despair. It was only yesterday that I thought I'd lost Julian again, only to learn that he's alive. And now, just when it seemed like the worst was over, fate has dealt us the cruelest blow of all.

The monsters who murdered Beth are going to take

Julian from me too.

"It's the only option we have, Nora." Peter's voice is soothing, like he's talking to a fractious child. "There is no other way. Esguerra is tough. He may be able to hang on for a while, no matter what they do to him."

I take a deep breath to regain control of myself. I can break down later, when I'm alone. "Nobody is tough enough to withstand nonstop torture." My voice is almost even. "You know that."

Peter inclines his head, conceding my point. From what I heard about his unique skills, he knows better than anyone how effective torture can be. As I look at him, an idea enters my head—an idea that I never would've entertained before.

"The terrorist they captured," I say slowly, holding Peter's gaze. "Where is he now?"

"He's supposed to be remitted into our custody, but for now he's still in Moscow."

"Do you think he might know something?" My hands twist in the skirt of my dress as I stare at Julian's torturer-in-chief. A part of me can't believe I'm about to ask him to do this, but my voice is steady as I say, "Do you think you could make him talk?"

"Yes, I'm sure I could," Peter says slowly, looking at me with something resembling respect. "I don't know if he'll know where they might go next, but it's worth a shot. I will fly out to Moscow immediately and see what I can find out."

"I'm coming with you."

His reaction is immediate. "No, you're not," he says, frowning at me. "I'm under explicit orders to keep you safe here, Nora."

"Your boss has just been captured and is about to be tortured and killed." My voice is sharp and biting as I enunciate every word. "And you think *my* safety is a priority right now? Your orders no longer apply because they have Julian. They no longer need me for leverage over him."

"Well, actually, they would love to have you for leverage over him. They could break him much faster if they had you as well." Peter shakes his head, his expression regretful but determined. "I'm sorry, Nora, but you need to stay here. If we do end up rescuing your husband, he would be very displeased to learn that I allowed you to be in danger."

I turn away, shaking, terror and frustration mingling together and feeding on each other until it feels like I will burst from it all. I feel helpless. Utterly and completely useless. When I had been taken, Julian came for me. He rescued me—but I can't do the same for him.

I can't even get off the estate.

"Nora . . ." It's Rosa. I can feel her hand on my arm as I blindly stare out the window, my mind running through all the dead ends like a rat in a maze. "Nora, please . . . Come, let's get you a bite to eat . . ."

I shake my head in curt denial and pull my arm away, keeping my gaze trained on the green lawn

291

outside. There's something nibbling at the edge of my brain, some errant, half-formed thought that I can't quite grasp. It has to do with something Peter said, something he mentioned in passing . . . I hear him leaving the room, his footsteps quiet in the hallway, and suddenly it hits me.

Spinning around, I sprint after him, ignoring the shock on Rosa's face as I push her out of the way. "Peter! Peter, wait!"

He stops in the hallway, giving me a cool look as I skid to a stop next to him. "What is it?"

"I know," I gasp out. "Peter, I know exactly what to do. I know how to get Julian back."

His expression doesn't change. "What are you talking about?"

I draw in a gulping breath and begin to explain my plan, speaking so fast I'm tripping over the words. I can see him shaking his head as I speak, but I persist anyway, driven by a sense of urgency more intense than anything I've ever experienced. I need to convince Peter that I'm right. Julian's life depends on it.

"No," he says when I'm done. "This is insane. Julian would kill me—"

"But he might be *alive* to kill you," I interrupt. "There's no other option. You know that as well as I do."

He shakes his head, and the look he gives me is genuinely regretful. "I'm sorry, Nora—"

"I will give you the list," I blurt out, grasping at the

only straw I can think of. "I will give you the list of names before your three years are up if you do this. Julian will hand it over as soon as he gets it into his hands."

Peter stares at me, his expression changing for the first time. "You know about the list?" he asks, his voice pulsing with such anger that I have to fight the urge to step back. "The list Esguerra promised me?"

I nod. "I do." Under any other circumstances, I would be terrified to provoke this man, but I'm beyond fear at the moment. A recklessness born of desperation drives me now, giving me uncharacteristic courage. "And I know that you won't get it if Julian dies," I continue, pressing my point. "All this time you've been working for him will be in vain. You'll never be able to get revenge on the people who killed your family."

His impassive look disappears completely, his face transforming into a mask of blazing fury. "You don't know shit about my family," he roars, and this time I do take a step back, my self-preservation instinct belatedly kicking in as I see his hands tightening into fists. "You fucking dare taunt me with them?"

He takes a step toward me as I back away, my heart hammering in my chest. Then, with a sharp, violent motion, he twists and punches the wall, his fist breaking through the drywall. I flinch, jumping back, and he punches the wall again, taking his rage out on it as he undoubtedly wants to do on me.

"Peter . . ." My voice is low and soothing, like I'm

talking to a wild animal. I can see Rosa and Ana in the doorway, looking terrified, and I try to diffuse the situation. "Peter, I'm not taunting you—I'm just pointing out the facts. I want to help you, but first you need to help me."

He glares at me, his chest heaving with rage, and I see him struggling to regain control. I'm shaking on the inside, but I keep my gaze steady on his face. *Don't show fear. Whatever you do, don't show fear.* To my intense relief, his breathing gradually begins to slow, the fury twisting his features ebbing as he brings himself back from whatever dark place his mind was in.

"I'm sorry," he says after a few moments, his voice strained. "I shouldn't have reacted like that." He takes one deep breath, then another, and I see his usual controlled mask sliding into place. "How do I know you'll be able to keep your promise about the list?" he says in a more normal tone of voice, his anger seemingly gone. "You're asking me to do something that Esguerra will hate. How do I know he'll come through with the list if I do this?"

"I will make him give it to you." I have no idea how I can *make* Julian do anything, but I don't let any of my doubts show. "I swear to you, Peter. Help me with this, and you can have your revenge before your three years here are up."

He stares at me, and I can practically feel his internal debate. He knows my arguments are sound. If he does what I ask, he stands a chance of getting that list of names sooner. If Julian dies, he won't get the list at all.

"Fine," he says, apparently reaching a decision. "Get ready then. We're leaving in an hour."

* * *

When we land in a small airport near Chicago, there is a thick layer of snow on the ground, making me grateful that I decided to wear my old Uggs. It's already evening, and the wind is bitterly cold, biting through my winter coat. I barely register the discomfort, however, all my thoughts consumed by the ordeal to come.

There is no bulletproof car waiting for us. Nothing to draw attention to our arrival. Peter calls a taxi for me, and I get into the back of the car by myself, while he heads back to the plane.

The driver, a kindly middle-aged man, tries to chat me up, likely in the hopes of figuring out who I am. I'm sure he thinks I'm a celebrity of some kind, arriving on a private jet like that. I give monosyllabic responses to all his questions, and he quickly catches on to my desire to be left alone. The rest of the drive passes in silence as I stare out the window at the night-darkened roads. My head pounds from stress and jet lag, and my stomach roils with nausea. If I hadn't forced myself to eat a sandwich on the plane, I would probably be passing out from exhaustion.

When we get to Oak Lawn, I direct the taxi to my parents' house. They're not expecting me, but that's for the best. It makes the whole thing look more authentic, less like a setup.

The driver helps me unload a small suitcase I packed for the occasion, and I pay him, tipping him an extra twenty bucks for my earlier rudeness. He drives off, and I wheel my suitcase to the door of my childhood home.

Stopping in front of the familiar brown door, I ring the doorbell. I know my parents are home because I see the lights in the living room. It takes them a couple of minutes to get to the door—a couple of minutes that feel like an hour in my exhausted state.

My mom opens the door, and her jaw goes slack with astonishment as she sees me standing there, my hand resting on the handle of the suitcase.

"Hi Mom," I say, my voice shaking. "Can I come in?"

CHAPTER TWENTY-FIVE

❖ JULIAN ❖

At first, there is only darkness and pain. Pain that tears at me. Pain that shreds me from within. The darkness is easier. There is no pain in that, only oblivion. Still, I hate the nothingness that consumes me when I'm in that dark void. Hate the blankness of non-existence. As time passes, I come to crave the pain because it's the opposite of that blankness—because feeling something is better than feeling nothing.

Gradually, the dark void recedes, lessens its hold on me. Now, alongside the pain, there are memories. Some good, some bad—they come at me in waves. My mother's gentle smile as she reads me a bedtime story. My father's hard voice and harder fists. Running through the jungle after a colorful butterfly, as happy and carefree as only a child can be. Killing my first man in that jungle. Playing with my cat Lola, then fishing and laughing with a bright-eyed, twelve-year-old girl . . . with Maria.

Maria's body broken and violated, her light and innocence forever destroyed.

Blood on my hands, the satisfaction of hearing her murderers' screams. Eating sushi in the best restaurant in Tokyo. Flies buzzing over my mother's corpse. The thrill of closing my first deal, the lure of money pouring in. More death and violence. Death I cause, death I revel in.

And then there is *her.*

My Nora. The girl I stole because she reminded me of Maria.

The girl who is now my reason for existing.

I hold the image of her in my mind, letting all the other memories fade into the background. She's all I want to think about, all I want to focus on. She makes the hurt go away, makes the darkness disappear. I may have brought her suffering, but she's brought me the only happiness I've known since my early years.

As time crawls by, I become aware of other things. Besides the pain, there are sounds and sensations. I hear voices and feel a cold breeze on my face. My left shoulder burns, my broken arm throbs, and I'm dying of thirst. Still, I seem to be alive.

I twitch my fingers to verify that fact. Yes, alive. Almost too weak to move, but alive.

Fuck. The rest of the memories flood in, and before I even open my eyes, I know where I am, and I know I probably shouldn't have fought the darkness. Oblivion would've been better than this.

"Welcome back," a man's voice says softly, and I open my eyes to see Majid's smiling face hovering over me. "You've been under long enough. It's time for us to begin."

* * *

They drag me along a hard cement floor of what appears to be some kind of a construction site. From the looks of it, it's going to be an industrial building, and the room they haul me into has no windows, only a doorway. I think about fighting, but I'm too weak from my injuries to have any chance of success, so I decide to bide my time and conserve what little strength I have left. I'm guessing I will need it to cope with what they have in store for me.

They begin by stripping me naked and stringing me up with a rope that they loop over a beam in the unfinished ceiling. They're not gentle about it, and the cast on my left arm breaks as they tie my wrists together and draw my bound arms up over my head. The agonizing pain in my injured arm and shoulder makes me pass out, and it's not until they throw ice-cold water on my face that I regain consciousness again.

In a way, I admire their methods. They know what they're doing. Take away a man's clothes, and he immediately feels more vulnerable. Keep him cold, weak, and injured, and he's already at a disadvantage, his psyche as battered as his body. They are starting off on the right foot. If I hadn't put others through this myself, I would've been begging and pleading right about now.

As it is, my body is in a complete fight-or-flight mode. The knowledge that I'm so close to death—or at least to excruciating pain—makes my heart pound with a sickeningly fast rhythm. I don't want to give them the satisfaction of seeing me shake, but I can feel small tremors running over my skin, both from the cold water they poured on me in an already-freezing room and from a surfeit of adrenaline. They've strung me up so high that only the tips of my toes touch the ground, and with the majority of my weight being supported by my tied wrists, my wounded arm and shoulder are already screaming in agony.

As I hang there, trying to breathe through the pain, Majid approaches me, a smug smile creasing his face. "Well, if it isn't Esguerra himself," he drawls, his British accent making him sound like some Middle Eastern version of James Bond. "How nice of you to pay our corner of the world a visit."

I don't say anything, just gaze at him contemptuously, knowing that will irritate him more than anything. I know what he's going to demand, and I have no intention of giving it to him—not when he's going to kill me in the most painful way possible anyway.

Sure enough, my lack of response provokes him. I can see the flare of rage in his eyes. Majid Ben-Harid thrives on the fear and misery of others. I understand that about him because I'm the same way. And because we're such kindred souls, I know how to spoil the fun for him. He's going to destroy my body, but he won't enjoy it quite as much as he'd like.

I won't let him.

It's small consolation for the fact that I'm going to die a torturous death, but it's all I've got at the moment.

His smug smile gone, Majid steps toward me. "I see you're not up for chitchat," he says, bringing a large butcher knife up to my face. "Let's cut to the chase then." He runs the tip of the blade down my cheek, cutting just deep enough for blood to run down my chin in a thin trickle. "You give me the location of your explosive factory, as well as all the security details, and I"—he leans so close that I can see the black of his pupils in the mud-brown irises of his eyes—"I will make your death quick. If you don't . . . well, I'm sure I don't need to elaborate on the alternative. What do you say? Do you want to make it easy for us or hard?

Because the outcome will be the same either way."

I don't respond, and I don't flinch away, not even when that blade continues its painful, cutting journey down my neck, chest, and stomach, leaving a bloody trail wherever it touches my skin.

It doesn't matter what I choose because Majid has no intention of honoring any promises he makes to me. He'll never give me a quick death—not even if I hand-deliver the explosive to him tomorrow. I've caused too much damage to Al-Quadar over the past few months, foiled too many of their plans. As soon as I give him what he wants, he'll take me apart in the most excruciating manner possible, just to show his troops how he metes out punishment to those who cross him.

That's what I would do in his place, at least.

The knife stops just below my ribs, the sharp point digging into my flesh, and I can see Majid's eyes gleaming with vicious pleasure. "Well?" he whispers, pressing it in a fraction of an inch. "Play or no play, Esguerra? It's really up to you. I can begin by harvesting some organs, just to make it extra profitable for us—or if you'd prefer, I can start lower, with your wife's favorite part . . ."

I suppress an instinctive male urge to shudder at that last bit and keep my expression calm, almost amused. I know he won't do anything too damaging at first—because if he did, I would bleed out right away. I've already lost too much blood, so it won't take much to send me under. The last thing Majid would want is to deprive himself of a conscious victim. If he's serious about getting that explosive, he'll have to start small and work up to the brutality he just threatened me with.

"Go ahead," I say coolly. "Do your best."

And giving him a mocking smile, I wait for the torture to begin.

CHAPTER TWENTY-SIX

❖ NORA ❖

The evening of my arrival home is a nonstop stream of crying, hugs, and questions about what happened and how I managed to come back.

I tell my parents as much of the truth as I can, explaining about the plane crash in Uzbekistan and Julian's subsequent capture by the terrorist group he's been fighting. As I speak, I can see them battling shock and disbelief. Terrorists and planes downed by missiles are so far outside of the normal paradigm of their lives that I know it's hard for them to process. It was difficult for me once, too.

"Oh, Nora, honey . . ." My mom's voice is soft and sympathetic. "I'm so sorry—I know you loved him, despite everything. Do you know what's going to happen now?"

I shake my head, trying to avoid looking at my dad. He thinks this is a good development; I can see it on his face. He's relieved that I'm most likely rid of the man he considers to be my abuser. I'm certain both of my parents think Julian deserves this, but my mom is at least attempting to be sensitive to my feelings. My dad, though, can hardly hide his satisfaction at this turn of events.

"Well, whatever happens, I'm glad you came home." My mom reaches out to take my hand. Her dark eyes are swimming with fresh tears as she gazes at me. "We're here for you, honey, you know that, right?"

"I do, Mom," I whisper, my throat tight with emotion. "That's why I came back. Because I missed you . . . and because I couldn't be alone on that estate."

That much is true, but that's not the real reason I'm here. I can't tell my parents the real reason.

If they knew I came home to get kidnapped by Al-Quadar, they would never forgive me for that.

* * *

Despite my exhaustion, I barely sleep that night. I know it'll take some time for Al-Quadar to respond to my presence in town, but I'm still consumed by dread and nervous anticipation. Every time I drift off, I have nightmares, only in these dreams it's not Beth who's being cut into pieces—it's Julian. The bloody images are so vivid that I wake up nauseated and shaking, my bedsheets drenched with sweat. Finally, I give up on sleep altogether and pull out the art supplies I brought with me in my suitcase. I'm hoping that painting will prevent me from dwelling on the fact that my nightmares may be playing out at this very moment in some Al-Quadar hideout thousands of miles away.

As the light of the rising sun filters into the room, I stop to examine what I painted. It looks abstract at first—just swirls of red, black, and brown—but a closer inspection reveals something different. All the swirls are faces and bodies, people tangled together in a paroxysm of violent ecstasy. The faces reveal both agony and pleasure, lust and torment.

It's probably my best work to date, and I hate it.

I hate it because it shows me how much I've changed. How little of the old me remains.

"Wow, honey, this is amazing . . ." My mom's voice startles me out of my musings, and I turn around to see her standing in the doorway, gazing at the painting with genuine admiration. "That French instructor of yours must be really good."

"Yes, Monsieur Bernard is excellent," I agree, trying to keep the weariness out of my voice. I'm so tired that I just want to collapse, but that's not an option at the moment.

"You didn't sleep well, did you?" My mom furrows her forehead, looking worried, and I know I didn't succeed in hiding my tiredness from her. "Were you thinking about him?"

"Of course I was." A sudden swell of anger sharpens my voice. "He's my husband, you know."

She blinks, clearly taken aback, and I immediately regret my harsh tone. This situation is not my mom's fault; if anyone is blameless in all this, it's my parents. My temper is the last thing they deserve . . . particularly since my desperate plan will likely cause them even more anguish.

"I'm sorry, Mom," I say, going over to give her a hug. "I didn't mean it like that."

"It's okay, honey." She strokes my hair, her touch so gentle and comforting that I want to weep. "I understand."

I nod, even though I know she can't possibly comprehend the extent of my stress. She can't—because she doesn't know that I'm waiting.

Waiting to be taken by the same monsters who have Julian.

Waiting for Al-Quadar to snap at the bait.

* * *

The morning drags by. It's a Saturday, so both of my parents are home. They're happy about that, but I'm not. I wish they were at work today. I want to be alone if—no, *when*—Majid's goons come for me. It had been relatively safe to spend the night, since Al-Quadar would need time to put whatever plan they have into action, but now that it's morning, I don't want my parents near me. The security detail Julian put in place around my family would ensure their safety, but those same bodyguards may also interfere with my abduction—and that's the last thing I want.

"Shopping?" My dad gives me a strange look when I announce my intention to hit the stores after breakfast. "Are you sure, honey? You just got home, and with everything going on—"

"Dad, I've been in the middle of nowhere for months." I give him my best men-just-don't-get-it look. "You have no idea what that's like for a girl." Seeing that he's unconvinced, I add, "Seriously, Dad, I could use the distraction."

"She's got a point," my mom chimes in. Turning toward me, she gives me a conspiratorial wink and tells my dad, "There's nothing like shopping to take a woman's mind off things. I'll go with Nora—it'll be just like the old times."

My heart sinks. I can't have my mom coming along if the point is to have my parents away from potential danger. "Oh, I'm sorry, Mom," I say regretfully, "but I already promised Leah I'd meet her. It's spring break, you know, and she's home." I had seen an update to that effect on Facebook earlier this morning, so I'm only partially lying. My friend is indeed in town—I just hadn't made any plans to see her today.

"Oh, okay." My mom looks hurt for a moment, but then she shakes it off and gives me a bright smile. "No worries, honey. We'll see you after you catch up with your friends. I'm glad you're distracting yourself like that. It's for the best, really . . ."

My dad still looks suspicious, but there is nothing he can do. I'm an adult, and I'm not exactly asking for their permission.

As soon as breakfast is over, I give them each a kiss and a hug and walk over to the bus stop on 95th street to get on the bus going to the Chicago Ridge Mall.

* * *

Come on, take me already. Fucking take me already.

I have been wandering through the mall for hours, and to my frustration, there is still no sign of Al-Quadar. They either don't know that I'm here, or they don't care about me now that they have Julian.

I refuse to entertain the latter possibility because if it's true, Julian is as good as dead.

The plan has to work. There is no other alternative. Majid simply needs more time. Time to sniff out that I'm here alone and unprotected—a convenient tool that they can use to force Julian to give them what they want.

"Nora? Holy shit, Nora, is that you?" A familiar voice yanks me out of my thoughts, and I turn around to see my friend Leah gaping at me with astonishment.

"Leah!" For a second, I forget all about the danger and rush forward to embrace the girl who had been my best friend for ages. "I had no idea you would be here!" And it's true—despite my lie to my parents this morning, I had not expected to run into Leah like that. In hindsight, though, I probably should have, since we used to hang out at this mall nearly every weekend when we were younger.

"What are you doing here?" she asks when we get the hug out of the way. "I thought you were in Colombia!"

"I was—I mean, I am." Now that the initial excitement is over, I'm realizing that running into Leah could be problematic. The last thing I want is for my friend to suffer because of me. "I'm just here for a brief visit," I explain hurriedly, casting a worried look around. All seems to be normal, so I continue, "I'm sorry I didn't tell you I was home, but things were kind of hectic and, well, you know how it is . . ."

"Right, you must be busy with your new husband and stuff," she says slowly, and I can feel the distance between us growing even though we haven't moved an inch. We haven't spoken since I told her about my marriage—just exchanged a few brief emails—and I see now that she still questions my sanity . . . that she no longer understands the person I've become.

I don't blame her for that. Sometimes I don't understand that person either.

"Leah, babe, there you are!" A man's voice interrupts our conversation, and my heart jumps as a familiar male figure approaches Leah from behind me.

It's Jake—the boy I once had a crush on.

The boy Julian stole me from that fateful night in the park.

Only he's not a boy anymore. His shoulders are heavier now; his face is leaner and harder. At some point in the past few months, he's become a man—a man who only has eyes for Leah. Stopping next to her, he bends down to give her a kiss and says in a low, teasing voice, "Babe, I got you that present . . ."

Leah's pale cheeks turn beet-red. "Um, Jake," she mumbles, tugging on his arm to draw his attention to my presence, "look who I just ran into."

He turns toward me, and his brown eyes go round with shock. "Nora? What—what are you doing here?"

"Oh, you know . . . just—just some shopping . . ." I hope I don't sound as dumbfounded as I feel. *Leah and Jake? My best friend Leah and my former crush Jake?* It's as if my world just tilted on its axis. I had no idea they were dating. I knew Leah broke up with her boyfriend a couple of months ago because she mentioned it in an email, but she never told me she'd hooked up with Jake.

As I look at them, standing next to each other with identical uncomfortable expressions on their faces, I realize it's not altogether illogical. They both go to the University of Michigan, and they have an overlapping circle of friends and acquaintances from our high school. They even have a traumatic experience in common—having their friend/date abducted—that could've brought them closer together.

I also realize in that moment that all I feel when I look at them is relief.

Relief that they seem happy together, that the darkness from my life didn't leave a permanent stain on Jake's. There's no regret for what might have been, no jealousy—only an anxiety that grows with every minute Julian spends in Al-Quadar's hands.

"I'm sorry, Nora," Leah says, giving me a wary look. "I should've told you about us earlier. It's just that—"

"Leah, please." Pushing aside my stress and exhaustion, I manage to give her a reassuring smile. "You don't have to explain. Really. I'm married, and Jake and I only had one date. You don't owe me any explanations . . . I was just surprised, that's all."

"Do you want to, um, grab some coffee with us?" Jake offers, sliding his arm around Leah's waist in a gesture that strikes me as unusually protective. I wonder if it's me he's protecting her from. If so, he's even smarter than I thought.

"We could catch up since you're in town and all," he continues, and I shake my head in refusal.

"I'd love to, but I can't," I say, and the regret in my voice is genuine. I desperately want to catch up with them, but I can't have them near me in case Al-Quadar chooses this particular moment to strike. I have no idea how the terrorists would get to me in the middle of a crowded mall, but I'm certain they'll find a way. Glancing down at my phone, I pretend to be dismayed at the time and say apologetically, "I'm afraid I'm already running late . . ."

"Is your husband here with you?" Leah asks, frowning, and I see Jake's face turning white. He probably didn't consider the possibility of Julian being nearby when he extended his invitation to me.

I shake my head, my throat tightening as the horrible reality of the situation threatens to choke me again. "No," I say, hoping I sound halfway normal. "He couldn't make it."

"Oh, okay." Leah's frown deepens, a puzzled look entering her eyes, but Jake regains some of his color. He's obviously relieved that he won't be confronted by the ruthless criminal who's caused him so much grief.

"I really have to run," I say, and Jake nods, his grip on Leah's waist tightening to keep her close.

"Good luck," he says to me, and I can tell he's glad I'm leaving. He's been raised to be polite, however, so he adds, "It was good seeing you," though his eyes say something different.

I give him an understanding smile. "You too," I say and, waving goodbye to Leah, I head for the mall exit.

* * *

I forget about Jake and Leah as soon as I step out into

the parking lot. Painfully alert, I scan the area before reluctantly pulling out my phone and calling for a cab. I would hang out at the mall longer, but I don't want to chance running into my friends again. My next stop will be Michigan Avenue in Chicago, where I can browse some high-end stores while praying that I get taken before I completely lose my mind.

The cold wind bites through my clothes as I stand there waiting, my thigh-length peacoat and thin cashmere sweater offering little protection from the chilly temperature outside. It takes a solid half hour before the cab finally pulls up to the curb. By that time, I'm half-frozen, and my nerves are stretched so tightly I'm ready to scream.

Yanking the door open, I climb into the back of the car. It's a clean-looking cab, with a thick glass partition separating the front seat from the back and the windows in the back lightly tinted. "The city, please." My voice is sharper than it needs to be. "The stores on Michigan Avenue."

"Sure thing, miss," the driver says softly, and my head snaps up at the hint of accent in his voice. My eyes lock with his in the front mirror, and I freeze as a bolt of pure terror shoots down my spine.

He could've been one of a thousand immigrants driving a cab for a living, but he's not.

He's Al-Quadar. I can see it in the cold malevolence of his gaze.

They have finally come for me.

It's what I have been waiting for, but now that the moment is here, I find myself paralyzed by a fear so intense, it chokes me from within. My mind flashes into the past, and the memories are so vivid, it's almost as if I'm there again. I feel the pain of barely healed stitches in my side, see the dead bodies of the guards at the clinic, hear Beth's screams . . . and then I taste vomit at the back of my throat as Majid touches my face with a blood-covered finger.

I must've gone as pale as a sheet because the driver's gaze hardens, and I hear the faint click of car door locks being activated.

The sound galvanizes me into action. Adrenaline pumping in my veins, I dive for the door and jerk at the handle while screaming at the top of my lungs. I know it's useless, but I need to try—and, more importantly, I need to give the appearance of trying. I can't sit calmly while they take me back to hell.

I can't let them find out that this time I want to go back there.

As the car begins moving, I continue wrestling with the door and banging on the window. The driver ignores me as he peels out of the parking lot at top speed, and none of the mall visitors seem to notice anything wrong, the tinted windows of the car hiding me from their gaze.

We don't go far. Instead of getting out onto the highway, the car swings around to the back of the building. I see a beige van waiting for us, and I struggle harder, my nails breaking as I claw at the door with a desperation that's only partially feigned. In my rush to rescue Julian, I hadn't fully considered what it would mean to be taken by the monsters of my nightmares—to go through something so horrific again—and the terror that swamps me is only slightly lessened by the fact that this situation is of my own doing.

The driver pulls up next to the van, and the locks click open. Pushing open the door, I scramble out on all fours, scraping my palms on rough asphalt, but before I can get to my feet, a hard arm clamps around my waist and a gloved hand slaps over my mouth, muffling my screams.

I hear orders being barked out in Arabic as I'm carried to the van, kicking and struggling, and then I see a fist flying toward my face.

There's an explosion of pain in my skull, and then there's nothing else.

CHAPTER TWENTY-SEVEN

❖ JULIAN ❖

I drift in and out of consciousness, the periods of wakeful agony interspersed with short stretches of soothing darkness. I don't know if it's been hours, days, or weeks, but it feels like I've been here forever, at the mercy of Majid and the pain.

I haven't slept. They don't let me sleep. I gain respite only when my mind shuts down from the torment, and they have ways of bringing me back when I'm under for too long.

They waterboard me first. I find it funny, in a kind of perverse way. I wonder if they're doing it because they know I'm part-American, or if they just think it's an efficient method of breaking someone without inflicting severe damage.

They do it a few dozen times, pushing me to the brink of death and then bringing me back. It feels like I'm drowning over and over again, and my body fights for air with a desperation that seems out of place given the situation. It wouldn't be such a bad thing if they accidentally drowned me; my mind knows that, but my body struggles to live. Every second with that wet rag on my face feels like an eternity, the trickle of water somehow more terrifying than the sharpest blade.

They pause every once in a while and throw questions at me, promising to stop if only I would answer. And when my lungs feel like they're bursting, I want to give in. I want to put an end to this—yet something inside me won't let me. I refuse to give them the satisfaction of winning, of letting them kill me while knowing that they achieved what they wanted.

As my body strains for air, my father's voice comes to me.

"Are you going to cry? Are you going to cry like your mama's pretty boy or face me like a man?"

I'm four years old again, cowering in the corner as my father kicks me repeatedly in the ribs. I know the right answer to his question—I know I need to face him—but I'm scared. I'm so scared. I can feel the wetness on my face, and I know it will make him angry. I don't mean to cry. I haven't truly cried since I was a baby, but the pain in my ribs makes my eyes water. If my mother were here, she'd hold me and kiss me, but she doesn't come near me when my father is in this kind of mood. She's too afraid of him.

I hate my father. I hate him, and I want to be like him all at once. I don't want to be scared. I want to be the one with the power, the one everyone's afraid of.

Rolling up into a little ball, I use the bottom of my shirt to wipe the betraying moisture off my face, and then I get to my feet, ignoring my fear and the ache in my bruised ribs.

"I'm not going to cry." Swallowing the knot in my throat, I look up to meet my father's angry gaze. "I'm never going to cry."

Curses in Arabic. More wetness on my face.

My mind is violently wrenched back to the present as I convulse, gagging and sucking in air when the soaked rag is removed. My lungs expand greedily, and through the ringing in my ears, I hear Majid yelling at the man who almost killed me.

Well, fuck. Looks like this portion of the fun is over.

They start with the needles next. Long, thick needles that they drive under my toenails and fingernails. I'm able to bear this better, my mind divorcing itself from my tortured body and taking me back to the past.

I'm nine now. My father brought me to the city for negotiations with his suppliers. I'm sitting on the steps, guarding the entrance to the building, a gun tucked into my belt underneath my T-shirt. I know how to use this gun; I already killed two men with it. I threw up after the first one, earning myself a beating, but the second kill had been easier. I didn't even flinch when I pulled the trigger.

A few teenage boys walk out onto the street. I recognize their tattoos; they're part of a local gang. My father probably used them at some point to distribute his product, but right now they appear to be bored and at loose ends.

I watch as they meander up and down the street, kicking at some broken bottles and ribbing each other. A part of me envies their easy camaraderie. I don't have a lot of friends, and the boys I occasionally play with all seem to be afraid of me. I don't know if it's because I'm the Señor's son, or if they've heard things about me. I don't usually mind their fear—I encourage it, in fact— but sometimes I wish I could just play like a regular kid.

These teenage boys haven't heard about me, though. I can tell because when they spot me sitting there, they smirk and walk toward me, thinking they've found easy prey to bully.

"Hey," one of them calls out. "What's a little boy like you doing here? This is our neighborhood. You lost, kid?"

"No," I say, replicating their smirks. "I'm about as lost as you . . . kid."

The boy who spoke to me swells up with anger. "Why you little shit—" He starts toward me, and immediately *freezes when I point my gun at him without blinking.*

"Try it," I invite him softly. "Come closer, why don't you?"

The boys begin to back away. They're not completely dumb; they see that I know how to handle the weapon.

My father and his men come out at that moment, and the boys scatter like a pack of rats.

When I tell my father what happened, he nods approvingly. "Good. You don't back down, son. Remember that—you take what you want, and you never back down."

Cold water in my face, followed by a brutal slap, and I'm back in the present. They have me tied to a chair now, my wrists bound behind my back and my ankles tied to the chair legs. My fingers and toes throb with agony, but I'm still alive—and for now unbroken.

I can see the frustrated fury on Majid's face. He's not happy with the progress thus far, and I have a feeling he's about to amp up his efforts.

Sure enough, he approaches me, his knife clutched in his fist. "Last chance, Esguerra . . ." He stops in front of me. "I'm giving you one last chance before I start cutting off some useful body parts. Where is the fucking factory, and how do we get in?"

Instead of answering, I gather whatever little saliva remains in my mouth and spit at him. The red-tinted spittle splatters all over his nose and cheeks, and I watch with satisfaction as he wipes it off with his sleeve, his body vibrating with rage at the insult.

I don't have a chance to enjoy his reaction for long, though, because he fists his hand in my hair and yanks on it, causing my neck to bend painfully backwards.

"Let me tell you what's about to happen, you piece of shit," he hisses, pressing the blade against my jaw. "I'm going to start with your eyes. I'm going to cut your left eyeball in half—and then I'm going to do the same with your right. And when you're blind, I'm going to start trimming your dick, inch by inch, until there's only a tiny stub left . . . Do you understand me? If you don't start talking now, you will never see or fuck again."

Fighting the urge to throw up, I remain silent as he pushes the knife upward, toward the thin skin under my left eye. The blade cuts through my cheek on the way, and I feel the warmth of the blood trickling down my cold skin. I know he's not bluffing, but I also know that giving in will not change the outcome. Majid will torture me to get answers—and once he gets them, he will torture me even more.

Glaring at my lack of reaction, Majid presses the knife deeper into my skin. "Last fucking chance, Esguerra. Do you want to keep your eye or not?"

I don't respond, and he drags the knife higher, causing my eyelids to squeeze shut reflexively.

"All right then," he whispers, enjoying my body's involuntarily panic as I try to jerk out of his reach . . . and then I feel a nauseating explosion of pain as the blade punctures through my eyelid and penetrates deep into my eye.

* * *

I must've lost consciousness again because there's more cold water being thrown at me. I'm shivering, my body going into shock from the excruciating agony. I can't see anything out of my left eye—all I feel there is a burning, leaking emptiness. My stomach roils with bile, and it takes all of my effort not to vomit all over myself.

"How about the second eye, Esguerra, hmm?" Majid smiles at me, his bloodied knife held tightly in his fist. "Would you like to be blind while we take your dick off, or would you rather see it all? Of course, it's not too late to stop all this . . . Just tell us what we want to know, and we might even let you live—since you're so brave and all."

He's lying. I can hear it in the gloating tone of his voice. He thinks he's got me nearly broken, so desperate to stop the pain that I will believe anything he says.

"Fuck you," I whisper with my remaining strength. *You don't back down. You never back down.* "Fuck you and your pathetic little threats."

His eyes narrow with rage, and the knife flashes toward my face. I squeeze my remaining eye shut, preparing for the agony . . . but it never comes.

Surprised, I peel open my uninjured eyelid and see that Majid got distracted by one of his minions. The man seems excited, pointing toward me as he chatters in rapid Arabic. I strain to make out some of the words I know, but he's speaking too fast. Judging by the smile spreading across Majid's face, however, whatever he's saying is good news for Majid—which means it's probably bad news for me.

My supposition is confirmed when Majid turns toward me and says with a cruel smirk, "Your other eye is safe for now, Esguerra. There is something I *really* want you to see in a few hours."

I glare at him, unable to hide my hatred. I don't know what he's talking about, but the pit of my stomach tightens as the terrorists file out of the windowless room. There's only one thing that would persuade me to give in—and she is safe and sound in my compound. They can't possibly be talking about Nora, not with all the security I have around her. It's some new mind game they're playing with me, trying to make me think they have something worse in store for me than what I've already suffered. It's a delay tactic, a way to prolong my suffering—nothing more.

I have no intention of falling for their trick, but as I wait there, bound and in the worst pain of my life, I'm not strong enough to stop the anxiety from creeping up on me. I should be grateful for this respite from torture, but I'm not.

I would gladly let Majid cut off every one of my limbs if only I could be certain that Nora is safe.

I don't know how much time passes while I wait in

torment, but finally I hear voices outside. The door opens, and Majid drags in a small figure dressed in a pair of Uggs and a man's shirt that hangs down to her knees. Her hands are bound behind her back, and there is a bloody stain on the underside of her left arm.

My stomach drops and cold horror spreads through my veins as Nora's dark eyes lock on my face.

My worst fear has come to pass.

They have the only person who matters to me in the whole fucking world.

They have my Nora—and this time, I can't rescue her.

CHAPTER TWENTY-EIGHT

❖ NORA ❖

Trembling from head to toe, I stare at Julian, my chest squeezing with agony at the sight. There is a rough, dirty-looking bandage on his shoulder, with blood seeping out of it, and his naked body is a mass of cuts, bruises, and scrapes. His face is even worse. Below the old bandage on his forehead, there isn't a spot left that isn't discolored or swollen. The most horrifying thing of all, however, is the huge bleeding gash running through his left cheek and all the way up into his eyebrow—a mess of ragged flesh where his eye used to be.

Where his eye *used* to be.

They cut out his eye.

I can't even begin to process that at the moment, so I don't try. For now, Julian is alive, and that's all that matters.

He's tied to a metal chair, his legs bound apart and his arms restrained behind his back. I can see the shock and horror on his bloodied face as he takes in my presence, and I want to tell him that everything will be all right—that this time I am saving *him*—but I can't. Not yet.

Not until Peter has a chance to get here with the reinforcements.

My bruised cheekbone is throbbing where they hit me, and the underside of my left arm is burning with pain from the open wound there. They stripped off my clothes and cut out my birth control implant while I was knocked out, probably fearing that it was a tracker of some kind. I hadn't expected that—I figured, if anything, they would find one of the real trackers—but it worked out even better than I'd hoped. After cutting out the implant and seeing that it was nothing more than a simple plastic rod, they must've dismissed me as a threat, thinking that I am exactly what I was pretending to be: a naïve girl who went to see her parents, oblivious of any remaining danger. It makes me glad that I had the foresight to leave the bracelet tracker at the estate, so as not to arouse their suspicions.

To my relief, it doesn't seem like they touched me much in other ways. At least, if they did anything more than cop a feel while I was unconscious, I feel no evidence of it. There is no soreness or stickiness between my legs, no pain of any kind. My skin is crawling at the knowledge that they had me naked, but it could've easily been much worse. When I woke up, I was already wearing someone's shirt and my own Ugg boots. They must be saving all the drama for when I'm in front of Julian.

This was the part of my plan that Peter found most risky: that time from my capture until my arrival at their hideout.

"You know that they can search every inch of you and find all three of the tracking devices Julian placed on you," he told me before we left the estate. "And then you'll both be lost to us. You do understand what they will do to you to make Julian talk, right?"

"Yes, I do, Peter." I gave him a grim smile. "I understand perfectly. There is no other choice, though, and the trackers are tiny, the insertion wounds nearly invisible at this point. They may find one or two, but I doubt they'll find all three—and if they do, by the time they do, you may have a fix on their location."

"Maybe," he said, his eyes speaking volumes about his opinion on my sanity, "or maybe not. There are a hundred things that can go wrong between the time you get taken and when they bring you to Julian."

"It's a risk I'll have to take," I told him, bringing the

discussion to an end. I knew how dangerous it would be for me to act as a human tracking device to locate the terrorists, but I couldn't see any other way to get to Julian in time—and judging by his current state, I was nearly too late as is.

I see Julian attempting to compose himself, to hide his visceral reaction to my presence, but he's not entirely successful. After the initial shock passes, his jaw tightens, and his undamaged eye begins to glitter with violent rage as he takes in my semi-dressed state. His powerful muscles bunch, straining against the restraints. He looks like he wants to rip apart everyone in the room, and I know that the ropes tying him to the chair are the only thing preventing him from launching a suicidal attack on our captors. The other terrorists must be thinking the same thing, because two of them step closer to Julian, clutching their weapons just in case.

Looking delighted with this turn of events, Majid laughs and drags me to the middle of the room, his grip on my arm excruciatingly tight. "You know, your dumb little whore all but fell into my lap," he says conversationally, fisting his hand in my hair and forcing me down to my knees. "We found her shopping in your absence, like all those greedy American bitches. Figured we'd bring her here, so you can see her pretty little face before I carve it up . . . Unless you want to start talking?"

Julian remains silent, glaring at Majid with

murderous hatred, while I take small, shallow breaths to cope with my terror. My eyes are watering from the pain in my scalp, and the fear pulsing through me feels almost like a living thing. With my hands restrained behind my back, there's nothing I can do to prevent Majid from hurting me. I have no idea how long it's going to take Peter to arrive, but there's every chance he might not make it in time. I can see the rust-colored stains on the blade hanging loosely from Majid's belt, and nausea rises in my throat as I realize that it's Julian's blood.

If we're not rescued soon, it will be my blood, too.

To my horror, Majid reaches for that blade, still holding my hair in that painful grip. "Oh, yes," he whispers, pressing the flat edge against my neck, "I think her head will make a nice little trophy—after I cut it up a bit, of course . . ." He pushes the knife upward, and I freeze in terror as I feel the blade cutting into the soft skin under my chin, followed by the stomach-churning sensation of warm liquid trickling down my neck.

The growl that emanates from Julian doesn't resemble anything human. Before I can do more than gasp, he surges forward, using the balls of his feet to propel himself and the chair off the floor. His action is so sudden and violent that the two men standing next to him don't react in time. Julian literally crashes into one of them, bringing the armed terrorist down to the floor, and, with one twist of his body, drives the metal leg of the chair into the man's throat.

The next few seconds are a blur of blood and screams in Arabic. Majid releases his hold on me and yells out some orders, galvanizing the others into action as he springs into the fray himself.

Still tied to the chair, Julian is dragged off the injured man's body, and I watch in horrified fascination as the man Julian attacked writhes on the floor, clutching his throat as rattling, gurgling sounds escape from his mouth. He's dying—I can see it in the weakening spurts of blood coming from the ragged wound in his neck—yet his agony doesn't seem to touch me. It's as though I'm watching a movie instead of observing a human being bleeding to death in front of my eyes.

Majid and the other terrorists rush to his aid, trying to staunch the flow of blood, but it's too late. The man's frantic grip on his throat eases, his eyes glazing over, and the stench of death—of evacuated bowels and violence—fills the room.

He's dead.

Julian killed him.

I should be disgusted and appalled, but I'm not. Maybe those emotions will hit me later, but for now, all I feel is a strange mixture of gladness and pride: gladness that one of these murderers is dead, and pride that Julian was the one to kill him. Even tied up and weakened by torture, my husband managed to take down one of his enemies—an armed man who was stupid enough to stand within Julian's lethal reach.

My lack of empathy disturbs me on some level, but I don't have time to dwell on it. Whether Julian intended to create a distraction or not, the end result is that nobody is paying attention to me at the moment—and as soon as I realize it, I spring into action.

Jumping to my feet, I cast a frantic glance around the room. My gaze lands on a small knife on a table near the wall, and I leap toward it, my pulse racing. The terrorists are all gathered around Julian on the other side of the room, and I hear grunts, curses, and the sickening sound of fists hitting flesh.

They're punishing Julian for this murder—and, for now, ignoring me.

Turning my back to the table, I manage to palm the knife and wedge the blade underneath the duct tape they wrapped around my wrists. My hands are trembling, causing the sharp blade to nick my skin, but I ignore the pain, trying to saw through the thick tape before they realize what's happening. My grip is slippery with sweat and blood, but I persist, and finally, my hands are free.

Shaking, I survey the room again, and spot an assault rifle leaning negligently against the wall. One of the terrorists must've left it there in the confusion resulting from Julian's unexpected attack.

My heart throbbing in my throat, I inch along the wall toward the weapon, desperately hoping that the terrorists won't glance in my direction. I have no idea what I'm going to do with one gun against a roomful of men armed to their teeth, but I have to do something.

I can't stand by and watch them beat Julian to death.

My hands close around the weapon before anyone notices anything, and I suck in a shaking breath of relief. It's an AK-47, one of the assault rifles I practiced with during my training with Julian. Gripping the heavy weapon, I lift it and point in the direction of the terrorists, trying to control the adrenaline-induced trembling in my arms. I've never shot at a person before—only at beer cans and paper targets—and I don't know if I have what it takes to pull the trigger.

And as I'm trying to work up the courage to act, a blinding explosion rocks the room, knocking me off my feet and onto the floor.

* * *

I don't know if I hit my head or was merely dazed by the explosion, but the next thing I'm aware of is the sound of gunfire outside the walls. The entire room is filled with smoke, and I cough as I instinctively attempt to get to my feet.

"Nora! Stay down!" It's Julian, his voice hoarse from the smoke. "Stay down, baby, do you hear me?"

"Yes!" I yell back, intense joy filling every cell of my body as I realize that he's alive—and in a good enough condition to speak. Keeping low to the ground, I peer out from behind the table that fell next to me, and see

Julian lying on his side on the other end of the room, still tied to the metal chair.

I also see that the smoke is coming in from the vent in the ceiling, and that the room is empty except for the two of us. The battle, or whatever is happening, is taking place outside.

Peter and the guards must have arrived.

Almost crying with relief, I grab the AK-47 lying next to me, lower myself onto my stomach, and begin to belly-crawl toward Julian, holding my breath to avoid inhaling too much smoke.

At that moment, the door swings open, and a familiar figure steps into the room.

It's Majid—and in his right hand, he's holding a gun.

He must've realized that Al-Quadar were losing and came back to kill Julian.

A surge of hatred rises in my throat, choking me with bitter bile. This is the man who murdered Beth . . . who tortured Julian and would've done the same thing to me. A vicious, psychotic terrorist who had undoubtedly murdered dozens of innocent people.

He doesn't see me there, all his attention on Julian as he lifts his gun and points it at my husband. "Goodbye, Esguerra," he says quietly . . . and I squeeze the trigger of my own weapon.

Despite my prone position, my aim is accurate. Julian had me practice shooting sitting, lying down, and even running at some point. The assault rifle bucks in my shaking arms, slamming painfully against my shoulder, but the two bullets hit Majid exactly where I intended—in his right wrist and elbow.

The shots throw him back against the wall and knock the gun out of his grasp. Screaming, he clutches at his bleeding arm, and I get up, heedless of the danger posed by the bullets flying outside. I can hear Julian yelling something at me, but his exact words don't register through the ringing in my ears.

In this moment, it's as though the entire world fades away, leaving me alone with Majid.

Our eyes meet, and for the first time, I see fear in his dark, reptilian gaze. He knows that I am the one who shot him, and he can read the cold intent on my face.

"Please, don't—" he begins saying, and I squeeze the trigger again, discharging five more bullets into his stomach and chest.

In the brief silence that follows, I watch as Majid's body slides down the wall, almost in slow motion. His face is slack with shock, blood dribbling out of the corner of his mouth, and his eyes are open, staring at me with a kind of numb disbelief. He moves his lips, as though to say something, and a rattling gurgle escapes his throat as more blood bubbles up out of his mouth.

Lowering the gun, I step closer to him, drawn by a strange compulsion to see what I have wrought. Majid's eyes plead with mine, begging for mercy without words. I hold his gaze, stretching out the moment . . . and then I aim the AK-47 at his forehead and pull the trigger again.

The back of his head explodes, blood and bits of brain tissue splattering against the wall. His eyes glaze over, the whites around the irises turning crimson as blood vessels burst in his eyes. His body goes limp, and the smell of death, sharp and pungent, permeates the room for the second time today.

Except it's not Julian who's the killer this time.

It's me.

My hands are steady as I lower the weapon again, watching the blood trickle down the wall behind Majid. Then I walk toward Julian, kneel down beside him, and carefully place the gun on the floor as I begin to work on untying his ropes.

Julian is silent as I free him from his bonds, and so am I. The sounds of gunfire outside are beginning to die down, and I'm hoping that means Peter's forces are winning. Either way, though, I'm ready for whatever may come, a strange calm engulfing me despite our still-precarious situation.

When Julian's arms and legs are free, he kicks the chair away and rolls onto his back, his right hand closing around my wrist. His left arm, still partially in a cast, is immobile at his side, and there's more blood on his face and body from the beating he just received. His grip on my wrist, however, is surprisingly strong as he pulls me closer, forcing me down on the floor next to him.

"Stay down, baby," he whispers through swollen

lips. "It's almost over . . . Please, stay down."

I nod and stretch out next to him on the right, being careful not to aggravate his injuries. With the door open, some of the smoke in the room is beginning to clear out, and I can breathe freely for the first time since the explosion.

Julian releases my wrist and slides his arm under my neck, gathering me against him in a protective embrace. My hand accidentally brushes against his ribs, causing him to hiss in pain, but when I try to scoot back, he merely holds me tighter.

When Peter and the guards step through the door a few minutes later, they find us lying in each other's arms, with Julian pointing the AK-47 at the door.

CHAPTER TWENTY-NINE

❖ JULIAN ❖

"How is she?" Lucas asks, sitting down on the chair next to my bed. There is a thick bandage on his head, and he has to use crutches for his broken leg. Other than that, he's already on the mend. He was unconscious in another room when Al-Quadar attacked the Uzbekistani hospital and thus missed all the fun.

"She's . . . okay, I think." I press a button to get the bed into a half-sitting position. My ribs ache at the motion, but I ignore the discomfort. Pain has been my constant companion since the crash, and I'm more or less used to it at this point.

Ever since our rescue from that construction site in Tajikistan five days ago, Nora and I have been recuperating in a special facility in Switzerland. It's a private clinic staffed with top doctors from all over the world, and I've had Lucas personally supervise the security here. Of course, with the most dangerous cells of Al-Quadar eliminated, there's less of an immediate threat, but it still pays to be cautious. I've had all of my injured men transferred here as well, so they could recover faster and in a nicer environment.

The room Nora and I share is state-of-the-art, equipped with everything from video games to a private shower. There are two adjustable beds—one for me and one for Nora—with Egyptian cotton sheets and memory foam mattresses on each. Even the heart-rate monitors and IV drips positioned around the beds look sleek, more decorative than medical. The whole setup is so luxurious, I can almost forget I'm in yet another hospital.

Almost, but not quite.

If I never set foot inside a hospital again, I will die a happy man.

To my tremendous relief, all of Nora's injuries turned out to be minor. The wound on her arm needed a few stitches, but the blow to her face left only a nasty bruise on her cheekbone. The doctors also confirmed that she hadn't been sexually assaulted, despite her state of undress. Within a few hours of our arrival here,

Nora was pronounced healthy and ready to go home.

I, on the other hand, am a bit worse off, though not nearly as fucked up as I could've been.

They've already performed two operations on me—one to minimize the scarring on my face, and the second one to put a prosthetic eye into the vacant eye socket, so I don't resemble a cyclops. I will never be able to see out of my left eye again—at least not until bionic eye technology advances further—but the surgeons have assured me that I'm going to look nearly normal once everything is healed.

My other injuries aren't too bad either. They had to reset my broken arm and wrap it in a new cast, but the gunshot wound in my left shoulder is healing nicely, as are my cracked ribs. I still have some crusted blood under my fingernails and toenails from the needle torture, but it's gradually getting better. The beating Majid's men gave me at the end bruised my kidneys a bit. However, thanks to Peter's prompt arrival, I escaped other internal injuries and more broken bones. When all is said and done, I will have a few more scars—and potentially some weakness in my left arm—but my appearance won't scare little children.

I'm grateful for that. I've never been particularly vain about my looks, but I want to make sure that Nora still finds me attractive, that I don't disgust her with my touch. She's assured me that my scars and bruises don't bother her, but I don't know if she really means it. Because of my injuries, we haven't had sex since our rescue, and I won't know how she truly feels until I have her in my bed again.

In general, I'm not sure how Nora has been feeling for the past five days. With all the surgeries and doctors in the way, we haven't had a chance to talk about what happened. Whenever I bring it up, she changes the topic, as though she wants to forget the whole thing. I would let her—except she's also been unusually quiet. Withdrawn in some way. It's as if the trauma she's gone through has caused her to retreat within herself . . . to shut down her emotions in some manner.

"So she's handling it?" Lucas asks, and I know he's talking about Majid's death. All of my men know about the way Nora gunned him down, and about her role in my rescue. They admire her for being so brave, whereas I'm battling a daily urge to throttle her for risking her life. And Peter—well, that's a whole other matter. If he hadn't disappeared promptly after bringing us to the clinic, I would've torn his head off for placing her in that kind of danger.

"She is," I say in response to Lucas's question. My concerns about Nora's mental state are not something I want to share with him. "She's handling it about as well as can be expected. The first kill is never easy, of course, but she's tough. She'll get through it."

"Yes, I'm sure she will." Reaching for his crutches, Lucas gets up and asks, "How soon do you want to head back to Colombia?"

"Goldberg says we can leave tomorrow. He wants

me to stay here one more night, to make sure everything is healing properly, and then he'll oversee my care back at the compound."

"Excellent," Lucas says. "I will make the arrangements then."

He hobbles out of the room, and I reach for my laptop to check on Nora's whereabouts. She went to get a snack from the cafe on the first floor of the clinic, but she's already been gone longer than ten minutes, and I am beginning to get worried.

Logging in, I pull up the report from the trackers and see that she's standing in the hallway, about fifty feet away from the room. The dot showing her location is stationary; she must be chatting with someone there.

Relieved, I close the laptop and place it back on the bedstand.

I know my fear for her is excessive, but I can't control it. Seeing Majid's knife at Nora's throat had been the worst experience of my life. I had never been so terrified as when I saw the blood trickling down her smooth skin. I literally saw a wall of red at that moment, the rage pumping through me giving me a surge of strength I hadn't known I possessed. Killing that terrorist hadn't been a conscious decision; the need to protect Nora had overwhelmed both my instinct for self-preservation and common sense.

If I had been thinking more clearly, I would've come up with some other way to get Majid's attention away from Nora until the reinforcements could arrive.

I had begun to suspect the rescue plan as soon as Majid mentioned shopping. It made a terrible kind of sense: Nora knew that my enemies would want her as leverage, and she knew that she had the trackers. I couldn't believe that she would put herself out there like that—or that Peter would let her—but it was the only thing that could explain how Al-Quadar were able to lay their hands on her in my absence.

Instead of staying safe at the estate, Nora risked her life to save mine.

Knowing what Majid was capable of, she faced her nightmares to rescue *me*—the man she has every reason to hate.

I don't know if I believed that she truly loved me until that moment . . . until I saw her standing there, scared, yet determined, her small body swathed in a man's shirt ten sizes too big for her. Nobody had ever done anything like that for me before; even when I was a child, my mother would slink away at the first sign of my father's temper, leaving me to his tender mercies. Other than the guards I hired, nobody had ever protected me. I had always been on my own.

Until her.

Until Nora.

As I'm remembering how fierce she looked with her gun pointed at Majid, the door to the room opens, and the subject of my musings walks in.

She's wearing a pair of jeans and a brown long-sleeved top, her thick hair caught in a ponytail behind her back and her feet clad in ballet-type flats. The bruise on her cheekbone is still there, but she covered it up with some makeup today, probably so she could video-chat with her parents without worrying them. She's been talking to them almost daily since our arrival at the clinic. I think she feels guilty about scaring them with her disappearance again.

She's also munching on an apple, her white teeth biting into the juicy fruit with evident enjoyment.

My heart begins to thump heavily in my ribcage as my chest expands with joy and relief. It's like that every time I see her now, my reaction the same whether she's been gone fifteen minutes or several hours.

"Hi." She walks over and gracefully perches on the right side of my bed. Leaning down, she presses her soft lips to my cheek in a brief kiss, then lifts her head to smile at me. "Want some apple?"

"No, thanks, baby." My voice turns husky as her touch makes me painfully aware of the fact that I haven't fucked her since leaving the estate. "It's all yours."

"All right." She bites into the apple. "I ran into Dr. Goldberg in the hallway," she says after swallowing. "He said you're getting better, and we can go home tomorrow."

"Yes, that's right." I watch her tongue flick out to clean up a tiny piece of fruit from her lower lip, and a bolt of heat tightens my balls. I am definitely getting better—or at least my cock believes that I am. "We'll leave as soon as he okays it."

Nora bites off another piece of apple and chews it slowly, studying me with a peculiar expression.

"What is it, baby?" Reaching for her free hand, I bring her delicate palm up to my face and rub the back of her hand against my cheek. I know I'm probably scratching her soft skin with my stubble—I haven't shaved in over a week—but I can't resist the lure of her touch. "Tell me what's on your mind."

She puts the apple core down on a napkin on the bedstand. "We should talk about Peter," she says quietly. "And about the promise I made to him."

I tense, my grip on her palm tightening. "What promise?"

"The list." Her fingers twitch in my grasp. "The list of names you promised him for the three years of service. I told him I'd give it to him as soon as you had it—if he helped me rescue you."

"Fuck." I stare at her in disbelief. I had been wondering how she'd persuaded Peter to disobey a direct order, and here is my answer. "You promised you'd help him get revenge if he assisted you in that insanity?"

Nora nods, her eyes trained on mine. "Yes. It was the only thing I could think of at the time. He knew that if you died, he wouldn't get the list at all—and I told him he'd get it earlier if he helped me."

My eyebrows snap together as a wave of fury rolls through me. That Russian motherfucker put my wife in mortal danger, and that's not something I can ever forgive or forget. He might've saved my life, but he had risked Nora's in order to do it. If he hadn't disappeared after carrying out the rescue, I would've killed him for that. And now Nora wants me to give him that list?

Not fucking likely.

"Julian, I promised him," she insists, apparently sensing my unvoiced reply. Her gaze is filled with uncharacteristic determination as she adds, "I know you're mad at him, but the whole plan was my idea— and he didn't want to do it at first."

"Right. Because he knew your safety should've been his top priority." Realizing I'm still squeezing her palm, I release her hand and say harshly, "The bastard's lucky he's still alive."

"I understand that." Nora gives me a level look. "So does Peter, believe me. He knew you'd react like this— which is why he left after dropping us off here."

I inhale, trying to hang on to my temper. "And good riddance to him. He knows I'll never trust him now. I ordered him to keep you safe on the estate, and what did he do?" I glare at her as the memory of her getting dragged into that windowless room, bloodied and scared, scrapes at my brain. "He fucking hand-delivered you to Majid!"

"Yes, and by doing so, saved your life—"

"I don't care about my fucking life!" I sit up all the way, ignoring the jolt of pain in my ribs. "Don't you get it, Nora? *You* are the only person I care about. *You—*

not me, not anyone else!"

She stares at me, and I see her large eyes beginning to glisten with moisture. "I know, Julian," she whispers, blinking. "I know that."

I look at her, and the anger drains out of me, replaced by an inexplicable need to make her understand. "I don't know if you do, my pet." My voice is quiet as I reach for her hand again, needing its fragile warmth. "You are everything to me. If something happened to you, I wouldn't want to survive—I wouldn't want a life that doesn't have you in it."

Her lips tremble, the tears pooling in her eyes before spilling over. "I know, Julian . . ." Her fingers curl around my palm, squeezing it tightly. "I know, because it's the same for me. When I thought your plane went down"—she swallows, her voice breaking—"and then afterwards, when I heard the gunshots during our call . . ."

I draw in a breath, her distress making my chest hurt. "Don't, baby . . ." I bring her hand up to my lips and kiss the inside of her palm. "Don't think about it anymore. It's over—there's nothing more to fear. Majid is gone, and we're on the verge of completely eradicating Al-Quadar . . ."

As I speak, I see her expression flattening, her gaze growing strangely shuttered. It's as if she's trying to pull back her emotions, to build some kind of a mental wall to protect herself. "I know," she says, and her lips stretch into the kind of empty smile I've often seen her wear since our rescue. "It's done. He's dead."

"Are you sorry about that?" I ask, lowering her hand. I need to understand the source of her withdrawal, to get to the bottom of whatever is causing her to shut down like this. "Are you sorry you killed him, baby? Is that why you've been upset the last few days?"

She blinks, as if startled by my question. "I'm not upset."

"Don't lie to me, my pet." Releasing her hand, I gently grasp her chin and look into her shadowed eyes. "Do you think I don't know you by now? I can see that you've been different since Tajikistan, and I want to understand why."

"Julian . . ." Her voice holds a pleading note. "Please, I don't want to talk about this."

"Why not? Do you think I don't get it? Do you think I don't know what it's like to kill for the first time and live with the knowledge that you took a human life?" I pause, watching for a reaction. When I see none, I continue, "We both know that Majid deserved it, but it's normal to feel like shit afterwards. You need to talk about it, so you can begin to come to terms with everything that happened—"

"No, Julian," she interrupts, the careful blankness of her gaze giving way to a sudden flare of anger. "You *don't* get it. I know Majid deserved to die, and I'm not sorry that I killed him. I have no doubt that the world is a better place without him."

"So what is it then?" I'm beginning to suspect where this is heading, but I want to hear her say it.

"I killed him," she says quietly, looking at me. "I stood next to him, looked him in the eye, and pulled the trigger. I didn't kill him to protect you, or because I had no other choice. I killed him because I wanted to." She pauses, then adds, her eyes glittering, "I killed him because I wanted to see him die."

CHAPTER THIRTY

❖ NORA ❖

Julian stares at me, the expression on his bandaged face unchanged at my revelation. I want to look away, but I can't, his grip on my chin forcing me to hold his gaze as I lay bare the awful secret that's been eating at me since our rescue.

His lack of reaction makes me think he doesn't fully understand what I'm saying.

"I killed him, Julian," I repeat, determined to make him comprehend now that he forced me to talk about this. "I murdered Majid in cold blood. When I saw him step into the room, I knew what I wanted to do, and I did it. I shot the weapon out of his hand—and when he was unarmed, I shot him again in the stomach and chest, making sure not to hit him in the heart, so he'd live a couple of minutes longer. I could've killed him right away, but I didn't." My hands squeeze into fists on my lap, my nails digging painfully into my skin as I confess, "I kept him alive because I wanted to look him in the face when I took his life."

Julian's unbandaged eye gleams a deeper blue, and I feel a wave of burning shame. I know it doesn't make sense—I know I'm talking to a man who's committed crimes far worse than this—but I don't have the excuse of his fucked-up upbringing. Nobody forced me to become a killer. When I shot Majid that day, I did it of my own initiative.

I killed a man because I hated him and wanted to see him die.

I wait for Julian to respond, to say something either dismissive or condemning, but he asks softly instead, "And how did you feel when it was over, my pet? When he lay there dead?" His hand releases my chin and moves down to rest on my leg, his large palm covering most of my thigh. "Were you glad to see him like that?"

I nod, dropping my gaze to escape his penetrating stare. "Yes," I admit, a shudder rippling through me as I remember the almost-euphoric high of seeing the bullets from my gun tearing through Majid's flesh. "When I saw the life leave his eyes, I felt strong.

Invincible. I knew he could no longer hurt us, and I was glad." Gathering my courage, I look up at him again. "Julian . . . I blew a man's brains out—and the scary thing is I don't regret it at all."

"Ah, I see." A smile tugs at his partially healed lips. "You think you're a bad person because you feel no guilt over killing a murderous terrorist—and you believe you should."

"Of course I should." I frown at the inappropriate amusement in his voice. "I killed a man—and you yourself said that it's normal to feel shitty about it. You felt bad after your first kill, right?"

"Yes." Julian's smile takes on a bitter edge. "I did. I was a child, and I didn't know the man I was forced to shoot. He was someone who had double-crossed my father, and to this day, I have no idea what kind of person he was . . . whether he was a hardened criminal or just someone who got mixed-up with bad company. I didn't hate him—I had no opinion about him, really. I killed him to prove that I could do it, to make my father proud of me." He pauses, then continues, his expression softening, "So you see, my pet, it was different. When you killed Majid, you rid the world of evil, whereas I . . . well, that's a whole other story. You have no reason to feel bad about what you did, and you're smart enough to know it."

I look at him, my throat tightening as I imagine eight-year-old Julian pulling that trigger. I don't know what to say, how to assuage his guilt over that long-ago event, and anger at Juan Esguerra fills my chest. "You know, if your father were alive, I would shoot him too," I say savagely, causing Julian to let out a delighted chuckle.

"Oh, yes, I'm sure you would," he says, grinning at me. The expression should've looked grotesque on his bruised and swollen face, but somehow it looks sexy instead. Even beat-up, bandaged like a mummy, and with several days' worth of dark stubble on his jaw, my husband radiates an animal magnetism that transcends mere looks. The doctors told us that his face will be nearly normal once everything is healed, but even if it isn't, I strongly suspect Julian will be just as seductive with an eye patch and some scars.

As though in response to my thoughts, his hand on my thigh moves higher, toward the juncture between my legs. "My fierce little darling," he murmurs, his grin fading as a familiar heated gleam appears in his uncovered eye. "So delicate, yet so ferocious . . . I wish you could've seen yourself that day, baby. You were magnificent when you faced Majid, so brave and beautiful . . ." His fingers press roughly on my clit through my jeans, and I suck in a startled breath, my nipples hardening as a surge of liquid need dampens my sex.

"Yes, that's right, baby," he whispers, his fingers moving upward to my zipper. "You with that weapon was the sexiest thing I've ever seen. I couldn't take my eyes off you." The zipper slides down with a metallic hiss, the sound strangely erotic, and my core clenches with a sudden desperate ache.

"Um, Julian . . ." My breathing is uneven, my heartbeat speeding up as Julian's hand delves into the open fly of my jeans. "What—what are you doing?"

His lips curve in a wicked half-smile. "What does it look like I'm doing?"

"But . . . but you can't . . ." The sentence devolves into a moan as his fingers boldly push into my underwear and cup my sex, his middle finger slipping between my wet folds to massage my throbbing clit. The heat that blasts through my nerve endings feels almost like an electric spark, every hair on my body standing up in response to the zing of pleasure. I gasp, feeling the tension gathering inside me, but before I can reach my peak, Julian's fingers withdraw, leaving me hovering on the edge.

"Take off your clothes, then climb on top," he orders hoarsely, pulling back the blanket to reveal a hospital gown tented with a massive erection. "I need to fuck you. Now."

I hesitate for a moment, worried about his injuries, and Julian's jaw tightens in displeasure.

"I mean it, Nora. Take those clothes off."

Gulping, I jump off the bed, unable to believe that I feel the compulsion to obey him even now. His left arm is in a cast, he can barely move without pain, and yet my instinctive response is to fear him—to want him and fear him at the same time.

"And lock the door," he commands as I begin to pull my shirt up. "I don't want to be interrupted."

"Okay."

Leaving my shirt on, I hurry over to the door to turn the lock that gives us privacy. Every step I take reminds me of the pulsing heat between my legs, my tight jeans rubbing against my sensitized clit and adding to my arousal.

When I return, Julian is in a semi-reclining position on the bed, his gown untied at the front and his hand stroking his erect cock. There is a stiff bandage around his ribs, but it does nothing to detract from the raw power of his muscular body. Even wounded, he manages to dominate the room, his appeal as magnetic as ever.

"Good girl," he murmurs, watching me with a heavy-lidded stare. "Now strip for me, baby. I want to see your sexy little ass wriggling out of those jeans."

I sink my teeth into my lower lip, the heat in his gaze turning me on even more. "All right," I whisper, and turning my back to him, I bend forward and slowly pull down my jeans, making sure to sway my hips from side to side as I expose my thong-clad ass to his eyes.

When the jeans are all the way down to my ankles, I turn back to face him and kick off my shoes, then step out of my jeans, leaving them lying on the floor. Julian watches my movements with undisguised lust, his breathing becoming heavy as the tip of his cock starts to glisten with moisture. He's no longer touching himself, his hands clutching the sheets instead, and I know it's because he's close to coming, the hard column of his sex jutting up in defiance of gravity.

Keeping my eyes trained on him, I proceed to take off my shirt, pulling it up over my head in a slow, teasing motion. Underneath, I'm wearing a silky white bra that matches my thong. I bought several outfits online earlier in the week, and I'm glad I decided to get a few nicer underwear sets. I love to see that look of uncontrollable hunger on Julian's face—the expression that says he would move mountains to have me at that moment.

As the shirt falls to the floor, he says roughly, "Come here, Nora." His gaze devours me, consumes me. "I need to touch you."

I inhale, my sex flooding with wetness as I take a couple of steps toward the bed, pausing in front of him. He reaches for me, smoothing his palm over my ribcage, and then moves his hand higher, toward my bra. His fingers close around my left breast, kneading it through the silky material, and I gasp as he pinches my nipple, causing it to stiffen further.

"Take the rest of your clothes off." His hand leaves my body, making me feel bereft for a moment, and I hurriedly unclasp my bra and push the thong down my legs before stepping out of it.

"Good. Now straddle me."

Biting my lip, I climb onto the bed, straddling Julian's hips. His cock brushes against the inside of my thighs, and I grasp it in my right hand, guiding it toward my aching entrance.

"Yes, that's it," he mutters, reaching out to grip my hip as I begin to lower myself onto his shaft. Releasing his cock, I use my palms to brace myself on the bed, and he groans, "Yes, take me in, my pet . . . All the way . . ." Using his grip on my hip, he pushes me lower, forcing his cock deeper into me, and I moan at the exquisite stretching sensation, my body adjusting to being filled and penetrated by his thick length.

It feels like the sweetest of reliefs, the pleasure-pain of his possession acute and achingly familiar all at once. As I watch him, drinking in the look of tormented pleasure on his face, it suddenly dawns on me that this could just as easily not be happening—that instead of lying underneath me, Julian could be six feet underground, his powerful body mangled and destroyed.

I am not cognizant of having made any sounds, but I must have, because Julian's eye narrows, his hand tightening on my hip. "What is it, baby?" he asks sharply, and I realize that I've begun to shake, chills wracking my body at the image of him lying there cold and broken. My desire evaporates, replaced by remembered terror and dread. It's as if I've been doused with ice water, the horror of what we've been through bubbling up and choking me from within.

"Nora, what is it?" Julian's hand slides up to my throat, gripping the nape of my neck to bring my face closer to his. His eye bores into me as my hands clutch convulsively at the sheets on each side of his chest. "What is it? Tell me!"

I want to explain, but I can't speak, my throat closing up as my heartbeat spikes, cold sweat drenching my body. All of a sudden, I can't breathe, toxic panic clawing at my chest and constricting my lungs, and I begin to hyperventilate as black dots encroach on the edges of my vision.

"Nora!" Julian's voice reaches me as if from afar. "Fuck . . . Nora!"

A stinging blow across my face snaps my head to the side, and I gasp, my hand flying up to cradle my left cheek. The shock of pain startles me out of my panic, and my lungs finally begin working, my chest expanding to let in much-needed air. Panting, I turn my head to stare incredulously at Julian, the darkness in my mind receding as reality pushes back in.

"Nora, baby . . ." He's gently rubbing my cheek now, soothing the pain he inflicted. "I'm so sorry, my pet. I didn't want to slap you, but you looked like you were having a panic attack. What happened? Do you want me to call for a nurse?"

"No—" My voice breaks as sobs rise up, bursting out of my throat. Tears begin to flow down my face as I realize that I completely freaked out—and that it happened during sex. Julian's cock is still buried inside me, only slightly softer than before, and yet I am shaking and crying, like a crazy person. "No," I repeat in a choked voice. "I'm all right . . . Really, I'll be fine . . ."

"Yes, you will be." His voice takes on a hard, commanding tone as his hand moves down to grip my throat. "Look at me, Nora. Now."

Unable to do anything else, I obey, meeting his gaze with my own. His eye glitters a bright, fierce blue. As I look at him, my breathing begins to slow, my sobs easing and my desperate panic fading. I am still crying, but silently now, more as a reflex than anything else.

"Okay, good," Julian says in that same harsh tone. "Now you're going to ride me—and you will not think of whatever got you so upset. Do you understand me?"

I nod, his instructions calming me further. As my anxiety melts away, other sensations start to creep in. I become aware of the clean, familiar scent of his body, the crisp feel of his leg hair pressing against my calves . . .

The way his cock feels inside me, warm, thick, and hard.

My body responds again, further distracting me from my panic. Taking a deep breath, I begin to move, rising up and then lowering myself onto his shaft, my core growing wet and soft as pleasure starts to curl low in my belly.

"Yes, just like that, baby," Julian murmurs, his hand sliding down my body to press against my clit, intensifying the tension growing inside me. "Fuck me. Ride me. Use me to forget your demons."

"Yes," I whisper. "I will." And keeping my eyes on his face, I pick up the pace, letting the physical pleasure carry me away from all the darkness, the inferno of our passion burning away the memories of icy horror within.

When we come, it's within seconds of each other, our bodies as attuned to each other as our souls.

* * *

That evening I go to sleep in Julian's bed, not my own. The doctors okayed it after cautioning me not to jostle his ribs or face during the night.

I lie on his right, my head pillowed on his uninjured shoulder. I should be asleep, but I'm not. My mind is buzzing, humming like a beehive. A million thoughts are running through my head, my emotions oscillating from elation to sadness.

We're both alive and more or less intact. We're together again, having both survived against all odds. I no longer have any doubts that in some fucked-up way, we're meant to be. For better or worse, we fit each other now, our twisted, damaged parts locking together like a jigsaw puzzle.

I have no idea what the future holds, whether things can ever truly be all right again. I still need to convince Julian to honor my promise to Peter—and I need to ask the doctors for a morning-after pill, given the fact that neither one of us remembered to use protection earlier today. I don't know if it's possible to get pregnant so quickly after losing the implant, but it's not a risk I'm willing to take. The possibility of a child—of a helpless baby subjected to our kind of life—horrifies me now more than ever.

Maybe I will change my mind with time. Maybe in a few years, I will feel differently. Less scared. For now, though, I am sharply cognizant of the fact that our life will never be a fairy tale. Julian is not a good man—and I'm no longer a good woman.

That should worry me . . . and maybe tomorrow it will. At this moment, however, feeling his warmth surrounding me, I am only aware of a deepening sense of peace, of a certainty that this is right.

That this is where I belong.

Raising my hand, I trace my fingers across his half-healed lips, feeling the sensual shape of them in the darkness.

"Will you ever let me go?" I murmur, remembering our long-ago conversation.

His lips twitch in a faint smile. He remembers too. "No," he replies softly. "Never."

We lie in silence for a few moments, and then he asks quietly, "Do you want me to let you go?"

"No, Julian." I close my eyes, a smile curving my own lips. "Never."

SNEAK PEEKS

Thank you for reading *Keep Me*. I hope you enjoyed this dark story. If you did, please mention it to your friends and social media connections. I would also be grateful if you helped other readers discover the series by leaving a review.

Nora & Julian's story continues in *Hold Me*. Please visit my website at www.annazaires.com to sign up for my new release email list and to learn more about my upcoming books.

And now please turn the page for a little taste of *Hold Me*, *Close Liaisons*, and some of my other works.

EXCERPT FROM *HOLD ME*

Author's Note: *Hold Me* is the conclusion of Nora & Julian's story. The following excerpt is from Julian's point of view.

* * *

A gasping cry wakes me up, dragging me out of restless sleep. My uninjured eye flies open on a rush of adrenaline, and I jackknife to a sitting position, the sudden movement causing my cracked ribs to scream in protest. The cast on my left arm bangs into the heart-rate monitor next to the bed, and the wave of agony is so intense that the room spins around me in a sickening swirl. My pulse is pounding, and it takes a moment to realize what woke me.

Nora.

She must be in the grip of another nightmare.

My body, coiled for combat, relaxes slightly. There's no danger, nobody coming after us right now. I'm lying next to Nora in my luxurious hospital bed, and we're both safe, the clinic in Switzerland as secure as Lucas can make it.

The pain in my ribs and arm is better now, more tolerable. Moving more carefully, I place my right hand on Nora's shoulder and try to gently shake her awake. She's turned away from me, facing in the opposite direction, so I can't see her face to check if she's crying. Her skin, however, is cold and damp from sweat. She must've been having the nightmare for a while. She's also shivering.

"Wake up, baby," I murmur, stroking her slender arm. I can see the light filtering through the blinds on the window, and I know it must be morning. "It's just a dream. Wake up, my pet . . ."

She stiffens under my touch, and I know she's not fully awake, the nightmare still holding her captive. Her breathing is coming in audible, gasping bursts, and I can feel the tremors running through her body. Her distress claws at me, hurting me worse than any injury, and the knowledge that I'm again responsible for this—that I failed to keep her safe—makes my insides burn with acidic fury.

Fury at myself and at Peter Sokolov—the man who allowed Nora to risk her life to rescue me.

Before my cursed trip to Tajikistan, she had been slowly getting over Beth's death, her nightmares becoming less frequent as the months wore on. Now, however, the bad dreams are back—and Nora is worse off than before, judging by the panic attack she had during sex yesterday.

I want to kill Peter for this—and I might, if he ever crosses my path again. The Russian saved my life, but he endangered Nora's in the process, and that's not something I will ever forgive. And his fucking list of names? Forget it. There is no way I'm going to reward him for betraying me like this, no matter what Nora promised him.

"Come on, baby, wake up," I urge her again, using my right arm to lower myself back down on the bed. My ribs ache at the movement, but less fiercely this time. I carefully shift closer to Nora, pressing my body against hers from the back. "You're okay. It's all over, I promise."

She draws in a deep, hiccuping breath, and I feel the tension within her easing as she realizes where she is. "Julian?" she whispers, turning around to face me, and I see that she's been crying after all, her cheeks coated with moisture from her tears.

"Yes. You're safe now. Everything is fine." I reach over with my right hand and trail my fingers over her jaw, marveling at the fragile beauty of her facial structure. My hand looks huge and rough against her delicate face, my nails ragged and bruised from the needles Majid used on me. The contrast between us is glaring—though Nora is not entirely unscathed either. The purity of her golden skin is marred by a bruise on the left side of her face, where those Al-Quadar motherfuckers hit her to knock her out.

If they weren't already dead, I would've ripped them apart with my bare hands for hurting her.

"What did you dream about?" I ask softly. "Was it Beth?"

"No." She shakes her head, and I see that her breathing is beginning to return to normal. Her voice, however, still holds echoes of horror as she says hoarsely, "It was you this time. Majid was cutting out your eyes, and I couldn't stop him."

I try not to react, but it's impossible. Her words hurl me back to that cold, windowless room, to the nauseating sensations I've been trying to forget for the past several days. My head begins to throb with remembered agony, my half-healed eye socket burning with emptiness once again. I feel blood and other fluids dripping down my face, and my stomach heaves at the recollection. I'm no stranger to pain, or even to torture—my father believed that his son should be able to withstand anything—but losing my eye had been by far the most excruciating experience of my life.

Physically, at least.

Emotionally, Nora's appearance in that room probably holds that honor.

It takes all of my willpower to wrench my thoughts back to the present, away from the mind-numbing terror of seeing her dragged in by Majid's men.

"You did stop him, Nora." It kills me to admit this, but if it weren't for her bravery, I would probably be decomposing in some dumpster in Tajikistan. "You came for me, and you saved me."

I still have trouble believing that she did that—that she voluntarily placed herself in the hands of psychotic terrorists to save my life. She didn't do it out of some naïve conviction that they wouldn't harm her. No, my pet knew exactly what they were capable of, and she still had the courage to act.

I owe my life to the girl I abducted, and I don't quite know how to deal with that.

"Why did you do it?" I ask, stroking the edge of her lower lip with my thumb. Deep down, I know, but I want to hear her admit it.

She gazes at me, her eyes filled with shadows from her dream. "Because I can't survive without you," she says quietly. "You know that, Julian. You wanted me to love you, and I do. I love you so much I would walk through hell for you."

I take in her words with greedy, shameless pleasure. I can't get enough of her love. I can't get enough of her. I wanted her initially because of her resemblance to Maria, but my childhood friend had never evoked even a fraction of the emotions Nora makes me feel. My affection for Maria had been innocent and pure, just like Maria herself.

My obsession with Nora is anything but.

"Listen to me, my pet . . ." My hand leaves her face to rest on her shoulder. "I need you to promise me that you will never do something like that again. I'm obviously glad to be alive, but I would sooner have died than had you in that kind of danger. You are *never* to risk your life for me again. Do you understand me?"

The nod she gives me is faint, almost imperceptible, and I see a mutinous gleam in her eyes. She doesn't want to make me mad, so she's not disagreeing, but I have a strong suspicion she's going to do what she thinks is right regardless of what she says right now.

This obviously calls for more heavy-handed measures.

"Good," I say silkily. "Because next time—if there is ever a next time—I will kill anyone who helps you against my orders, and I will do it slowly and painfully. Do you understand me, Nora? If anyone so much as endangers a hair on your head, whether it's to save *me* or for any other reason, that person will die a very unpleasant death. Do I make myself clear?"

"Yes." She looks pale now, her lips pressed together as if to contain a protest. She's angry with me, but she's also scared. Not for herself—she's beyond that fear now—but for others. My pet knows I mean what I say.

She knows I'm a conscienceless killer with only one weakness.

Her.

* * *

Please visit my website at www.annazaires.com to learn more and to sign up for my new release email list.

ANNA ZAIRES

EXCERPT FROM *CLOSE LIAISONS*

Author's Note: *Close Liaisons* is the first book in my erotic sci-fi romance trilogy, the Krinar Chronicles. While not as dark as *Twist Me* and *Capture Me*, it does have some elements that readers of dark erotica may enjoy.

* * *

A dark and edgy romance that will appeal to fans of erotic and turbulent relationships . . .

In the near future, the Krinar rule the Earth. An advanced race from another galaxy, they are still a mystery to us—and we are completely at their mercy.

Shy and innocent, Mia Stalis is a college student in New York City who has led a very normal life. Like most people, she's never had any interactions with the invaders—until one fateful day in the park changes everything. Having caught Korum's eye, she must now contend with a powerful, dangerously seductive Krinar who wants to possess her and will stop at nothing to make her his own.

How far would you go to regain your freedom? How much would you sacrifice to help your people? What choice will you make when you begin to fall for your enemy?

* * *

Breathe, Mia, breathe. Somewhere in the back of her mind, a small rational voice kept repeating those words. That same oddly objective part of her noted his symmetric face structure, with golden skin stretched tightly over high cheekbones and a firm jaw. Pictures and videos of Ks that she'd seen had hardly done them justice. Standing no more than thirty feet away, the creature was simply stunning.

As she continued staring at him, still frozen in place, he straightened and began walking toward her. Or rather stalking toward her, she thought stupidly, as his every movement reminded her of a jungle cat sinuously approaching a gazelle. All the while, his eyes never left hers. As he approached, she could make out individual yellow flecks in his light golden eyes and the thick long lashes surrounding them.

She watched in horrified disbelief as he sat down on her bench, less than two feet away from her, and smiled, showing white even teeth. No fangs, she noted with some functioning part of her brain. Not even a hint of them. That used to be another myth about them, like their supposed abhorrence of the sun.

"What's your name?" The creature practically purred the question at her. His voice was low and smooth, completely unaccented. His nostrils flared slightly, as though inhaling her scent.

"Um . . ." Mia swallowed nervously. "M-Mia."

"Mia," he repeated slowly, seemingly savoring her name. "Mia what?"

"Mia Stalis." Oh crap, why did he want to know her name? Why was he here, talking to her? In general, what was he doing in Central Park, so far away from any of the K Centers? *Breathe, Mia, breathe.*

"Relax, Mia Stalis." His smile got wider, exposing a dimple in his left cheek. A dimple? Ks had dimples? "Have you never encountered one of us before?"

"No, I haven't." Mia exhaled sharply, realizing that she was holding her breath. She was proud that her voice didn't sound as shaky as she felt. Should she ask? Did she want to know?

She gathered her courage. "What, um—" Another swallow. "What do you want from me?"

"For now, conversation." He looked like he was about to laugh at her, those gold eyes crinkling slightly at the corners.

Strangely, that pissed her off enough to take the edge off her fear. If there was anything Mia hated, it was being laughed at. With her short, skinny stature and a general lack of social skills that came from an awkward teenage phase involving every girl's nightmare of braces, frizzy hair, and glasses, Mia had more than enough experience being the butt of someone's joke.

She lifted her chin belligerently. "Okay, then, what is *your* name?"

"It's Korum."

"Just Korum?"

"We don't really have last names, not the way you do. My full name is much longer, but you wouldn't be able to pronounce it if I told you."

Okay, that was interesting. She now remembered reading something like that in *The New York Times*. So far, so good. Her legs had nearly stopped shaking, and her breathing was returning to normal. Maybe, just maybe, she would get out of this alive. This conversation business seemed safe enough, although the way he kept staring at her with those unblinking yellowish eyes was unnerving. She decided to keep him talking.

"What are you doing here, Korum?"

"I just told you, making conversation with you, Mia." His voice again held a hint of laughter.

Frustrated, Mia blew out her breath. "I meant, what are you doing here in Central Park? In New York City in general?"

He smiled again, cocking his head slightly to the side. "Maybe I'm hoping to meet a pretty curly-haired girl."

Okay, enough was enough. He was clearly toying with her. Now that she could think a little again, she realized that they were in the middle of Central Park, in full view of about a gazillion spectators. She surreptitiously glanced around to confirm that. Yep, sure enough, although people were obviously steering clear of her bench and its otherworldly occupant, there were a number of brave souls staring their way from farther up the path. A couple were even cautiously filming them with their wristwatch cameras. If the K tried anything with her, it would be on YouTube in the blink of an eye, and he had to know it. Of course, he may or may not care about that.

Still, going on the assumption that since she'd never come across any videos of K assaults on college students in the middle of Central Park, she was relatively safe, Mia cautiously reached for her laptop and lifted it to stuff it back into her backpack.

"Let me help you with that, Mia—"

And before she could blink, she felt him take her heavy laptop from her suddenly boneless fingers, gently brushing against her knuckles in the process. A sensation similar to a mild electric shock shot through Mia at his touch, leaving her nerve endings tingling in its wake.

Reaching for her backpack, he carefully put away the laptop in a smooth, sinuous motion. "There you go, all better now."

Oh God, he had touched her. Maybe her theory about the safety of public locations was bogus. She felt her breathing speeding up again, and her heart rate was probably well into the anaerobic zone at this point.

"I have to go now . . . Bye!"

How she managed to squeeze out those words without hyperventilating, she would never know. Grabbing the strap of the backpack he'd just put down, she jumped to her feet, noting somewhere in the back of her mind that her earlier paralysis seemed to be gone.

"Bye, Mia. I will see you later." His softly mocking voice carried in the clear spring air as she took off, nearly running in her haste to get away.

* * *

If you'd like to find out more, please visit my website at www.annazaires.com. All three books in the Krinar Chronicles trilogy are now available.

EXCERPT FROM *THE THOUGHT READERS* BY DIMA ZALES

Author's Note: If you'd like to try something different—and especially if you enjoy urban fantasy and science fiction—you might want to check out *The Thought Readers*, the first book in the *Mind Dimensions* series that I'm collaborating on with Dima Zales, my husband. But be warned, there is not much romance or sex in this one. Instead of sex, there's mind reading. The book is now available at most retailers.

* * *

Everyone thinks I'm a genius.

Everyone is wrong.

Sure, I finished Harvard at eighteen and now make crazy money at a hedge fund. But that's not because I'm unusually smart or hard-working.

It's because I cheat.

You see, I have a unique ability. I can go outside time into my own personal version of reality—the place I call "the Quiet"—where I can explore my surroundings while the rest of the world stands still.

I thought I was the only one who could do this—until I met *her*.

My name is Darren, and this is how I learned that I'm a Reader.

* * *

Sometimes I think I'm crazy. I'm sitting at a casino table in Atlantic City, and everyone around me is motionless. I call this the *Quiet*, as though giving it a name makes it seem more real—as though giving it a name changes the fact that all the players around me are frozen like statues, and I'm walking among them, looking at the cards they've been dealt.

The problem with the theory of my being crazy is that when I 'unfreeze' the world, as I just have, the cards the players turn over are the same ones I just saw in the Quiet. If I were crazy, wouldn't these cards be different? Unless I'm so far gone that I'm imagining the cards on the table, too.

But then I also win. If that's a delusion—if the pile of chips on my side of the table is a delusion—then I might as well question everything. Maybe my name isn't even Darren.

No. I can't think that way. If I'm really that confused, I don't want to snap out of it—because if I do, I'll probably wake up in a mental hospital.

Besides, I love my life, crazy and all.

My shrink thinks the Quiet is an inventive way I describe the 'inner workings of my genius.' Now that sounds crazy to me. She also might want me, but that's beside the point. Suffice it to say, she's as far as it gets from my datable age range, which is currently right around twenty-four. Still young, still hot, but done with school and pretty much beyond the clubbing phase. I hate clubbing, almost as much as I hated studying. In any case, my shrink's explanation doesn't work, as it doesn't account for the way I know things even a genius wouldn't know—like the exact value and suit of the other players' cards.

I watch as the dealer begins a new round. Besides me, there are three players at the table: Grandma, the Cowboy, and the Professional, as I call them. I feel that now almost-imperceptible fear that accompanies the phasing. That's what I call the process: phasing into the Quiet. Worrying about my sanity has always facilitated phasing; fear seems helpful in this process.

I phase in, and everything gets quiet. Hence the name for this state.

It's eerie to me, even now. Outside the Quiet, this casino is very loud: drunk people talking, slot machines, ringing of wins, music—the only place louder is a club or a concert. And yet, right at this moment, I could probably hear a pin drop. It's like I've gone deaf to the chaos that surrounds me.

Having so many frozen people around adds to the strangeness of it all. Here is a waitress stopped mid-step, carrying a tray with drinks. There is a woman about to pull a slot machine lever. At my own table, the dealer's hand is raised, the last card he dealt hanging unnaturally in midair. I walk up to him from the side of the table and reach for it. It's a king, meant for the Professional. Once I let the card go, it falls on the table rather than continuing to float as before—but I know full well that it will be back in the air, in the exact position it was when I grabbed it, when I phase out.

The Professional looks like someone who makes money playing poker, or at least the way I always imagined someone like that might look. Scruffy, shades on, a little sketchy-looking. He's been doing an excellent job with the poker face—basically not twitching a single muscle throughout the game. His face is so expressionless that I wonder if he might've gotten Botox to help maintain such a stony countenance. His hand is on the table, protectively covering the cards dealt to him.

I move his limp hand away. It feels normal. Well, in a manner of speaking. The hand is sweaty and hairy, so moving it aside is unpleasant and is admittedly an abnormal thing to do. The normal part is that the hand is warm, rather than cold. When I was a kid, I expected people to feel cold in the Quiet, like stone statues.

With the Professional's hand moved away, I pick up his cards. Combined with the king that was hanging in the air, he has a nice high pair. Good to know.

I walk over to Grandma. She's already holding her cards, and she has fanned them nicely for me. I'm able to avoid touching her wrinkled, spotted hands. This is a relief, as I've recently become conflicted about touching people—or, more specifically, women—in the Quiet. If I had to, I would rationalize touching Grandma's hand as harmless, or at least not creepy, but it's better to avoid it if possible.

In any case, she has a low pair. I feel bad for her. She's been losing a lot tonight. Her chips are dwindling. Her losses are due, at least partially, to the fact that she has a terrible poker face. Even before looking at her cards, I knew they wouldn't be good because I could tell she was disappointed as soon as her hand was dealt. I also caught a gleeful gleam in her eyes a few rounds ago when she had a winning three of a kind.

This whole game of poker is, to a large degree, an exercise in reading people—something I really want to get better at. At my job, I've been told I'm great at reading people. I'm not, though; I'm just good at using the Quiet to make it seem like I am. I do want to learn how to read people for real, though. It would be nice to know what everyone is thinking.

What I don't care that much about in this poker game is money. I do well enough financially to not have to depend on hitting it big gambling. I don't care if I win or lose, though quintupling my money back at the blackjack table was fun. This whole trip has been more about going gambling because I finally can, being twenty-one and all. I was never into fake IDs, so this is an actual milestone for me.

Leaving Grandma alone, I move on to the next player—the Cowboy. I can't resist taking off his straw hat and trying it on. I wonder if it's possible for me to get lice this way. Since I've never been able to bring back any inanimate objects from the Quiet, nor otherwise affect the real world in any lasting way, I figure I won't be able to get any living critters to come back with me, either.

Dropping the hat, I look at his cards. He has a pair of aces—a better hand than the Professional. Maybe the Cowboy is a professional, too. He has a good poker face, as far as I can tell. It'll be interesting to watch those two in this round.

Next, I walk up to the deck and look at the top cards, memorizing them. I'm not leaving anything to chance.

When my task in the Quiet is complete, I walk back to myself. Oh, yes, did I mention that I see myself sitting there, frozen like the rest of them? That's the weirdest part. It's like having an out-of-body experience.

Approaching my frozen self, I look at him. I usually avoid doing this, as it's too unsettling. No amount of looking in the mirror—or seeing videos of yourself on YouTube—can prepare you for viewing your own three-dimensional body up close. It's not something anyone is meant to experience. Well, aside from identical twins, I guess.

It's hard to believe that this person is me. He looks more like some random guy. Well, maybe a bit better than that. I do find this guy interesting. He looks cool. He looks smart. I think women would probably consider him good-looking, though I know that's not a modest thing to think.

It's not like I'm an expert at gauging how attractive a guy is, but some things are common sense. I can tell when a dude is ugly, and this frozen me is not. I also know that generally, being good-looking requires a symmetrical face, and the statue of me has that. A strong jaw doesn't hurt, either. Check. Having broad shoulders is a positive, and being tall really helps. All covered. I have blue eyes—that seems to be a plus. Girls have told me they like my eyes, though right now, on the frozen me, the eyes look creepy—glassy. They look like the eyes of a lifeless wax figure.

Realizing that I'm dwelling on this subject way too long, I shake my head. I can just picture my shrink analyzing this moment. Who would imagine admiring themselves like this as part of their mental illness? I can just picture her scribbling down *Narcissist*, underlining it for emphasis.

Enough. I need to leave the Quiet. Raising my hand, I touch my frozen self on the forehead, and I hear noise again as I phase out.

Everything is back to normal.

The card that I looked at a moment before—the king that I left on the table—is in the air again, and from there it follows the trajectory it was always meant to, landing near the Professional's hands. Grandma is still eyeing her fanned cards in disappointment, and the Cowboy has his hat on again, though I took it off him in the Quiet. Everything is exactly as it was.

On some level, my brain never ceases to be surprised at the discontinuity of the experience in the Quiet and outside it. As humans, we're hardwired to question reality when such things happen. When I was trying to outwit my shrink early on in my therapy, I once read an entire psychology textbook during our session. She, of course, didn't notice it, as I did it in the Quiet. The book talked about how babies as young as two months old are surprised if they see something out of the ordinary, like gravity appearing to work backwards. It's no wonder my brain has trouble adapting. Until I was ten, the world behaved normally, but everything has been weird since then, to put it mildly.

Glancing down, I realize I'm holding three of a kind. Next time, I'll look at my cards before phasing. If I have something this strong, I might take my chances and play fair.

The game unfolds predictably because I know everybody's cards. At the end, Grandma gets up. She's clearly lost enough money.

And that's when I see the girl for the first time.

She's hot. My friend Bert at work claims that I have a 'type,' but I reject that idea. I don't like to think of myself as shallow or predictable. But I might actually be a bit of both, because this girl fits Bert's description of my type to a T. And my reaction is extreme interest, to say the least.

Large blue eyes. Well-defined cheekbones on a slender face, with a hint of something exotic. Long, shapely legs, like those of a dancer. Dark wavy hair in a ponytail—a hairstyle that I like. And without bangs— even better. I hate bangs—not sure why girls do that to themselves. Though lack of bangs is not, strictly speaking, in Bert's description of my type, it probably should be.

I continue staring at her. With her high heels and tight skirt, she's overdressed for this place. Or maybe I'm underdressed in my jeans and t-shirt. Either way, I don't care. I have to try to talk to her.

I debate phasing into the Quiet and approaching her, so I can do something creepy like stare at her up close, or maybe even snoop in her pockets. Anything to help me when I talk to her.

I decide against it, which is probably the first time that's ever happened.

I know that my reasoning for breaking my usual habit—if you can even call it that—is strange. I picture the following chain of events: she agrees to date me, we go out for a while, we get serious, and because of the deep connection we have, I come clean about the Quiet. She learns I did something creepy and has a fit, then dumps me. It's ridiculous to think this, of course, considering that we haven't even spoken yet. Talk about jumping the gun. She might have an IQ below seventy, or the personality of a piece of wood. There can be twenty different reasons why I wouldn't want to date her. And besides, it's not all up to me. She might tell me to go fuck myself as soon as I try to talk to her.

Still, working at a hedge fund has taught me to hedge. As crazy as that reasoning is, I stick with my decision not to phase because I know it's the gentlemanly thing to do. In keeping with this unusually chivalrous me, I also decide not to cheat at this round of poker.

As the cards are dealt again, I reflect on how good it feels to have done the honorable thing—even without anyone knowing. Maybe I should try to respect people's privacy more often. As soon as I think this, I mentally snort. *Yeah, right.* I have to be realistic. I wouldn't be where I am today if I'd followed that advice. In fact, if I made a habit of respecting people's privacy, I would lose my job within days—and with it, a lot of the comforts I've become accustomed to.

Copying the Professional's move, I cover my cards with my hand as soon as I receive them. I'm about to sneak a peek at what I was dealt when something unusual happens.

The world goes quiet, just like it does when I phase in . . . but I did nothing this time.

And at that moment, I see *her*—the girl sitting across the table from me, the girl I was just thinking about. She's standing next to me, pulling her hand away from mine. Or, strictly speaking, from my frozen self's hand—as I'm standing a little to the side looking at her.

She's also still sitting in front of me at the table, a frozen statue like all the others.

My mind goes into overdrive as my heartbeat jumps. I don't even consider the possibility of that second girl being a twin sister or something like that. I know it's her. She's doing what I did just a few minutes ago. She's walking in the Quiet. The world around us is frozen, but we are not.

A horrified look crosses her face as she realizes the same thing. Before I can react, she lunges across the table and touches her own forehead.

The world becomes normal again.

She stares at me from across the table, shocked, her eyes huge and her face pale. Her hands tremble as she rises to her feet. Without so much as a word, she turns and begins walking away, then breaks into a run a couple of seconds later.

Getting over my own shock, I get up and run after her. It's not exactly smooth. If she notices a guy she doesn't know running after her, dating will be the last thing on her mind. But I'm beyond that now. She's the only person I've met who can do what I do. She's proof that I'm not insane. She might have what I want most in the world.

She might have answers.

* * *

If you'd like to learn more about our fantasy and science fiction books, please visit Dima Zales's website at www.dimazales.com and sign up for his new release email list.

ABOUT THE AUTHOR

Anna Zaires fell in love with books at the age of five, when her grandmother taught her to read. She wrote her first story shortly thereafter. Since then, she has always lived partially in a fantasy world where the only limits were those of her imagination. Currently residing in Florida, Anna is happily married to Dima Zales (a science fiction and fantasy author) and closely collaborates with him on all their works.

To learn more, please visit www.annazaires.com.

44143914R00218